LAST SUMMER

LAST SUMMER

THERESA WEIR

DOUBLEDAY

New York   London   Toronto   Sydney   Auckland

LOVESWEPT®

PUBLISHED BY DOUBLEDAY

a division of Bantam Doubleday Dell Publishing Group, Inc.
666 Fifth Avenue, New York, New York 10103

DOUBLEDAY and the portrayal of an anchor with a dolphin
and the word LOVESWEPT and the portrayal of the wave device
are trademarks of Doubleday, a division of
Bantam Doubleday Dell Publishing Group, Inc.

Book design by Patrice Fodero

Library of Congress Cataloging-in-Publication Data

Weir, Theresa, 1954–
    Last summer / Theresa Weir. — 1st ed.
        p.   cm.
    "November 1992."
    I. Title.
PS3573.E3976L37   1992
813'.54—dc20   92-10813
                                          CIP

ISBN 0-385-41782-9

Printed in the United States of America

November 1992

1   3   5   7   9   10   8   6   4   2

First Edition

Chapter 1

*J*ohnnie Irish adjusted his dark, wire-rimmed sunglasses, gave a nod to the pilot, then paused in the doorway of the charter plane.

Something had definitely been lost arriving by air, he decided. To get the full effect of Hope, Texas, a guy had to approach it by land. He had to cross miles and miles of desolate desert, tumbleweeds, and broken-down shanties. He had to see all the billboards boasting two-headed snakes and five-legged lambs.

As a teenager, Johnnie and some buddies had decided to take in one of those roadside attractions. They'd plunked down a buck fifty only to discover that the snake was pickled and the lamb was stuffed. From the highly visible black stitches, they'd also decided that the freak appendage had been added by some myopic seamstress. They'd quickly pointed out the flaws in loud, boisterous voices. Doubled up with laughter, tears streaming from their eyes, they'd been kicked out of the joint—which only made them laugh all the harder.

Johnnie had been kicked out of a lot of places since then. Bars. Hotels. Restaurants.

Towns.

Hope, Texas, in particular.

Three months ago, when he'd gotten the phone call asking him to be the main attraction in Hope's homecoming parade, he'd laughed out loud, right into the receiver. But then he thought it over awhile and the temptation proved too much. He'd been harboring a bitterness toward his hometown for a long time, and wouldn't revenge be sweet? So, fifteen years after being tossed out on his ass, he'd decided to come back.

Desert wind, not yet heated by the day, felt good against his skin. He'd forgotten how clear and untainted the air here was. He took a moment to pull some of that air deep into his lungs.

He could see the promised car waiting for him—the parade convertible. Standing beside it, shading her eyes with one hand, was a dark-haired woman. For a second, panic thumped in his chest while his mind spun backward to his childhood and all its horrors. For a second, he thought the woman standing by the car was his mother, then his head cleared and he remembered she was dead. He let out his breath in relief.

Maggie Mayfield watched as Johnnie Irish stepped from the plane. They had agreed to meet at the private airstrip in order to keep his arrival place secret.

Even from a distance she could see that his hair was too long, his jeans too faded. They weren't the kind of jeans that had been made to look old. These *were* old. They'd most likely been dark blue when purchased, but through the years they had faded and conformed to the contours of his body until they were a part of him. Besides the decrepit jeans, he was wearing a red and white baseball jacket and leather high-top sneakers.

She thought of all the ruffles and patent leather waiting along the parade route and felt a stab of irritation. He could have at least dressed up a little.

Right from the start, she'd been against inviting Johnnie Irish to their community. Hope was surrounded by mile after mile of desert. To the south, the nearest town, Little Burgundy, was forty-five miles away. Its claim to fame was a twin movie theater and a brand-new Piggly Wiggly. Some sixty miles to the north was Black River. Its only building was a combined tavern and gas station.

There was no fast lane in Hope, Texas. Sure, the kids drank, and Maggie knew that drugs had filtered their way into town. That kind of thing was everywhere. But she'd like to think it wasn't nearly as bad in Hope as it was other places.

So why had they rolled out the red carpet to welcome the very type of person they prided themselves in being without? Why had they invited Johnnie Irish into their midst when he was the embodiment of everything they didn't want in their town? The man stood for drugs and sex and alcohol. He was known for his loud, drunken parties and his flagrant disregard for the law and other people's property. In short, he was a bad example—the *worst* example for their young people—and she'd told the town council so.

"It isn't every town that can brag that they helped raise a movie star," George Bailey had argued.

"And think of the money he'll bring in," Mabel French had added. "Think of the excitement, the life! We need some excitement and life in Hope."

In the end they'd taken a vote and Maggie had lost six to one. And since she was the head of the parade committee, she now had the dubious honor of escorting their guest into town.

She watched as he strolled leisurely toward her, watched as a lizard skittered in front of him, across the cracked cement to disappear behind a tumbleweed.

Maggie had never had the desire to see a Johnnie Irish movie. Screwball comedies didn't appeal to her. Not that she was against silliness. She just preferred deeper, meaningful stories. But she'd seen a lot of magazine photos of him, plus interviews on a couple of morning shows. Enough to be prepared for Johnnie Irish's celebrity arrogance and celebrity good looks. She was even prepared in case he decided to turn his lady-killer charm in her direction—not that she thought he would. She wasn't his type. She was too flat, too straight up and down. Too plain.

From interviews she knew his voice would be deep and bluesy, with just a hint of a drawl left over from his Hope, Texas, days. She knew that his body and face would be fascinatingly perfect. Well, not mannequin perfect, or classically perfect. No, not classical. But then classical didn't make a woman's pulse quicken. Dangerous. Dangerous was what made a woman's pulse quicken.

From a certain angle, his nose appeared a little crooked, most likely broken in a fight. Beneath dark, slashing brows his eyes were as blue as the Texas sky, but not as clear. There was something in them . . . something secretive. Maybe a holding back . . . or maybe a seductive promise . . .

She'd always figured that the camera was kind to him. Some people just photographed well. Nobody could really *look* like that.

But now, as the distance closed between them, she discovered that the camera hadn't done him justice. And with dismay, she found herself falling victim to his looks just like one of her star-struck high school students. For the first time in years, she actually regretted the flatness of her chest.

He was a few yards away when her brain went comatose. She could feel her knees begin to tremble, her heart begin to pound in her ears.

And then he was there, standing in front of her, the rounded toes of his sneakers lined up opposite her leather taupe pumps. She looked up. She couldn't see his eyes through the dark sunglasses. She hated talking to someone who was wearing dark glasses. Worse yet were glasses with mirrors where all you saw was a distorted image of yourself.

As she fumbled in her mind, trying to dredge up her practiced words of greeting, her hair whipped across her mouth. She pulled back the lank strands, securing them at her neck with one hand. "I'm Maggie Mayfield. Welcome to Hope!" How eloquent. And it really wasn't Hope at all. They were ten miles from Hope.

"Hope." He braced his hands on his hips and did a slow pan of the stark, desert landscape. Nothing but sand and sky, scrub pine and yucca . . . and goatheads that stuck to the soles of your shoes. He rocked on his heels. "A nothing town in the middle of one giant litterbox."

What a perfectly horrid thing to say. Not exactly the words she'd expected. Certainly not the words she'd relate to the *Hope Chronicle* when they interviewed her tomorrow. But his opening comment had been good for one thing. Her knees stopped knocking and the roaring in her head ceased. Her brief star-struck moment was over. And now that her eyes were no longer clouded, she could see that Johnnie Irish was a little lax in the grooming department. What she had at first mistaken as carefully cultivated stubble was actually no more than wino neglect. And sure it was windy, but his hair looked as if he'd roared in on a Harley. And was that alcohol she smelled? Was the star of their homecoming parade drunk?

Maggie wasn't a native of Hope. She and her husband, Steven, had moved there because of his emphysema, but Maggie had quickly grown fond of the little town. Even after Steven's death she had stayed on. And now she couldn't help but jump to Hope's defense. "How can you talk that way about a town that helped shape who you've become?"

He shoved his hands into the front pockets of his jeans and looked down the highway that led to Hope, Texas. "That's why I *can* talk," he mumbled, more to himself than to her . . . or maybe he was speaking to the town itself. "I've got a right."

She didn't understand. Once again she thought about all the excited, expectant people waiting along Main Street. She thought about their months of preparation and how the whole town had gotten into the spirit of things. She thought about the huge banners draped across the street: HOPE WELCOMES JOHNNIE IRISH. JOHNNIE IRISH DAY. WELCOME HOME, JOHNNIE IRISH.

What a slap in the face.

People had come hours early just to get a good spot. At this very moment they were standing near curbs, waiting, camera in one hand, the colorful confetti they'd spent late-night hours shredding and cutting in the other.

They were waiting to welcome home a hero, not some over-grown brat hurling out insults instead of smiles.

"This whole thing will take an hour, tops," she told him, her voice loud and clear. "All you have to do is wave and smile. When the parade is over, we'll put you in a car and whisk you back to the plane."

He moved past her, reaching for the driver's door. "Okay, then. Let's go do it."

"Oh no you don't." She cut in front of him, guarding Cora Stevenson's classic Caddy. "I drive," she said, her gaze never wavering from his dark glasses.

She had the feeling that the eyes behind them were scanning her quite thoroughly. She didn't like the sensation. But she was glad she hadn't given in to the urge to conceal her nose freckles with makeup, or have her hair done. She certainly didn't want him to get the wrong idea and think she'd taken any extra care over her appearance because of him.

"I don't remember you," he said with childlike bluntness. "You from Hope?"

"I moved here a few years ago. But even if I'd always lived here, I doubt you would have remembered me. I'm sure we would have run in different circles."

One side of his sensual mouth turned up and he nodded slightly, as if agreeing. He took off his glasses, and now she could see why he'd chosen to wear the dark lenses in the first place: to hide the condition of his eyes—which a generous dose of red-chasing eyedrops wouldn't begin to cure. She thought of an apt description for the *Chronicle*. *The bright red of his jacket perfectly matched his eyes.*

And yet her sarcasm was tempered with something else—irritation, possibly. What made a person so self-destructive? Did he think so little of himself? Or was he just too caught up in the fast lane to stop?

"I know how we can settle this," he said. "We'll do the rock, paper, scissors thing. You win—you drive. I win—I drive. Ready? One, two—"

She just stood there, staring at him.

"Come on," he coaxed, holding out a fist between them. "You know how to play, don't you?"

"Of course I do." This was too ridiculous.

"One—"

Grudgingly she put her fist beside his.

He smiled. "Two. Three!"

His fist remained closed, hers open. He was rock, she was paper.

He flashed her another ornery grin and shrugged. "That crazy paper."

"Yeah," she agreed a little feebly, feeling somewhat bemused. "That crazy paper."

She wasn't really conscious of movement, but suddenly she was sliding behind the Cadillac's huge steering wheel. She started the engine, then maneuvered the boat of a car onto the deserted highway, cringing when the rear tires squealed as they made contact with pavement. It wasn't her fault. She wasn't used to driving anything with power, and she preferred it that way. Right now she longed for the familiarity of her Volkswagen Beetle.

Her passenger let out a taunting laugh. "Sure you don't want me to drive?"

"No thanks. I want to live long enough to spot Elvis working at the local A&W."

He laughed again. Who was the comedian here anyway? And what had gotten into her? She was never sarcastic.

He leaned forward and flipped on the radio, spinning the dial through several stations until he came to one he was apparently searching for. Then he settled back in the seat while rock music vibrated in the dashboard and the wild wind whipped his hair about his head. His right elbow was resting on the window frame while his hand weaved up and down, fingers pointing into the wind, riding the air currents.

"Who took the horny toad queen this year?" he yelled over the noise of the wind and the radio.

She had no answer for that, so she pretended not to hear him. Instead, she kept her eyes focused on the water mirages crawling across the pavement in front of them.

"Becky May was so honored, last I knew," he informed her. "It was actually a toss-up between her and Selma Johnson. They both spent quite a bit of their senior year on their backs."

He was more incorrigible than any of her students.

"Craig Ferguson still live around here?"

Something she could answer. "He's a car salesman at the Chevrolet dealership."

"No kidding? I always figured he'd end up discovering a cure for the common cold or something. Don't get me wrong. Craig was an okay guy. Kind of a pencil neck, but okay. Now, his old man was another story altogether." A pause. For effect? "Kicked me out of Hope High."

"What a surprise," Maggie drawled.

"He still principal?"

"Yes."

"The world keeps turning, but old Hopeless just stays the same."

"Sometimes it's all right to stay the same. Why change a good thing?"

He quit playing with the wind and turned toward her, his left arm draped across the back of the seat. "Humans need variety or else their brains stagnate. What do you do for excitement? For a buzz?"

She could tell him that she liked to play piano in a big empty room. She liked sharing quiet conversation with her friend Karen, and playing softball with Karen and her three kids. But those were joys, not the thrill-seeking he was talking about. "I don't feel the need for a buzz," she said. "I'm content."

"You're stagnant."

It was pointless. He was too mixed-up to understand, and that made her feel a little sorry for him.

They stopped at the edge of town so he could take his place on the car body, just in front of the trunk, his feet on the back-seat.

"Smile and wave," Maggie told him. "That's all you have to do."

He smiled and waved, demonstrating his remarkable skill. At that moment she could easily understand how he'd managed to charm the pants off so many women. Lucky for her, she was immune to that sort of thing. Lucky for her that she'd never been attracted to his type.

She put the car in gear. In another hour, she promised herself, this would all be over.

They had decided to put their town star near the middle of the parade, behind the Hope High marching band and directly in front of cute-as-a-button Susie Mapes and her twirling baton.

Getting into place was only a matter of edging into the opening that had been left for them. Maggie had the Cadillac in line just minutes before the police siren wailed, announcing the start of the parade.

She let out a pent-up breath. Everything was going like clock-work.

The band, comprised of horns and drums, played a most peculiar rendition of "Hey Jude," then went on to "You Are the Sunshine of My Life." The band instructor was new to Hope High, and it was her belief that the kids were happier playing golden-oldie Top Forty tunes. The problem was that Top Forty didn't always translate well to horns and drums.

The parade went smoothly, with waving and clapping and much confetti-tossing. Occasionally Maggie would glance over her shoulder to find her passenger behaving. He'd put his sunglasses back on and was smiling and waving, just as he'd promised.

They were almost to the halfway point—Clark Drugstore—when from the vicinity of the backseat and very near her right ear came the metallic sound of a pop top being pulled open, followed by a suspicious hissing fizz.

She looked over her shoulder. Johnnie Irish had his head tilted back, elbow high, guzzling a beer.

What happened next was strictly reflex. Maggie forgot all about the manual transmission. She slammed on the brakes. The car shuddered, bucked, and died. Johnnie Irish let out a curse. His hands flailed. Beer sloshed. Then he disappeared over the trunk.

Time seemed to crawl and fly at once. Maggie fumbled for the door handle, shouldered open the door, then realized the car was rolling backward. She slammed her foot down on the brake pedal, at the same time remembering to turn off the ignition and pull out the emergency brake—all the while praying that she hadn't run over Johnnie Irish.

She found him sprawled on his back, half under the car's huge chrome bumper, mouth open, eyes closed.

Out cold.

Susie Mapes was standing nearby, clutching her baton; her eyes huge, the tassels on her white boots trembling.

In the distance a few wobbly notes of "Take a Letter, Maria" could be heard drifting on the air. Then the notes died as the solo performer most likely realized something was amiss.

Maggie crouched down at Johnnie's side. He was beginning to show signs of consciousness. His eyelids fluttered. He let out a groan.

"Don't move," she told him.

The words were barely out of her mouth when he tried to lever himself up on both elbows, winced, put a hand to his head, then sank back to the ground, face pale. "You're one helluva driver, Maggie May," he gasped.

Just when she was feeling guilty, when she was feeling that this fiasco was all her fault, something beside him caught her eye.

A syringe.

Luckily her back was to the crowd that was rapidly gathering behind them. She scooped up the syringe, hiding it against her palm and wrist—not for Johnnie's sake, but the town's.

"I think you lost something." She pressed the capped and loaded syringe against his hand, which curled around it with familiarity.

"My fix," he mumbled, relief in his voice. "Thanks."

He could hardly move, but somehow—most likely from habit—he managed to pocket the needle inside his jacket.

Up until that point, in spite of everything Maggie knew about Johnnie Irish, in spite of everything he'd said and done, she had kind of liked him. But now she felt a keen sense of disappointment, and more than a little sorrow.

All her life she'd been guilty of giving people false nobilities. She foolishly tended to imagine them the way she wanted them to be, not the way they really were. And she had started to do the same with Johnnie. Because he was so good-looking, because he had charmed her with his ornery smile, she had begun to hope he was more than what he seemed. But she should have known better. Celebrities weren't like real people. Aside from the booze and drugs, acting messed them up. It made them so they couldn't tell the difference between what was real and what wasn't.

Behind her, Maggie could hear Susie, who before today had been one of Johnnie Irish's biggest fans, trying to explain what had happened. Her voice was teary and breathless and full of shocked disbelief. "He splashed beer in my hair, and he said the F word. . . ."

Maggie sat back on her heels. "I think we better have the ambulance swing by."

Above her, a banner billowed and filled with air, the enlarged letters mocking her and the town.

WELCOME HOME, JOHNNIE IRISH.

Welcome home, indeed.

On the ground, Johnnie Irish moaned and said, "I think I'm gonna puke."

Chapter 2

*T*wo hours later Johnnie walked out of Hope Medical Center with a slight concussion—which explained why he'd gotten sick— a couple of slightly bruised ribs, and no red carpet in sight. In fact, he'd guess that the town was probably organizing a lynching party about now.

His host, Maggie Mayfield, was long gone. He'd told her not to worry about hauling him around, he'd rent a car. She hadn't argued. And who could blame her? He could still see the disgust on her face when that syringe had rolled out. And since it was impossible for him to pass up an opportunity to shock, he'd played it up. There was something in him that, whenever somebody said, "Oh, you're bad," made him want to respond, "If you want bad, I'll show you bad."

Now that his moment in the sun was over, now that he was no longer the center of attention, negative or otherwise, he was beginning to wonder just what the hell had gotten into him, coming back to Hope. It had been a stupid idea. But then he'd had a lot of stupid ideas in his life. Still, he should have known better. Wasn't that what people were always telling him?

But when he'd plotted his revenge, he hadn't thought about

people like Maggie. He hadn't thought about little kids and baton twirlers. . . .

Truth was, Hope had a bad effect on him. Always had. And now that he was back, some of his bravado was fading. Some of the old feelings, the old insecurities, were creeping in, and he didn't like it. Not one bit. He didn't want to be the kid with chronic head lice wearing his classmates' hand-me-downs. He didn't even like to be reminded that such a kid had ever existed.

He shouldn't have come.

A small crowd of die-hard fans had gathered outside, and they now approached him, one teenager stepping forward with pencil and paper in his hand to ask shyly for an autograph. Quite a switch from Los Angeles, where Johnnie was used to being mobbed. Maybe it was because of what had happened this morning. Or maybe it was the town. "Reserved" was Hope's middle name. Hope Reserved Texas. Somebody—he couldn't remember who—had said you're never a real celebrity in your hometown, because people there know you for what you really are.

Maybe it was true.

Maybe the people of Hope knew about the restlessness that ate at him, that never went away. Maybe they knew that he was full of insecurities and self-doubt. But that as long as he kept moving, kept talking, kept stirring up trouble, the insecurities were covered by the noise and confusion.

When he finished signing the autographs, he headed for the rental car that had been left at the curb. A blue Chevy sports coupe.

He slid behind the wheel, started the engine, tested the gears, then pulled away from the curb with only minimal squealing.

He was anxious to be gone, but there were a few things he had to do first, a few places he had to go.

Funny, the things you forget. Like the weird layout of the town. Since Hope was perfectly flat, the streets had been gullied so when the occasional rain came, the water had someplace to go. All the streets running east and west had ditches that crossed the intersections. Driving north and south was a little like riding a weary roller coaster.

As he turned the final corner, he could see the railroad yard with its abandoned boxcars and rusty rails. It gave him a sick feeling in the pit of his stomach.

Why was he doing this to himself? Because he had to see, had to know that the house was empty. Sometimes he had dreams. . . .

He stopped the car in front of a one-story shanty—the place where he'd spent those so-called formative years. There was a "Condemned" sign in one window, the only window with any glass.

Actually the place hadn't changed all that much. The yard was bare dirt with a few crawling goatheads. Still there was the cement stoop where he'd spent cold nights curled up like a dog while his mother entertained inside. He used to watch her boyfriends come and go, praying none of them was his father, especially Brace Cahill, the town sheriff.

He could almost hear his mother's voice, screaming at him. "Don't tell him you're my kid, you hear me? Men don't want a lady with a kid. If it wasn't for you, I wouldn't be living in this dump. I'd be married to some rich man."

Johnnie had eventually gotten too big to lie on the stoop. That's when he'd taken to roaming the streets at all hours. That's when he'd started getting into trouble with the cops.

She'd been insane, his mother. As a kid, he hadn't seen it, hadn't known or understood.

What angered him was knowing that Hope had turned a blind eye on a child who had needed help, and in so doing had almost sealed his fate. But there had been one person who hadn't looked away, and he knew, without the slightest doubt, that if not for that person's encouragement he would have ended up in prison. Or dead, the way the high school principal had predicted all those years ago.

Harriet Lundy. He wondered if she was still around. She'd seemed old back then. She'd have to be ancient by now.

Afternoon sunlight poured in the picture window, spilling in dust-gathering rays to the carpeted floor. With arthritic hands, Harriet straightened the doily on the back of the recliner. Beside her, Kitty Yellow humped his back, curling around Harriet's thick black shoes.

"Do you think he'll come?" she asked the fat tabby. "I do hope he comes."

The cat looked up at her with green eyes and meowed.

Harriet's mind wasn't as good as it used to be. Sometimes she forgot things, important things. Sometimes she forgot what year it was, and the name of the president, and who wrote this particular play or that song. But she'd never forgotten Johnnie Irish. Ornery Johnnie Irish.

Time played tricks on her. Sometimes when Harriet thought about the past, it hardly seemed like the past at all, it was so vivid in her mind. Other times, she couldn't seem to recall what she had done just yesterday.

Hands braced on the arms of the rocker-recliner, she eased herself down into the chair. Then, with her toe, she pushed against the floor to start a gentle rocking. And she thought about the first time she'd seen Johnnie. . . .

It was the second week of school. Her drama class was acting scenes from *The Glass Menagerie* when Johnnie showed up in the doorway.

"I've been kicked out of algebra," he announced, his voice a challenge. Dark hair hung over angry blue eyes, and even though she was several yards away, she could smell the cigarette smoke—and very likely another kind of smoke—trapped in the fabric of his ragged jeans and stretched-out T-shirt.

"They told me to come here," he said. "Something about a creative outlet." His top lip curled.

I should have taken that job in New York, Harriet thought with dismay. She didn't know if she had the stamina to handle a boy like Johnnie. Under normal conditions . . . maybe. But she was still grieving over the death of the son she'd lost to the war.

Why have they put him in my drama class? she wondered resentfully. *Because nobody else wants him. And they knew you wouldn't argue about it.*

She'd had such high expectations for this particular class. It was the main reason she was still teaching. She'd wanted to put on one of the best play productions the community of Hope had ever seen. But now, with Johnnie Irish to turn things upside down . . .

His back was to her as he talked to a couple of other students. Her gaze fell to the toothbrush sticking out of his back pocket. That single image said everything she needed to know about Johnnie. She'd never been one to gossip, not like some of the others around her, but she'd heard rumors about the boy's mother, and if just a fraction of those rumors were true . . . well, it was very sad indeed.

Since she didn't have any more copies of *The Glass Menagerie*, she picked up her own tattered, highlighted, and well-thumbed copy. "Welcome to drama class," she told Johnnie. "We have an exciting semester planned." She handed him the play. "I'll have to order a new one for you, but until it comes you can use mine."

He took the book and held it in both hands, fingers to the spine, thumbs to the rolled edges. Then he smiled, a surprised smile, a sincere smile that lit up the blue of his eyes, as if he thought she'd done something really special.

"Thanks, Harry."

She'd been teaching so long that she thought nothing and no one could surprise her anymore. She was wrong.

She had expected Johnnie to lounge in the back of the room, hurling out sarcastic comments. Not so. He jumped into acting with an almost manic zest. He would play each part with exaggerated glee. For Laura's mother, his voice would trill higher and higher as he minced about the room in an imaginary dress. By the end of the hour, the entire class, herself included, would be weak and wilted from too much laughter.

He was a ham, but it was more than that. He was a ham with real talent. He was a natural mimic, and he had a remarkable memory. He could memorize entire scenes with little or no effort.

He was incorrigible. He was delightful. He was a breath of fresh air to her tired, grief-stricken soul. . . .

A knock sounded on the door. For one confused moment, Harriet thought it was the principal stopping by her classroom, or a student delivering a message from the office. But then she remembered she was home, not her comfortable home at the edge of town, but the small house her son had talked her into buying at the same time he'd convinced her to sell the old property. She remembered that she hadn't taught in years and years. And she remembered that Johnnie Irish was back in town.

The front door opened a crack and a voice, with achingly familiar irreverence, said, "Harry?"

Years fell away.

Harriet put a trembling hand to her breast, then to her head, to make sure her hair was in place. She was pushing herself to her feet when the door opened all the way.

He came in as he'd always come in, like a whirling dervish. But when he put his arms around her to give her a hug, he was careful of her old bones, and she was grateful for that.

She pulled back, an arm's length away, so she could get a good look at him. He wasn't a gangling teenager anymore, dressed in clothes that were dirty and ill-fitting. His long arms and long legs had filled out. But those startling blue eyes could belong to only one person.

She realized she was crying and reached up her sleeve for her hankie.

"Ah, Harry. Don't cry. I didn't come here to upset you."

"I'm not upset. I'm happy." She lifted her bifocals, wiped her eyes, and tucked the handkerchief away. "I'm so proud of you. So incredibly proud. I've seen every single one of your movies."

But even though he was a wonderful actor, she'd sensed that he was holding back. He wasn't giving a hundred percent. The opposite of comedy was tragedy, and she knew he could play them both equally well if only he would try. But that would mean reaching inside himself. It would mean exposing his soul to the public, and maybe he wasn't ready for that. Maybe he never would be. How could he reveal to others something he wouldn't even reveal to himself?

Years ago Harriet had come to understand why Johnnie was such a study in contrasts. Thanks to his mother, he had no sense of self-worth. In some way, making people laugh validated his existence, made him feel worthy. On the other hand, he liked to thumb his nose at the very same people, just to prove that he didn't need anybody.

It made her sad to know that he was still a hurt child.

At the kitchen table they talked and drank coffee.

"Remember that time Catfish fell off the stage and into the orchestra pit?" Johnnie asked, laughing.

Harriet tried to remember, but couldn't. She shook her head. "My memory's not as good as it used to be."

"Aw, come on. I bet you can still remember every line from every play you ever directed. I can still see you standing in the wings, your lips moving through the whole production." He drummed his fingers on the table and cast his eyes toward the ceiling. "Let me see, how about this."

He quoted some lines from *Our Town*, lines long familiar. Like an old song, or the tissue-wrapped scent of a brittle, pressed rose, the words spun her back to a happier time, a less lonely time, a time when old age happened to other people.

Chapter 3

*S*afe in her own living room, Maggie Mayfield kicked off her shoes, then reached under the hem of her red knit skirt, peeled off her panty hose, and tossed them to the floor. That accomplished, she collapsed into an overstuffed chair, arms and legs sprawled.

Thank God it was over.

Except for the occasional flutter of wayward confetti, all signs of the parade were gone. Banners had been torn down and stuffed into black plastic trash bags. Fire trucks were back in their garages. Streets that had been shoulder-to-shoulder people were empty. After months of preparation, the much awaited Hope homecoming parade was over, leaving an unpleasant taste in everyone's mouth.

She'd told them.

Hadn't she told them?

Inviting Johnnie Irish is a bad idea. That's what she'd said. But she wasn't going to gloat about being right. She wished she'd been wrong. She wished the parade had been a wonderful success. She wished that afterward Johnnie Irish had stood around signing autographs and making polite conversation. It would have been nice. Nice, but totally unrealistic.

Next year, if the parade committee still felt the need to sport a local hero, they should invite Mrs. Rutledge, who not only wrote but spoke in iambic pentameter. So far, she'd had three poetry journals—she always called them journals—printed locally. She hauled the books—journals—around in the back of her Rambler station wagon, hawking them at every function she could find. Not very exciting, but as far as Maggie knew, Mrs. Rutledge didn't guzzle and regurgitate beer in public.

Or what about that nice Mr. Pease? The man who'd invented some kind of pig castra—

A knock sounded at the door, four short syllables.

Maggie didn't want to have to talk to anybody. She was tired of trying to explain the workings of the celebrity mind to elderly women and outraged parents of small children. Maybe flying makes him sick, she'd told them. Maybe he came down with a particularly fast-acting virus. . . .

Rap, rap, rap, rap.

She sighed and shoved herself out of her chair, crossed the room, and opened the door.

When she saw who it was, she practically screamed and slammed the door. Instead, she kept a firm grip on the knob and planted herself in the opening.

Johnnie Irish was leaning against the porch rail with all the posturing of a street-smart kid. His hands were buried in the front pockets of his faded jeans. His shoulders, still clad in the baseball jacket, were hunched against some imaginary chill, or possibly the censure of the town. Eyes no longer hidden by dark glasses traveled over her, taking in her messy hair, wrinkled dress, and bare, size-eight feet.

She put one foot on top of the other in an attempt to make them look smaller. Then she shifted back to her previous position with both feet flat on the floor, telling herself she didn't care what Johnnie thought of her foot size.

He shoved his hip away from the railing. "Look, I—" His eyes shifted to the room behind her as he silently asked to be invited inside.

She chose to ignore his body language.

"Mind if I come in?"

Unconsciously she closed the door a little more while keeping herself wedged in the narrow opening. "Sorry. I'm fresh out of beer."

He laughed and nodded, apparently at her on-target barb. "That's okay. I make it a point to never drink after twelve noon." He smiled, and his thick black eyebrows lifted, giving him a kind of puppyish charm.

Maggie smiled—how could she help it? She liked puppies. She opened the door and stepped back.

He came in on springy sneakers. As he brushed past her, she could feel the nervous energy radiating from him, and she wondered at the wisdom of letting him inside. Was he high? Had he recently shot up the dope that had fallen from his pocket?

He browsed her living room like an appraiser or some psychic looking for power-emanating objects. He examined things with curious eyes and felt things with the careful touch of a blind person. Was he just rude? she wondered. Or too inexperienced with the real world to know that his actions reflected an amazing lack of manners?

She watched as he picked up a piece of pottery and turned it in his hand. "You make this?" he asked.

"Yes." How had he guessed?

He slid a well-shaped finger along the lip, as if memorizing the texture of the baked clay. She noted that his skin was curiously pale for a Californian. Did he come out only at night?

"Pottery's pretty cool," he said. "I tried to throw a pot once, but I got off center and the clay went zinging across the room."

If today's fiasco was any indication, he was off center quite frequently. "Using the wheel takes a lot of practice," she said.

He put the pottery back and moved on to an arrangement of framed pictures, all of people who were no longer in her life. There were a couple of photos of her parents, one of which had been taken on their fortieth anniversary. These he didn't touch, as if instinctively knowing they were special.

"I'm sorry about what happened today," he said. For all his earlier boldness, he kept his eyes focused on the pictures. "I never meant to screw up the parade." He shrugged. "Well, I meant to screw it up, but not quite so much."

His gaze moved past the photos of her parents to stop on a

small gold-framed one of Maggie and her husband. They had been playing tag football on his mother's lawn in Ohio. Steven had tackled her, rolling her to the ground, and his brother, Elliot, had caught the moment on film. It was a laughing, joyous picture, full of life.

"Your husband?" Johnnie asked, his eyes going from the picture to her bare ring finger.

"Yes."

He scanned the room, eyes tracking over last week's laundry, stacks of library books, partially graded papers, sheet music, and the hastily discarded panty hose, as if trying to find her missing husband somewhere in the mess.

Maggie had been through this kind of thing before. So much, in fact, that her response now seemed a little like the lines of a play that had been recited too many times. It no longer hurt to tell people that Steven was dead. In some strange way, as if by giving voice to her loss, it made it easier to deal with. "My husband died three years ago," she explained.

Johnnie's bland expression changed. It wasn't embarrassment or awkwardness she now read, not the things she was used to seeing in people's faces. This was more like an inexplicable flash of comprehension, then it was gone as quickly as it had come.

He turned away and began scrutinizing things again. Her books, and all the little knickknacks that were more than knickknacks because they were gifts her students had given her over the years.

"You're a teacher," he stated.

"Yes."

His long fingers reverently brushed across the leather spines of several volumes of plays. Thornton Wilder . . . Arthur Miller . . . Tennessee Williams. "Drama?"

"Yes."

"Then you took Harriet Lundy's place."

"Not actually. There was a Mr. Samuels before me." Harriet Lundy was almost a living legend. No one could take her place. Some people said she could have directed in New York, but had chosen to stay in Hope, teaching high school. "Did you have Harriet for a teacher?" Maggie asked. She was having a hard time visualizing Johnnie as a student in their school system.

"Yeah. My senior year. She was great. Better than great."

He turned back to the shelf. This time he pulled out a narrow softbound book. He held it up, eyebrows raised in question. "Sex education?"

She wanted to jerk the book from his hand, but she managed to refrain from doing anything so immature. "Something else I teach."

He laughed. "Bet you end up with some horny guys."

"They take it pretty seriously."

He slid the book back into place, then looked at his watch.

She was surprised that he wore one. He didn't seem like the type to pay much attention to a schedule.

"It's almost one o'clock," he said. "What do you say I buy you some lunch?"

It was the last thing she'd expected. Possibly the last thing she wanted. She had never been one to live her life afraid of what others might say or think, but maybe it was time to start. She'd seen Johnnie's performance at the parade. What would he do in a restaurant? Stick straws up his nose and tap-dance on the table?

"Thanks, but . . . I don't think so."

Electric blue eyes sized her up. "You don't like me, do you?"

With the exception of her gynecologist, she'd never met anyone so blunt. It made things very awkward. "I don't even know you."

"Doesn't matter. You've already formulated an opinion. You probably hated me before I ever stepped out of the plane this morning. Isn't that right?"

There was no need for words. Her answer was on her face.

"You thought, There he is, a dopehead who screws a new chick every night. Who is self-centered and egotistical and spoiled all the way through. Well, I want you to know something." He pointed a finger at her. "I don't owe this town a thing. You know why? Because Hope, Texas, never did jack shit for me. I resent this place for not only turning a blind eye but for telling me I was a loser before I ever had a chance to find out who I was."

He stopped, as if surprised by his own outburst. He let out a frustrated breath and swung away. "What am I talking to you for? Why the hell did I even come here?" But instead of leaving, he dropped to the couch.

Minutes ago he'd been keyed up and edgy. Now his high energy level had suddenly evaporated. He looked spent, incredibly fatigued. A fine sheen of perspiration covered his face. His skin was bloodless. His pale hands trembled.

Withdrawal?

He attempted to shove himself up from the couch, failed, then tried again. This time he made it. He stood there for a couple of seconds, swaying. Then he crumpled to the floor.

Maggie was near enough to keep his head from hitting anything as he went down, pulling her with him.

Oh God! He was so white, she thought, kneeling beside him as he lay sprawled on his back. She was trying to gather her thoughts enough to figure out what to do when, to her intense relief, he seemed to come around a little.

With closed eyes, one of his hands groped blindly inside his jacket, fumbling at his shirt pocket.

What was he searching for? Cocaine? Heroine?

"Sugar," he whispered. "Need sugar. . . ."

That's when it hit her. He was diabetic. The needle that had fallen from his pocket hadn't been filled with cocaine, but insulin. She had students who were diabetic and she knew how important it was to eat the right food at exactly the right time. Johnnie hadn't eaten lunch and now he was going into insulin shock.

Oh God.

She jumped to her feet and ran to the kitchen. She yanked open the cupboard door and pulled out the sugar canister.

Empty.

She jerked open the junk drawer. Her fingers scrambled frantically across coupons, clothespins, a screwdriver, pliers, and twist ties to finally close around a half-eaten roll of Lifesavers.

Heartbeats later she was back at Johnnie's side, candy in hand.

Lemon.

Hard floor under his back.

His entire body was wet, soaked with a cold sweat.

Someone was talking to him while rubbing something hard and lemon-flavored across his lips.

Candy. Sugar.

And Maggie Mayfield.

Grounded now, Johnnie felt a little relieved. It was always a relief when the thing you most dread finally happened. When it was finally over.

He tried to open his eyes, but it was too much of an effort. He didn't want anybody feeding him like a baby, so he closed his teeth over the piece of candy, managing to shove the feeding fingers away at the same time. He crunched, swallowed, then waited for the sugar to counteract the insulin.

In another minute he was able to open his eyes.

This morning, when she'd picked him up at the airstrip, Maggie Mayfield's eyes had been almost gold. Now, in the shadows cast by walls, they were amber.

And scared. Scared to death.

His gaze dropped to the tattered roll in her hand. "Guess that's why they call 'em Lifesavers," he whispered weakly, managing a feeble smile.

She didn't smile back. Too scared. It probably wasn't every day somebody almost went comatose in her living room. He thought about the stuff he'd told her just before he'd blacked out. What the hell had gotten into him? It wasn't like him to talk about his childhood like that. But sometimes a high level of insulin sent his head to a weird place.

"That was just erotic as hell," he told her, relieved that his voice sounded stronger. He wanted to lighten things up and coax a smile from her.

"Why didn't you tell me you were diabetic?" she asked.

"Bad for my bad-ass image."

She rolled her eyes and let out an exasperated breath—or was it relief? "You're a real brat, you know it?"

"Thank you," he said, with just the right amount of humility. He was glad to see her reacting again.

It had to be some kind of record, he decided. Passing out twice in the same day. Of course the first one really didn't count. He hadn't passed out all by himself. It had something to do with his head making contact with concrete.

He should get up and out of this poor woman's life, but he was afraid he might not be able to walk very far. And if he did make it to the car, he sure as hell wouldn't be able to drive, not until he had something to eat. "Got any food in this joint?" he asked.

She was already moving. "Stay right there and I'll get you a sandwich and some milk."

She must have been aware of the importance of his getting food rapidly, because in hardly more than a minute she was back, putting a plate and glass of milk on the corner of the coffee table. He figured she probably had some students with diabetes. Too many kids had it.

He didn't even attempt to drag himself onto the couch. Instead, he sat cross-legged on the floor while she sat across from him in the lounger, her feet tucked under her, watching every move he made.

He lifted the sandwich to his mouth, annoyed to see that his hand trembled. Had she caught that? Probably.

He concentrated on getting some of the sandwich down, took a drink of milk, then wiped his upper lip. "Don't worry. I'm not going to slip away again," he assured her. "Twice in one day's my limit. In fact, once a day is rare. This has only happened to me a couple of times, and both those times people just figured I'd overdosed." He laughed and she winced, reminding him that she'd assumed the same thing.

"Your color is . . ." He watched as she searched for a polite description. ". . . better," she finally said.

He knew his color was never good. Even though he lived in Los Angeles, it was usually the moon he saw and not the sun.

He took another bite of sandwich, feeling better by the minute, more like his old self, enough to start taking more alert note of his surroundings.

She had a great body, he decided. Not curves and softness, but streamlined, like an athlete. "You a runner?" he asked around a mouthful of bread and bologna and salad dressing. He would have preferred ketchup, but he wasn't going to complain.

"A runner?" She shook her head. "Why would you think that?"

"You're kinda built like one. Compact. Those long legs . . ."

She actually looked uncomfortable. He hadn't meant to embarrass her, but he couldn't quit staring. He was used to all sorts of women and he knew Maggie probably wouldn't be considered beautiful by some people's standards, but she had the kind of creamy skin the camera loved. And those eyes. Tranquil and wise, maybe too wise. She'd suffered in her life, and he suddenly realized he didn't like thinking about her suffering.

He wondered how it was for her, a widow, living in a little dogpatch of a town, far from anyplace and anywhere. How did she stand it? Why did she stay? He'd go nuts.

When he finished his sandwich, he thanked her and got up to leave.

"You probably won't believe this, but I *am* sorry about the parade." He meant it. He knew the apology didn't fit his usual "now I need your approval, now I don't" pattern of behavior. He normally didn't exit a scene caring whether someone liked him or not. That was reserved for the first and second acts. But he wanted Maggie May to like him, vaguely concluding that it was because she was no threat to him since he was never going to see her again.

"That's okay." She waved his words away. "It'll give the town something to talk about for the next couple of weeks. And the story will get more outrageous and exciting with each telling."

"Still hate me?" he asked.

"I never hated you."

"Still mad at me, then?"

She shook her head and smiled. She had a great smile.

"Was it better than running into Elvis at the A&W?"

She laughed. "Better than Elvis."

She had a great laugh, an unrestrained laugh that was kind of a surprised whoop. He collected laughs. He would remember hers.

He left, pausing long enough to cast a glance over his shoulder as he headed down the narrow sidewalk. She was leaning in the doorway, watching him go. She waved, and he waved back, feeling a bit of regret because he wouldn't ever see her again. He wouldn't be coming back here, and she probably wouldn't be leaving.

He drove to the airstrip and was boarding the plane when something made him pause and turn. Before him was nothing but sand and sky. The vastness of it caused a constriction of wonder to tighten in his chest. He'd forgotten how big the desert was, how blue and endless its sky.

When he was younger, he'd liked poetry. For a time he'd even kept a tattered red notebook full of scribbles that he'd kept hidden in an abandoned house next door. One day he accidentally forgot and left the book on the floor next to his bed. After school he'd come home to find his mother and Brace Cahill reading it out loud, sloshing beer on the printed pages and laughing themselves breathless over words that had been deep and meaningful to him. Words about the desert and the sky. About places far away.

That night he'd crawled into the bedroom closet, unscrewed the wooden panel near the floor, and stuffed the notebook in with the bathroom pipes that ran inside the wall. He never touched the notebook again. And since then he'd never read or written any poetry.

The unpleasant memory reminded him that he was in a hurry, reminded him that he was glad to be leaving his hometown behind.

Chapter 4

$\mathcal{E}$xcept for receiving a potted catalpa tree, Maggie didn't hear from Johnnie Irish again. Not that she'd expected to.

But to her self-disgust, she couldn't quit thinking about him. Often, before she was aware of the direction of her thoughts, she would visualize him as he'd looked the day he'd come to Hope, the same vignettes playing over and over in her mind. In one, she saw him in profile, sitting in the passenger seat of Cora's Cadillac, his hair whipping about his head, one hand riding the wind. In another, she would see him sprawled on his back on her floor, his face pale in contrast to the darkness of his hair. And she would recall the way his lips had felt against her fingertips as she'd brushed the sugared candy across them. Soft. Warm.

One night she gave in and rented a Johnnie Irish movie. The videotape jacket proclaimed it to be the screwball comedy of the year, but after watching it Maggie felt a keen sense of disappointment. Not in the movie—it had been wonderful, Johnnie had been wonderful—but toward whoever had planned its marketing.

They just hadn't gotten it. They hadn't seen beyond the simple plot. They hadn't seen that the movie was painted in several subtle layers. They hadn't seen beyond Johnnie's good looks; they hadn't seen that he could act, *really* act.

She was surprised to find that his humor wasn't so much verbal as physical, more like Chaplin. It was done with facial expressions and body language. A cocked eyebrow, the way he moved. His timing was perfect, his movements precise and smooth as a ballet dancer's, too graceful to be considered slapstick.

She was reluctantly impressed.

But it didn't last. Johnnie Irish suddenly made the cover of almost every tabloid in the country. She couldn't go through a checkout lane without coming face-to-face with him. He was still living in the fast lane, either hosting or attending wild parties, a different woman on his arm every week. One article told about how he'd driven a car into a motel swimming pool, another how he'd been carried out of a bar.

Not the type of person to dwell on. Certainly not a person to moon over like some lovesick teen.

She must forget about him.

Time passed. Summer came and went. Then fall. The winter was mild, as winters were in Hope. Spring came again.

Yes, she must forget about him.

Total darkness.

Comforting darkness. Coaxing, warm, all-encompassing darkness.

Scuffling feet.

A random thought. *OD'd again.*

Hard floor under him. People yelling. Hands ripping open his shirt. Cold metal pressed against his naked chest.

"Clear."

A crushing, snapping, white-hot pain. Johnnie's body bucked. His lungs remembered what they were supposed to do. Air rushed in.

"Got a heartbeat."

A mask was strapped over his nose and mouth.

"Let's get him to the hospital."

Rolling. Rolling away.

• • •

When Johnnie woke up in the hospital and found out that he was still alive, his first reaction was one of disappointment. Not that he'd tried to kill himself, as everybody was probably saying. It was just that his system was delicate. It could abuse only so many substances at a time.

But it was kind of scary to think about how easily death had seduced him, how appealing it had seemed.

It was no excuse, but the last year had been a real bitch. He'd worked hard, making two movies back-to-back. The last one, *Canadian Geeks*, had been filmed in a remote region of Canada where all the equipment and crew had to be flown in. They'd lived in Quonset huts that were so cold the drinking water froze overnight.

The script had called for Johnnie to go snowshoeing wearing nothing but a pair of baggy boxer shorts—purely physical, visual comedy, something Johnnie loved doing. After ten hours, Johnnie had been borderline hypothermic, but he'd felt good about the final take. He'd always been a big fan of Charlie Chaplin, and even though he knew he could never equal the Great One's ability to project thought through facial expressions and body language, Johnnie felt he'd done a fair job.

Before the filming was over, most of the crew had come down with colds, some with pneumonia, Johnnie included. Then came time for the movie's screening.

Johnnie had never had people walk out on a screening before, so it was a new experience for him. He'd wanted to jump up and tell them to wait, the funny part was coming. They'd love the snowshoe scene, if they'd just wait. But Johnnie had managed to keep his mouth shut—thanks to his agent, Sherman, who'd had him in a strong headlock.

The show ended up being yanked before it had a chance to go national. Johnnie's first real bomb. His first experience with mass rejection. But what could people expect with a title like *Canadian Geeks*?

He quickly learned something he'd always suspected. You have a lot of friends on the way up, hardly any on the way down. And a guy could make ten fairly decent movies, but make one flop . . .

Goodbye, career. Goodbye, Hollywood.

But he didn't let it bother him for long. He got on with the business of partying too hard and sleeping too little. And making the tabloids too much.

He was seriously thinking of going to New York when a part came his way that he actually wanted. It was a comedy, but it had the potential to be a lot more. He knew, if played with just the right touch of pathos, the movie could be a classic.

He wanted the part more than he'd wanted anything in a long time. But in the end it went to a younger guy. One, they said, who had more screen appeal, more comedic appeal. One who didn't have a flop behind him. Because in Hollywood a guy was only as good as his last movie.

Back home in the Hollywood Hills, Johnnie tossed the dog-eared screenplay in the trash. He hadn't really wanted the part anyway.

From downstairs he could hear rock music, could feel its vibration under his bare feet. People came and went at his place. Most of the status seekers were long gone, but the die-hard moochers had remained.

Johnnie decided he'd join them. He went downstairs, cranked up the stereo even louder, and shouted, "Let's party!"

Everything after that was kind of a blur. At one point some cops stopped by and told him to turn down the music, explaining that they'd had several complaints from neighbors. Johnnie laughed and invited the boys in blue inside, but they weren't amused. They became authoritarian and Johnnie got mad. He called them a couple of choice names and the next thing he knew he was being hauled down to the police station.

Certainly not his first time in jail. Not that it ever got any easier. A cage was a cage. Restraint was restraint.

The town of Hope had introduced him to his first jail cell. At sixteen he'd been caught sleeping in the park and had been hauled in for breaking curfew.

After that first visit it just kind of became a habit. The old "if you want bad, I'll give you bad" thing. He'd ended up being arrested for several misdemeanors, from loitering to consumption of alcohol by a minor. By age eighteen he had all the graffiti memorized, and had added a few choice words of his own.

But it had been years since he'd heard that final click of the cell door. And this time it sounded a little too much like a gun's hammer falling into place. Panic set in. Plus an overpowering feeling of suffocation.

A short time later his system shut down.

Luckily Sherman had insisted upon being allowed inside the cell to see him. Sherman, for all his apparent easygoing ways, could be extremely persuasive when he set his mind to it. Once inside, Sherman had found Johnnie on the floor, with hardly a pulse.

Now here he was, hooked up to IVs, his blood monitored every hour in order to keep his insulin and mineral levels fine-tuned. He'd already gotten the obligatory lecture from his doctor. About how lucky he was to be alive, and how he'd better start learning to discipline his life. Either that or die.

A knock sounded on the door and Sherman stepped into the room. In one hand was his usual diet soda, in the other a bag of doughnut holes. He started to offer the bag to Johnnie, remembered he couldn't have any, and offered the diet cola instead. Johnnie shook his head.

"You look a little better than you did the other night," Sherman said. "You're breathing anyway. Sorry, but the newspapers got their hands on the story. I tried to keep it from them, but there were too many people involved. I've seen interviews with the ambulance driver and the emergency room staff. Hell, I've even seen an interview with the night janitor."

"Forget it, Sherm," Johnnie said, trying to act as though bad press didn't bother him.

Sherman grabbed the remote control and plopped down on the foot of the bed. "What's on the tube?" He flipped through a series of stations, pausing now and then to throw in a comment. "Jake Fisher—he was great in that movie, wasn't he?" He clicked the remote, this time pausing when he came to the face of a well-known comedy actor. "They keep trying to get him to carry his own movie. They don't understand that his comedy comes from playing off somebody else."

In a town where agents were thought of as necessary evils or beneficial parasites, Sherman broke all the stereotypes. Even though he was showing signs of middle age, Johnnie still thought he'd look more at home digging post holes on a farm than breathing west coast smog. Last year, as a joke, Sherman's kids had gotten him a T-shirt that said, "Let's do lunch." He wore it on Sunday afternoons when he was in the backyard grilling hamburgers.

Not that he wasn't a little Hollywood. Everybody in the area had at least one big secret, and Sherman was no exception. His secret was so terrible that he'd made Johnnie swear never to reveal it. The six-foot-four strapping jock cried at movies.

It didn't matter what kind of movie. Any would do. Love stories, dog stories, cop stories. He cried. If you were sitting in a theater and heard somebody honking his nose, there was a good chance the honker was Sherman.

Sherman finally exhausted the channels, flicked off the remote, and tossed it on the bedstand. "Something's gotta give," he said. "You've got to get away, that's all there is to it."

Sherman was right, but sometimes Johnnie felt as though his life were a series of false starts. All of them ending with his running to something new, something better. Sometimes he wondered what would happen if he just toughed it out. And anyway, it was easy for Sherman to give advice. He had a wife who was his best friend. He had decent kids and parents he could visit at Christmas or whenever he felt like it. He was probably the most stable, normal guy Johnnie knew.

"Where would I go?" Johnnie asked, shifting his weight, consciously making an effort to lighten his voice. He was an actor, right? "To Tibet to find my inner self?"

"I'm not kidding." Sherman ran his fingers through his straight, straggly hair.

He wasn't that much older than Johnnie, but his thinning hair was getting some gray in it, a reminder of Johnnie's own vanishing youth. Someday he'd be sitting in a retirement home, watching his old movies—if he lived that long, which he seriously doubted.

"When I saw you on the floor of that jail cell," Sherman said, shaking his head at the memory, "*my* heart almost stopped. You almost *died*, man."

What would Sherman think if Johnnie told him it wasn't dying that scared him? It was living. It was the possibility that someday someone would see behind his protective cloak of comedy and not like what was there.

"Come on," Johnnie said, deciding things were getting too deep. "You don't have the right attitude. You're supposed to take things like that in stride. You're supposed to be cool and cutthroat. Not get bent out of shape because a client OD'd."

"You're more than a client. You know that."

Johnnie wanted to believe him, but nobody could be sure about anybody in this business. He locked his hands under his head and stared up at the tiled ceiling. If Sherman was on the level, then the guy had left himself open for a ton of grief. The tough preyed on the weak. That's just the way it was. "Do you ever think that maybe we're not cut out for this?" Johnnie asked.

"I'm cut out for it, but I damn well wonder about you," Sherman said. "My mom and dad busted their butts farming. They looked sixty when they were forty. There's no way I'm doing that."

It wasn't like them to talk about feelings, but Johnnie guessed when you share a life-and-death experience with someone, when that someone was responsible for saving your life, it changed the rules. "Do you ever miss the farm?" he asked.

"You know what I miss the most? Being able to go to sleep at night with the doors unlocked. That's what I miss. And sometimes when I'm on the freeway during rush hour I wonder what the hell I'm doing there. Then I remember how tough my folks had it and it all makes sense again."

They joked about what they'd both be doing if they weren't in the movie business. Johnnie told him about his prison theory.

Sherman said he'd be a carhop at a park-and-eat, or maybe the guy who sifted the cigarette butts out of sand ashtrays.

"I shouldn't have given you that script," Sherman said, finally steering things back to the problem at hand. "But it was *so perfect*. I couldn't see anybody but you playing the lead. I still can't."

Johnnie waved his words away. "I didn't give a rip about that part."

It was a lie and they both knew it.

"What really gets me is knowing what a botch Peterson will make of it," Sherman said. "He'll play it straight slapstick. The show will come out, do halfway decent, then it will be gone and forgotten. Makes me sick. We had a perfect little classic right there in our hands."

"Forget about it, Sherman. Something else will come along."

But Johnnie wasn't sure. And he knew Sherman wasn't sure. It had been a part in a million. There would be other parts, but it would be rare to find one with the same kind of spark, the same kind of magic.

"I swore I wouldn't bring up the screenplay. I came here to try to talk you into taking some time off." Sherman rubbed the back of his neck and avoided eye contact. "Maybe you could look up that therapist you went to a few years back."

"Forget it." Johnnie didn't believe in psychoanalysis, at least not for himself. He'd never have gone to a therapist in the first place if one of his producers hadn't insisted. What a waste.

What good did it do to dwell on the past? What good did it do to cry over things that had already happened? That you couldn't do anything about? It smacked of self-pity. And he didn't feel sorry for himself. Like old Abe said, a man was happy as he made up his mind to be.

"No shrink," he told Sherman.

"Okay, then at least take some time off. Disappear for a while. Give people a chance to forget about the last movie, and about what happened the other night."

Johnnie had to admit it sounded good. God, but he was tired. Weary of the whole game. He didn't feel like facing anybody. It wasn't really running away if you came back, he reasoned. And it would be good for him to breathe some pure air for a change, and see clear sky.

But where would he go to find that clear sky?

Unharmonious notes from the ancient upright echoed through the Hope opera house, jarring Maggie all the way to her dental fillings.

It was the first day of play rehearsal and things weren't going well. Disaster about summed it up. Just days earlier Maggie's piano player had fallen down and broken both her wrists, so Maggie had been forced to recruit Mrs. Malcolm. If only she'd known that Mrs. Malcolm was fast on her way to total deafness. The poor woman was always several notes ahead of or behind the children—when she was playing the same song at all.

While Mrs. Malcolm beat out an awkward, unmetered tune, Maggie faced the stage, almost shouting the song to the children, trying to get them to sing in unison in spite of Mrs. Malcolm. They snarled the words along with her, reminding her more of the munchkins from the Lollipop Guild in *The Wizard of Oz* than angelic children.

She was about to cry uncle when suddenly the music actually began to sound like music. Somehow the kids and Mrs. Malcolm had finally bonded, they were in sync, they were actually singing and playing the same notes at the same time.

When the song was over, Maggie turned to give the woman some well-deserved praise. Her breath caught. Her smile froze.

Sitting beside a relieved-looking Mrs. Malcolm was Johnnie Irish.

His hair was still shaggy and long and as dark as she remembered. He still made her heart beat in that ridiculous schoolgirl way.

Here he was, back in Hope. Or Hopeless, as he had called it. *Why?*

"What's the matter?" he asked with exaggerated innocence. He stood, revealing a Charlie Chaplin T-shirt and faded jeans.

"Haven't you ever heard anybody play by ear before?" He bent at the waist, then proceeded to bang the side of his head against the piano keys.

The children onstage collapsed with laughter. The ones waiting their turn in the front row doubled over in their seats and clutched their stomachs.

Johnnie's comedy routine was brief, but not brief enough. By the time he stopped, Mrs. Malcolm was already heading for the door.

Without looking back, she waved a hand in the air. "I'm going home to watch Oprah!"

In her desperation to stop the woman, Maggie caught her foot on a wooden folding chair, dragging it across the floor with her. "Mrs. Malcolm!" Piano players were like gold. "Mrs. Malcolm!"

But Mrs. Malcolm didn't hear her. The door opened and closed. Mrs. Malcolm was gone.

Maggie swung back to Johnnie. "Now look what you've done!"

She motioned toward the back door. "You don't know how hard it was to get her here in the first place."

Johnnie stood watching her, not looking the least upset. Of course he wasn't. What did this have to do with him? What did he have to lose? Nothing! And why did he have to create chaos wherever he went?

"Don't worry." He locked the fingers of both hands, stretched out his arms, and popped his knuckles. "I'll play."

"You?" He had to be kidding.

"Sure."

"Oh yeah, maybe today. But what about tomorrow and the next day? What about a month from now?"

Her mind jumped back to plan A, the one she'd formulated before finding Mrs. Malcolm. Maggie would have to play piano herself, plus direct.

Oh Lord.

"I'll play for as long as you need me. Every day if you want."

Sure, she thought, not believing him for a second. She let out a breath and pulled back her hair from her forehead . . . and realized that the kids' attention was riveted on them, watching everything that was going on. Maggie got a grip on herself. "Okay. Since you chased Mrs. Malcolm away, I'd say the least you can do is get us through the rest of this rehearsal."

"The very least."

He took a seat at the piano, flipping back imaginary tails. With his back rigid, he straightened the sheet music, flexed his fingers . . . then jumped to his feet and broke into a raucous impersonation of Jerry Lee Lewis, pounding the keys until the piano rocked, shaking his head until his hair hung over his eyes.

Pandemonium was the word of the moment. The children, who had only just collected themselves, collapsed like limp dolls, holding their stomachs and rolling on the floor and in the aisles.

Maggie wanted to laugh. Oh, how she wanted to laugh. She finally had to look away to hide a smile, but when she turned back she was in control. Her lips formed a straight line. Her arms were crossed severely beneath her breasts.

Johnnie stopped his one-man show. He glanced over at her, then put up his hands as if to ward her off. "Okay, okay. Just breaking the ice. It'll be all business from now on. I swear."

His words brought back memories of another time when he'd promised to behave for the Hope parade. And who could forget how that had turned out? She still had nightmares about it. But she needed a piano player, and things couldn't get much worse.

In the end his playing wasn't too bad. It wasn't wonderful, but the song was recognizable, and he didn't race ahead, then slow to a crawl the way Mrs. Malcolm had done. Yes, except for the few annoying times Johnnie jumped in and tried to direct, the rest of the afternoon went pretty smoothly, all things considered.

When practice was over and the doors were locked, Johnnie glanced around the parking lot. It was deserted except for a rental car. "Need a ride?"

"No thanks. I like to walk."

"Oh, come on."

She didn't know why he was there, but her instinct for survival, her common sense, was screaming at her to stay away from him, as far away as possible.

"Thanks anyway," she said. "But I need the exercise." She started to thank him for playing piano, but decided against it. He shouldn't be thanked for creating chaos. And now she would have to get in touch with Mrs. Malcolm again and beg her to come back. Maybe if she promised to tape Oprah's show for her . . .

Johnnie was still watching her, as if unaware that it was time for them to go their own directions.

Now that they were outside in the sunlight, Maggie noticed that, if possible, he looked even more unhealthy today than he had the day of the parade. His skin was pale, almost transparent, his eyes dark. Deep inside she felt a tug of fear.

Had he been sick? Was he sick now?

"I have to go," she said, not wanting to be the one to worry about him.

He fell into step beside her. "I'll walk you home. I haven't walked anybody home in years."

She could hardly tell him no. A sidewalk was public property. And he seemed so fragile.

He smiled, and the fear she'd felt earlier intensified, radiating a little deeper.

She lived only a couple of blocks away. Maybe she walked a little faster than usual, or maybe Johnnie's light banter made the time go more quickly than it ever had before. Whatever the reason, they were soon approaching her yard.

"I see you planted the tree."

She looked to where the catalpa tree grew strong and straight. She'd never planted a tree before. It had been a new experience for her. She'd never had much luck with growing anything, so she'd been surprised and pleased when it continued to thrive. "No one's ever given me a tree," she said.

"You looked like a tree person."

He said the most surprising things.

She couldn't have said how it happened, because she could swear she hadn't invited him inside, but somehow he was in her house and she was handing him a glass of iced tea. He took a couple of swallows, then set it aside. His eyes, as he watched her, had the same luminous quality she'd noticed in his movie.

"You turn me on," he said.

He did have a way of saying the most unexpected things.

In a matter of two steps, he had her against the wall, the length of him pressed to her.

Why was he doing this? Why had he singled her out? A widow. A teacher. Someone who hardly needed more than a training bra. What kind of game was he playing?

There was nothing threatening in his manner. Quite the opposite. He seemed almost guileless in his sudden advances. No artful seduction. Just *you turn me on*.

She had to remind herself that he came from a world of pleasure-seeking and instant gratification, where people gave no thought to the consequences of their actions.

Why should that knowledge make her sad?

His mouth was so near. Hadn't she thought about that mouth too much over the past year? At the most inconvenient times? And it wasn't just her thoughts. He'd somehow managed to infiltrate her very habits, her likes and dislikes. Just last week someone had offered her a Lifesaver and she'd told them that lemon was her favorite flavor, when in truth it was cherry.

His face was only inches away, his mouth . . .

He lowered his head. Then his lips made contact with hers. And the very softness sent a rush of warmth through her. His kiss was lazy, tender.

But he was an actor, she reminded herself. He would know how to kiss all sorts of ways. Soft . . . Hard . . .

To him, this was a game. She was a temporary amusement, and the last thing she wanted was to be someone's entertainment.

She turned her face away and shoved at his chest. "Please leave."

"What?" His voice held disbelief.

"Leave."

"You don't have to worry. I've got rubbers."

She didn't know whether to laugh or get mad. She could see that it would do no good to explain. He wouldn't understand. He lived in a world where sex and love were two completely different things.

In the end she couldn't get mad or laugh. Instead, she felt a deep sadness, a sadness she was fast becoming accustomed to feeling in her mercurial dealings with Johnnie Irish.

To save herself, she pushed him toward the door.

Chapter 5

*J*ohnnie was careful not to let the door hit him in the ass on the way out. After it had slammed shut, he stood on the porch awhile, going over what had just happened.

She'd turned him down. He'd never been turned down before. Not that he wanted to go to bed with every woman he met. He was selective about his partners. He'd just never had a woman tell him no before.

It was humbling.

And challenging.

He hadn't sought her out. He hadn't gone to the opera house with the intention of looking up Maggie Mayfield.

He'd arrived in Hope, dropped off his stuff at a small apartment that perfectly suited his needs, then immediately proceeded to get bored. He'd been checking out the town when he'd wandered into the opera house, surprised to find the door unlocked, more surprised to find people inside, especially somebody he knew, or kind of knew. The rest had just happened, the way things had a way of happening in his life. With no real forethought. He'd seen Mrs. Malcolm struggling along, the poor woman unable to hear the kids' voices because of her own piano playing. It had contained the makings of a great comic skit.

As soon as he'd realized what was going on, he hadn't been able to resist stepping in to help her out. Old damsel in distress.

But Maggie May hadn't appreciated it.

He smiled to himself, a perverse orneriness creeping through him. Years ago he'd liked to tease girls and make them scream. Not because he was cruel, but because deep down he knew they really enjoyed the attention. Some would even pout if he ignored them for too long.

Leave me alone. Don't leave me alone.

He was getting those same conflicting messages from Maggie. He'd seen her eyes dilate, heard her quick intake of breath, seen the pulse flutter in her neck. She'd wanted him, but she'd told him no. Why?

Because she was a good girl.

But someday he was going to tease her until she screamed. Someday, before leaving Hope, he was going to get Maggie to say yes.

He headed back for the opera house where he'd left his car. This time he noticed things he'd been too busy to notice before.

The street where Maggie lived was lined with houses that were practically identical except for color, which varied anywhere from white to maroon. All of them were small, square, one-bedroom homes built for singles or newlyweds just starting out. Some had yards of dirt and sandburs and cacti. Some were lush green due to avid and obsessive watering. Maggie's yard fell somewhere in between. Green here and there, sand here and there, showing that she tried but wasn't fanatical about keeping up appearances.

Johnnie had once helped script a short feature called *Green Grass* where the central character's neighbor was a yard freak. Every free hour of his life was spent keeping his yard trimmed and edged and watered—while his relationship with his family crumbled.

If a person wanted green grass he should live somewhere else. The desert wasn't supposed to have grass. That's why it was the desert.

Johnnie was halfway to the opera house when he spotted someone heading his direction. A tall, gangly man shuffled toward him on the sidewalk, a shopping bag in one hand, head down, eyes glued to his shoes.

The distance between them closed.

They met.

Johnnie said hi.

The man mumbled something, and, never looking up, continued on his way.

It was then that Johnnie realized he knew him. It was Phil. Phil Harmonic.

During high school they'd played in a band together. Phil played harmonica, so Johnnie had come up with the nickname Phil Harmonic, much to Phil's unamusement. But Johnnie hadn't done it to be mean. It had just been one of those stupid kid things.

Johnnie yelled after him.

Phil stopped and slowly turned around, no sign of recognition in his gaunt face.

But it had to be him. Same straight, lank hair, same slouching posture. Same face, only older. "Phil. How's it going? It's me—Johnnie."

Phil stared blankly. "Johnnie . . . ?"

"We played in a band together, remember? In high school."

Nothing seemed to register.

"In Jake's garage."

"Jake?"

"Yeah."

Jake had been a piano wizard. He took weekly lessons, and after each one he'd give a quick repeat lesson to Johnnie, free of charge. Johnnie learned fast, and pretty soon he was teaching Jake keyboard licks.

"I don't play music anymore." Phil smiled a sweet but alarmingly vacant smile. "I just listen."

"What kind of music do you listen to?" Johnnie asked. "Are you still into hard rock?"

Phil shook his head. He stepped closer and opened the shopping bag he was carrying, tilting it so Johnnie could see inside. It held a couple of tattered album jackets and what looked like a kid's plastic record player, along with a spiral-topped sketch pad.

"Birdsongs," Phil explained. "I listen to birdsongs." He put his bag on the walk, bracing it between his legs. He reached inside and pulled out the sketch pad, carefully turning the pages one at a time.

It was full of drawings of birds. Birds in flight, birds nesting, birds perched on tree limbs. All meticulously and lovingly drawn.

Years ago Phil had played the harmonica, but his real talent had been art. He could duplicate anything he saw, making things look like an enhanced photograph. Back before copiers, he'd duplicate dollar bills to use in change machines.

Done showing off his artwork, Phil shut the sketch pad and asked, "Would you like to hear some birdsongs?"

Johnnie nodded, all the while wondering what the hell had happened to his old friend.

Phil settled himself cross-legged in the middle of the sidewalk, took out the record player, and put on a thick, scratched, 33⅓ record. With long-nailed fingers, he set the needle in the record's groove, then turned on the player. The disc revolved at about 23⅓ revolutions per minute.

"The batteries are low," Phil said as they listened to a man's sluggish voice explain about the song of the cardinal.

The cardinal's song is a series of whistles, sometimes sounding like a boy calling for his dog, at other times more varied. Remember the memory phrase, whoit-whoit-whoit-whoit.

Phil mimicked the sound, then continued to listen, head cocked to one side, his face a study of joyful satisfaction.

Johnnie thought back to the time right before he'd been kicked out of Hope. Phil had been heavy into drugs, dropping acid and mescaline and shooting heroine—whatever he could get his hands on.

Johnnie had tried to get Phil to slow down, but lecturing him about it only seemed to make him more determined to mess himself up. Now Johnnie wondered if the drugs were to blame for the new Phil. Could someone really fry his brain?

Johnnie tried to draw him into conversation, but Phil seemed too enraptured with the lazy warbles coming from the portable player to give Johnnie more than an occasional grunt or monosyllabic reply.

Johnnie gave Phil a pat on the shoulder. "See you around." Phil didn't look up and Johnnie walked away.

Poor Phil. Poor Phil Harmonic.

The next day Johnnie was back at the opera house. By the time he arrived, rehearsal was already under way.

He slipped quietly in the side door, giving himself time to soak in the nostalgia of a building he had always loved.

It hadn't changed. That had been the first thing he'd noticed yesterday. At one time they'd talked about remodeling, but it would have been a desecration. Like putting shag carpet in Andrew Jackson's Hermitage or a satellite dish on top of the Sistine Chapel.

The entire theater was made of wood, with a balcony running along the two side walls. The floor was inlaid like a gym, with oak chairs that could be folded and stored away whenever space was needed for dances or penny carnivals, or whatever.

The place still smelled the same, of mildew and age. Of trunks and closets packed with greasepaint-stained costumes.

As a teenager, standing inside the theater had always made him acutely conscious of time and the fragility of life. He experienced the same sensation now. He could feel the ghosts of people who had been there before him, many of whom no longer existed, at least in the physical sense.

Unlike film, the stage actors' youth and talent hadn't been preserved on celluloid, but their presence could still be felt. Some Broadway theaters even kept a ghost light burning in honor of the actors gone by.

He stepped away from the shadows of the balcony and moved down the aisle.

Maggie Mayfield stood at the piano, plunking out notes with one hand while trying to give directions with the other. Her hair was pulled back in a ponytail. She was wearing a baggy sweatshirt, along with jeans and sneakers, looking annoyingly healthy, like somebody who belonged in a yogurt or bean sprout commercial.

She definitely turned him on.

When she looked over her shoulder, she actually seemed a little glad to see him, but she probably would have been glad to see anybody with ten fingers and a rudimentary knowledge of the keyboard.

A couple of kids spotted him, giggled, and nudged each other.

Something Johnnie had learned years ago was once you established yourself as a comedian, you were pretty much set. You really didn't have to be very funny after that, because people got to the point where they associated you with funny. That's all it took. Humor was a strange thing. Humor was a great thing.

He hated to disappoint the kids, but he needed to score some points with Maggie, so he tossed them a smile and a wave, then guided Maggie from behind the piano where he then sedately took a seat.

Johnnie be good.

The play was a musical adaptation of *The Pied Piper*, with lots of singing and dancing. It looked like mass confusion to Johnnie. They had a helluva long way to go.

In between songs he gave Maggie a big smile that said, *See, I can behave.*

She answered with raised eyebrows. *Oh yeah?*

She was warming to him. He could tell.

Everything went fine until they were about halfway through practice. But this time it wasn't Johnnie who disrupted things, it was Harriet Lundy.

She bustled into the opera house, looking every bit a woman with a purpose. Johnnie gave her a smile, finished the piece he was playing, then got up from the piano.

"Harry. What a nice surprise."

It was good to see her out and about. Yesterday he'd stopped by her house and she hadn't seemed quite herself. She had been confused, sometimes forgetting that he was even there.

She slipped off her gauzy scarf and hung it over the back of a chair. "Am I late?" She cast a glance around the room. "I don't know what happened. I've never been late for a rehearsal before."

It took him a few seconds to grasp what was going on. She was mixed-up. Just like yesterday. "That's okay," he said, his mind racing ahead, wondering how he should handle this. "We were just killing time, working on a few of the tougher numbers."

"Well, then, let's get busy." She clapped her hands and strode toward the stage the way Johnnie had seen her do years ago. Confident and enthused.

"I hope you've got Act One, Scene One memorized," she announced, "because today we're going to do it without our playbooks."

The kids didn't let out a peep. Even the redheaded rabble-rouser on the end had quit shoving the boy next to him. Johnnie had been hoping for some help from Maggie, but she looked more nonplussed than the kids.

"Harry—" He went after his old teacher, reaching out to stop her.

"Don't worry." She gave his hand a firm squeeze, her strength a surprising change from yesterday's weak clasp. "Forget all about what happened," she said. "Don't think about anything but the play. And remember—you have real talent. That's something nobody can take from you."

Harriet opened the tattered playbook she'd been clutching. "Let's start with Act One, Scene One—at the bakery."

The kids shuffled their feet and kept their eyes downcast. One little girl with curly blond hair let out a scared sniffle.

"Where is Charlie?" Harriet demanded, her eyes searching the stage. Suddenly she seemed to notice the children. "What are all you children doing up there?" Uncertainty edged into her voice. "That isn't how the play opens."

"Harriet." Johnnie slipped the softcover from her fingers. *Flowers for Algernon*, the play Johnnie had done in high school. He tucked the book under his arm so he could take both of Harriet's hands. She was so frail. The bones under her parchment skin felt sharp and brittle. He repeated her name, drawing her gaze from the stage to him.

"Johnnie—" Her voice dropped to a loud whisper. "Those children . . . they look so young. Don't you think they look awfully young for high school?"

The pain and confusion in her eyes was killing him. Not Harry, who had taken on half the town for him. He had to be straightforward with her. He had to explain and hope she would understand.

"Harry, this isn't high school drama. It's a children's theater group."

Maggie had slid off the edge of the stage and was coming toward them. Johnnie was relieved to read compassion in her eyes, not impatience.

"This is Maggie Mayfield." He reached out to pull Maggie a little closer, experiencing an odd security in her presence. "She's the play's director."

"Maggie Mayfield?" Harriet's gray eyes clouded with confusion. "Are you any relation to the Mayfields who live west of town?"

"No."

"You're the new drama teacher?"

"Yes, I am."

As they watched, Harriet seemed to piece together some of the forgotten years, and as she did, she seemed to shrink a little. Johnnie could almost see her thoughts turn inward.

"But I don't teach anymore." She spoke the words slowly to herself, as if trying to memorize an unfamiliar line. Her eyes searched and found Johnnie's. "Do I?"

"To me, you'll always be a teacher."

She smiled.

Johnnie didn't realize how tense he'd been until that moment, until he felt his muscles relax, felt relief radiate through him.

"You always did know just what to say to me, didn't you?" she asked.

"How did you get here, Mrs. Lundy?" Maggie asked.

"Why . . ."

That confusion again. Johnnie hated the uncertainty in her eyes. As he watched, he could see the exact moment she remembered.

"I drove," she said proudly. "My husband taught me to drive, you know. We had the '48 then. I'll never forget the time I ran into the side of the garage. We'd only had the car a month. I thought Harold would be mad, but he laughed." She picked up her scarf and draped it over her head. With stiff, arthritic fingers, she struggled to tie it under her chin. "Imagine that. A man who would laugh when his wife ran into the garage . . ."

Johnnie watched in distress as Harry tried to master the knot. Totally unadept at such things, he was nonetheless about to help when Maggie came to the rescue.

"That's a wonderful story," Maggie said, tying the ends of Harriet's scarf. "I can't think of many men who would take something like a bashed fender so good-naturedly."

"Harold's like that. Softhearted."

She'd slipped into the present tense again.

"Always gives the paperboy some extra money. Harold plants flowers, you know. All kinds of flowers. Have you ever known a man who planted flowers?"

Maggie was shaking her head. "No. He sounds very special."

"Oh, he is."

Harriet had been a widow as long as Johnnie had known her. When he was a kid, he'd never given it much thought. She'd seemed old to him then, but now he realized she couldn't have been much more than fifty when he'd first met her.

"Come on, Harry," Johnnie said, putting an arm around her, careful of her frailness. "How about letting me give you a ride home?"

She looked up at Johnnie, then back at Maggie. "Before I married Harold, I told myself there was something special about a man who plants flowers."

Johnnie dug in his pocket for his car keys. He handed them to Maggie. "I'll take Harriet home in her car. Can you pick me up at her house when you're done here?"

Maggie nodded and walked them to the door.

Harriet's car turned out to be a green Oldsmobile with manual everything and a steering wheel so big that driving was more like maneuvering a riverboat. Johnnie didn't know how Harriet had found the strength to back it out of her garage, let alone drive the two miles to the opera house.

The car was low on gas so he docked at a nearby station, where he filled it up and checked the oil. By the time he got Harriet home, she seemed more worried than confused.

"Sometimes I forget things," she said after they were inside. "Sometimes I even think Harold is still alive."

On top of the television, placed carefully on a rectangular doily, were three photographs.

"My husband and sons," Harriet explained, picking up the frames one at a time, then replacing them. "Harold was killed in World War II. Parker died in Vietnam. He didn't have to go, but he wanted to be like his father. And of course young men think they're indestructible."

Johnnie didn't know what to say.

"My other son lives in Albuquerque, but I never see him—only when he needs money." She sighed. "Some people say Vietnam was a senseless war, but it wasn't, was it, Johnnie?" She was watching him with fierce intensity, her eyes begging him to say the words she needed to hear.

"No," he said. "No, it wasn't."

She was quiet a moment, then she said, "I have Alzheimer's, you know."

It was what he'd expected, what he'd been afraid of.

"I was diagnosed last year. They gave me medicine to take, but sometimes I still get mixed-up."

"I'm sorry." He *was* sorry.

She took a deep, trembling breath. "I don't usually tell people, because I don't want them to pity me. But I suppose it's time they knew."

"Why don't you sit down and I'll fix you some iced tea or something."

She reached out and patted his hand. "Thanks, but I'm awfully tired all of a sudden." Talking about her illness seemed to have reminded her that she was old and worn-out. "If you don't mind, I think I'll go take a little nap." She called her cat, and the two of them disappeared into the bedroom.

After she had gone, Johnnie walked to the picture window. Hands shoved in the front pockets of his jeans, he stared outside, watching for Maggie. From his vantage point, he could see most of the yard, of which there was very little. No trees. No flowers.

He thought about the house Harry used to own. A two-story sandstone with giant gray pillars and a wraparound porch. The yard had been full of trees and birdhouses. And flowers. Lots of flowers . . .

Flowers for Algernon . . .

He hadn't thought about the play in years. But looking back, he could see that it had changed the course of his life. Harry had changed his life.

She'd insisted that he try out for the lead. He'd balked, saying he didn't want any more to do with school than he absolutely had to. But secretly he'd been flattered that she'd even considered him.

In the end he tried out and got it. At first he'd been wild with excitement. But then he discovered that some of the parents were complaining because they didn't think the part should have gone to him. And Johnnie began to think that having anything to do with the play had been a big mistake.

"Give the part to somebody else," he told Harriet. "I don't want it."

But her mind was set.

"I don't know why I'm doing this," he complained.

"Because you're good. Because when all this is over, when everybody else has gone on to do other things, you'll still be standing. Because you have talent. They can bully you into quitting, they can threaten to fire me, but they can never take away your talent."

In the face of such faith, how could he walk away? How could he let Harry down?

He stuck with the part, but his timing was off. The joy was gone. At night he had trouble sleeping, and during the day he couldn't eat. He wanted to quit. He wanted to party with his friends. But he stuck it out.

On the evening of the play, Harriet gave him a fierce smile. Then in a voice that was full of Katharine Hepburn determination said, "Go out there and do it. Do it for me." Her eyes were bright and fierce. "Do it for yourself."

The house wasn't full by any means, but it didn't matter. Halfway through the first act the audience faded away. Gone were the parents who had griped, gone was the memory of his mother belittling him for his grand delusions, his friends laughing and calling him a wimp.

He was somebody else, somebody who had nothing to do with Hope, Texas. He was Charlie.

Ever since he could remember, Johnnie had liked to make people laugh. He wasn't sure why. Deep down he supposed their laughter was something of a surrogate for the love and attention he'd never gotten at home. Or maybe it was the feeling of control it gave him in a life that had no control, no restrictions or boundaries.

He discovered that being onstage was kind of the same as making people laugh, the same kind of high, only different. Bigger.

A lot bigger.

Before meeting Harriet the only decisions Johnnie made dealt with what side of the street to walk on, or whether or not he should ditch school and get stoned.

But standing on that stage sparked something inside him, the beginning of a dream. Before that, the things he'd wanted in life had seemed so unattainable, so impossible, that he didn't dare consider them. Suddenly he was thinking of a life beyond Hope. Suddenly he was thinking that maybe he wasn't the loser everybody said he was.

The sound of a car engine brought him out of his reflections, back to the present. Back to Maggie Mayfield, who was pulling into the driveway. Back to Hope, a place he'd once walked away from without a glimmer of regret.

Chapter 6

*J*ohnnie had surprised her more than once, the first time being when he'd shown up for rehearsal after Maggie had practically thrown him out of her house. The second was in the calm, level-headed way he'd handled Harriet.

Now, as they both stood in Harriet's living room, Johnnie, someone she would classify as perpetually restless, seemed in no hurry to leave. Instead they waited for Harriet to wake up from her rest, staying long enough to make sure she wasn't confused.

Afterward, Johnnie drove Maggie home, and on the way he was quiet. When they got there, he didn't try to come in. He didn't get out of the car. He simply said, "See you around," and left.

Hours later, Maggie was still puzzling over him, trying to make sense of his presence in Hope. She had to admit that he'd done a fantastic job with the music. And the children adored him. But why wouldn't they? He spoke their language. Ironic that the play was an adaptation of *The Pied Piper*. But he'd been at it only two days. Would he stay until the play was finished? Would he give them a month? Did he have a month to give?

It didn't seem likely.

What was he doing in Hope?

She heard the sound of a rumbling engine and looked out the window in time to see her friend Karen getting out of her beater of a car.

A fellow high school teacher, Karen was one of the first people Maggie had met when she moved to Hope. Karen was one of those petite blondes who always dressed in pastels that complemented a peaches-and-cream complexion. She didn't do it to please anybody but herself. She certainly didn't do it to please a member of the opposite sex, because Karen was a man hater. She'd even cross-stitched a pillow that said a woman needs a man like a fish needs a bicycle, and she told the most horrendous stories, one of her favorites being how she'd used her ex-husband's toothbrush on the dog's teeth, then sweetly returned the brush to its owner.

Nobody could really blame her. The man had truly been one of the biggest jerks in Hope. Maybe in all of Texas.

Maggie waved through the window. Karen saluted with a rolled newspaper.

"I can't stay," she said when Maggie met her at the door. "I'm on my way to pick up Sara from ballet lessons, Timothy from basketball camp, and Melanie from her sleepover." She handed Maggie the folded newspaper. "But I just found out why Johnnie Trouble is back in town." She tapped at the paper. "Read this."

She was almost to her car when she shouted over her shoulder, "Call you tonight!"

Karen pulled away in a cloud of blue smoke and Maggie focused on the folded paper in her hand. Down near the bottom of the page, in a blocked-off section that was used for interesting tidbits, was the heading: "Failed Suicide Attempt Sends Johnnie Irish Packing."

Maggie felt a thud in the hollow of her stomach.

After an almost successful suicide attempt, Johnnie Irish slinks out of Tinseltown to hide his shame. And what drove him to want to end his life in the first place? A bad haircut? A fly in his soup? Or could it have been his latest flop?

Maggie stood there stunned while emotions poured over her. Sorrow, confusion, anger. But not surprise. No, not surprise. She had glimpsed a darkness in him, beneath his teasing smile.

Now she knew what he was doing in Hope. He was hiding.

The next day Johnnie was back for rehearsal looking incredibly sexy in a white T-shirt and black jeans. He was on his best behavior, seeming to go out of his way to make things run smoothly.

After practice was over and the children had gone, Johnnie stuck around, and even though Maggie dreaded any kind of confrontation, she knew she would find no better time to question him.

He stood leaning against the piano, legs crossed at the ankles, arms at his chest. "That little girl Sara. She's just cute as hell. Did you see the way she did the town-square bit? She stole the scene."

Karen's daughter, one of the shyest children Maggie had ever seen.

"I was worried about her at sign-up," Maggie told him. "I was afraid her mother was pushing her into acting in hopes of helping her overcome her shyness. I thought acting onstage might be too traumatic for her."

"You can't predict something like that. I know people who are big show-offs, but put them in front of a camera and they freeze. With somebody else, it can be just the opposite. Some people open up."

And where did he fit in? Someone who seemed at ease anywhere, yet was desperate enough to want to take his life?

She pulled a folding chair close and sat down. "Johnnie . . . we have to talk."

"I like to talk."

"I have to know about your plans."

"Plans?" One dark eyebrow lifted. "I don't have any plans."

"That's why we need to talk. I have to know if you're going to be around until the play is over."

He shrugged in a very noncommittal way, as if she'd asked him to stick around four more minutes instead of four more weeks. "Sure."

"How can I be certain?"

"Because I said so."

A person who tried to kill himself wasn't a stable individual. Johnnie should probably be under the care of a psychiatrist right now, not hiding out in Hope, playing piano for a children's theater.

Her silence seemed to irritate him. The relaxed posture disappeared. "Do you want me to sign a contract or something?"

"Johnnie . . . I know why you're here. I read about what happened."

There had been times in her life when she'd had the wind knocked out of her. That's how Johnnie looked now. As if someone had punched him in the stomach. His reaction took her totally by surprise. She hadn't expected him to care what she thought, or what she knew about him.

He turned away, one hand on the piano top, as if for support. She could see the tenseness of his muscles beneath his shirt.

"So," he said, "you've been reading the rags." He slowly lowered himself to the piano bench, his long fingers skimming over the ivory keys without making a sound.

He cleared his throat. "Just for the record"—he struck a single note—"I didn't try to kill myself." There was a long, thoughtful pause. He kept his head lowered, his eyes trained on the keyboard. "I just didn't try not to."

Which in his case, with his diabetes, was pretty much the same thing. What made someone like him so self-destructive?

During her years as a teacher Maggie had dealt with several class clowns, enough to know that they were all hiding something. They were all hurting inside. And she'd been around enough of them to know that they were almost always victims of neglect, if not abuse. She'd even come up with her own theory to explain their disruptiveness. She'd concluded that most children required so many hours of attention in their lives, and if they didn't get it, they became ravenous, demanding that attention any way they could, the more disruptive the better. But that didn't help when it came to understanding Johnnie. Not someone who had made so much of his life, who had the adoring attention of millions.

"Why?" she asked.

Once again she was given a glimpse of the tormented individual she'd seen briefly before. He banged a fist against the keyboard,

57

sending discordant notes through the hall. "Just drop it, okay? I came here to escape curiosity and speculation. What I do to myself is nobody's business but mine."

Someone needed to shake him up.

She jumped to her feet, the chair almost tipping over behind her. "What a self-centered attitude," she said, her voice raised. "It's my business if you're going to be playing for me. If you're going to be influencing my students. This is a big thing to them. If you're going to be a part of it, I want you to be a plus, not a minus. Do you want me to have to tell little Sara that Johnnie won't be playing piano today because he's dead?"

She sometimes spoke before thinking, and this was one of those times. She regretted her last sentence before it was finished.

He flinched, then shoved himself to his feet. "What the hell am I doing here?" He looked around, his expression incredulous, like someone who had sleepwalked and woken up to find himself in a strange place. "Just what *the hell* am I doing here? I'm an adult. I don't have to listen to some lecture from a sexually frustrated goody-two-shoes." He kicked the piano bench, then strode angrily out of the opera house, slamming the door behind him.

Maggie knocked on the door of Johnnie's second-story apartment. When no one answered, she knocked again.

She'd really messed up yesterday. Getting mad. Saying all the wrong things. It wasn't like her to lose her temper. She couldn't recall a time when she'd ever gotten mad at Steven. But Johnnie seemed to bring out the worst in her.

When no one answered her knock, she tried the knob. It turned. She opened the door a crack and called Johnnie's name.

From inside came a bored voice. "You're already halfway in. You may as well come the rest of the way."

He was standing with his back to her, wearing nothing but a pair of jeans. His head was bent as he concentrated on something in his hands.

The one-room apartment surprised her. It was pretty much a dive, totally unfurnished except for a single bed, a telephone, and a pile of dirty laundry. But of course there weren't all that many places to choose from in Hope.

She stepped closer. Now she could see that he had pricked his finger and was testing his blood. On the counter was a digital readout kit similar to ones she'd seen some of her diabetic students use.

Numbers flashed on the readout, then the machine emitted a single beep. Johnnie leaned closer, squinting his eyes. "Six hundred," he muttered. "Must've forgotten my shot this morning."

Her earlier resolve to remain impartial vanished. His blatant self-destruction frustrated and angered her. "You *forgot* to give yourself an insulin shot? How can you forget something as important as that?"

He turned, and now she could see that he must have pulled on his jeans when he'd heard her knock. The top buttons were undone. She could see the taut plane of his lower stomach, down past where underwear should have been but wasn't.

"Sometimes I don't remember," he said defensively. "Do you always remember to take your vitamins? Or maybe your birth control pills? Oh, I forgot. You don't have any use for birth control."

She chose to ignore the dig. "I take my vitamins every morning," she told him.

That didn't impress him. He turned away again, dismissing her. He dragged a box across the counter and dug out a syringe. Then he fumbled around some more, this time pulling out a glass vial. With his teeth he uncapped the syringe, then aimed the needle at the metal-banded end of the vial. His hands were shaking so much he couldn't get the needle in.

"Here, let me help."

"Ah don—" He spit out the syringe cap. It hit the counter, then rolled to the floor. "I don't need any damn help."

It was agonizing, watching him struggle to draw the insulin from the vial, watching the palsied shaking of his hands as he flicked a finger against the syringe, getting out any air bubbles.

"Shit."

He took a few faltering steps, then collapsed, managing to sprawl on his back across the bed, one arm thrown across his eyes. "Give me the shot," he gasped out. "Hurry."

He was clutching the loaded syringe in one hand.

She hated needles. Once one of her students had needed a

shot. Instead of giving it to him, Maggie had screamed for the school nurse. There was no school nurse today.

"Don't worry," he said breathlessly as she continued to hesitate. "I don't have any diseases." He let out a harsh, self-mocking laugh. "I get my blood tested all the time."

"That's not what I'm worried about." She slipped the needle from his grasp. His hand was dry. His entire body—everything she could see—was drained of color.

"I don't know if I can do this." She sank down on the bed next to him, her hip pressing against his side. "I've never given anybody a shot."

"Hurry."

Her gaze traveled over him. Arms, legs, stomach. "Where?"

"Anywhere. My stomach. Straight in, all the way."

"I don't want to hurt you!"

His arm dropped from his face. He tried to lift his head. It fell back against the mattress. "Hurt me!" he gasped. *"Please."*

She pinched some stomach flesh near his navel the way she'd seen the school nurse do. Cringing, she stuck in the needle. She was shaking almost as much as Johnnie, and when she pushed in the plunger the needle shifted, but he seemed oblivious to the pain.

Then it was over. Done.

Little by little, his color returned and his breathing became more regular.

"I hate this," he said with vehemence. He sat up and swung his feet to the floor, elbows on his knees.

They said diabetes was harder for men to accept than women. And it had to be especially hard for somebody like him.

"It's all a matter of acceptance and routine, isn't it?" she asked. "And routine isn't so bad."

"Maybe not for somebody like you."

He'd done it again. He couldn't seem to quit reminding her that she was a nobody. A boring nobody. It made her defensive too. "Isn't the real reason you hate being diabetic because it's something you have no control over?" she asked. "It's the one thing in your life you can't do anything about?"

He didn't answer. He just sat staring at her, a thoughtful expression on his face.

She got up from the bed. "I better go."

"Wait." He reached out and grabbed her wrist, stopping her. "Ouch."

He immediately let go. "I barely touched you."

"I have a low pain threshold."

Amazingly he laughed, and there was true delight in the sound. Then he became serious again. "I'm sorry. I didn't mean to hurt you *or* your feelings."

"It's the truth, isn't it? I'm boring and my life is boring. I don't need to party all night long—I don't want to," she told him. "And I don't like a lot of noise and I hate crowds." That settled it. "I'm a boring person who likes boring things."

She opened the door, then stopped for one final look. He was lying on his back, one hand behind his head, one knee bent, a bare foot on the mattress.

A tightness gathered in her throat. She shook her head. "I don't understand you."

She had to leave, had to get away. She was just outside the open door, a hand still on the knob, when his voice carried to her.

"Don't go."

She paused and looked over her shoulder, knowing in her heart that she should keep moving.

"Stay. Just for a while."

Most women went to him without question. But she couldn't do that. It wasn't in her to do that. "Why?" she asked.

He got up from the bed, buttoned his pants the rest of the way, and came to her. "To talk."

Up close, his eyes were a dark blue, shot with black. Up close, they looked sad. A little desperate.

She stepped back inside and shut the door.

"Want something to drink?" He crossed to the countertop refrigerator and peered inside. "I've got Diet Coke, Diet Coke, or Diet Coke."

Some of the tenseness left her. She smiled. "Do you have any Diet Coke?"

He laughed. "No, but I have . . ." He pulled out a can and held it up for her inspection. Diet Coke.

She nodded her approval.

He wiped the top with what appeared to be yesterday's T-shirt, popped open the pull tab, took a swallow, and handed it to her.

She took a sip, cold carbonation filling her mouth, going down her throat.

When she lowered the can, he was watching her with what she could only describe as a whimsical expression. He smiled and shook his head. "What is it about you?" he asked. "I get around you and suddenly I want to tell you all the things I never tell people." He paced to the only window in the room and looked out.

In the distance she could see the highway that led to Hope, or away from Hope, depending on one's perspective. On either side of the road were irrigated cotton fields. Past the fields, the landscape turned desert brown under a cloudless sky.

"Your husband . . . was he sick a long time before he died?" Johnnie asked.

She'd never mentioned Steven's illness to him. He must have asked somebody about it. "Several months."

"And you took care of him?"

"Until the end when he was in the hospital."

"But no shots?"

"No shots."

He nodded. "When you were a kid, did you ever dream you could fly?"

His mind was always clicking, jumping from one subject to another. "I think I may have once or twice."

"I used to dream it all the time," he said. "And the dreams seemed so real. I remember waking up and thinking that I'd actually flown somewhere. Now in my dreams I try to fly but I can't get off the ground. I wonder how come kids can fly, but grown-ups can't."

She felt an incredible tightness in her throat that she tried to swallow but couldn't. "I don't know." *Maybe because they've forgotten how.*

One hand on the windowsill, he continued to stare out into the distance, his eyes focusing on something in his mind. "Ever see a guy in town named Phil Craig?"

"The bird man?"

A pause. "Yeah."

"I feel so sorry for him. He sleeps in the park. People have tried to give him a place to stay, but he always says he doesn't want it.

He takes an occasional shower here or there. People give him food. They say he took too many drugs."

"I went to high school with him. I remember he used to have this bumper sticker on the back window of an old Buick station wagon. It said, 'I'd rather be a doper than a roper.' I used to think that was funny as hell."

He fell silent while continuing to stare out the window. "See out there, past that oil rig?" He pointed. "That's the pauper's graveyard. My mother's buried out there. Surprises you, doesn't it? A lot of people criticize me for not buying her a plot with a nice big marble tombstone, but I won't be a hypocrite."

Without taking her eyes from him, she set the cola can down on the counter.

"I used to have this cat I called Swagman. He was a stray I found in the train yard. I used to walk around town with him riding on my shoulder. He was smart as hell. He could do tricks like opening doors and turning off the radio. One day I came home from school and he wasn't around. Turned out my mother had taken him to the pound."

What kind of mother would have done such a thing? Maggie wondered, stepping closer.

"I hurried down to spring him, but when I got there, I found out I didn't have enough money. So I stole it. It was the first time I'd ever stolen anything. Funny thing was, when I got back to the pound, Swag was gone, accidentally put to sleep, and I ended up getting hauled to the police station for theft."

He swung away from the window and sank to the bed.

Maggie didn't know why he was telling her this. Maybe it was his way of opening up, of sharing a little bit of himself. Whatever the reason, she found the darkness in him suffocating, bewildering. She wanted to take it away.

She couldn't see his face. It was buried in his hands, but suddenly she needed to touch him. She put a hand on his shoulder. As soon as she made physical contact he turned to her, wrapped his arms around her, and pulled her close.

He mumbled something about wanting to hold her. Then, before she was fully aware of what was happening, he lay down on the bed, taking her with him, her back to the mattress. The length of him was pressed to her. One of his knees urged her legs apart until she felt the warmth of him between her thighs. His hand slid under her shirt to splay across her waist. She could feel the tingle of each finger against her flesh.

A protest was forming in her head when his mouth came down on hers, soft and wet and warm.

He confused her. He beguiled her. He made her limp and hot. He took her completely by surprise.

If she kissed him back just a little . . . what would it hurt?

It was easy. So easy, taking very little effort on her part. Slowly, erotically, his tongue outlined her lips. And when she opened for him, he slipped inside. At the same time, his hand trailed up her ribs to cup her bare breast.

"I could tell you weren't wearing a bra," he whispered. In half a second he shifted, shoving up her shirt. He bent his head to take her breast in his mouth, his tongue circling the nipple. He sucked, and she felt a corresponding pull deep in her abdomen.

Fast. He was so fast, she thought through a haze of amazement. His sensuality level was too high for her. She was caught up in it. Taken away by it. The fingers of both her hands were somehow threaded through his silky hair, whether to pull him away or hold him close, she didn't know.

She moaned and lifted her hips. The sound brought his mouth back to hers. He slid up her body, finding her lips and parting them, kissing her deeply, his tongue stroking hers, the taste of him familiar now. Then he deftly unbuttoned her jeans to slide his hand beneath the zipper, his fingers easing under her panties and across her taut abdomen. They didn't linger but slipped down through the curls. Lower and lower . . .

He stroked her with his fingers. Long strokes. Deep strokes. "You're ready," he murmured, sounding breathless and pleased.

How had this happened? He was practically a stranger. She hardly knew him. Hardly— He stroked her again, and again. Her hips moved to meet his touch.

She was a leaf, drifting, caught by a sudden gust and carried higher to fall once more. He made her want him . . . made her need him. . . .

He drew away a little. With both hands, he undid her zipper, then, hands inside her jeans, palms cupping her bottom, he slid down her pants.

"Johnnie—"

He placed a wet kiss just below her navel, his hair falling forward to brush across her overheated skin. Then he moved lower.

From somewhere came a flicker of self-preservation. In the back of her mind, she heard her own words. *A person shouldn't have sex for the sake of sex. It wasn't something a person did because it felt good.*

"Johnnie—"

They couldn't do this. *She* couldn't do this. She put a hand to his shoulders, digging in with her fingers. "Johnnie—" Her voice came out stronger this time, more forceful.

He looked up across an expanse of nakedness, a question in his dark eyes. His lips were flushed from kissing, his breathing ragged.

Heat rushed through her, collecting in her cheeks, in her face. Now that he'd stopped kissing her, now that some of the haze had lifted from her mind, she saw her shirt shoved above her breasts, her pants almost to her knees.

She thought about Steven.

Suddenly she wanted to cry. "I can't do this," she choked out around the tightness in her throat. "I'm sorry."

It was her fault. She'd led him on, let him go this far without a whimper of protest. She wouldn't blame him for being mad. He had every right.

All she wanted was to pull herself back together. But she didn't want him to watch. She tugged down her shirt and flung an arm across her hot face, waiting for him to turn away.

But he didn't.

She felt his hands on her hips, and her heart jumped. Would he force her? Some guys would think a girl owed them after going so far. Oh God. Surely he wouldn't force her?

She felt her panties being eased back into place.

"Lift your hips," he whispered.

She did, and her jeans slid to her waist. Then they were buttoned and zipped. Her shirt was smoothed down.

When he was done, she rolled to the wall, her knees drawn to her chest, the knuckles of one hand pressed to her trembling mouth.

She'd never made love to anyone but Steven. From the time they'd met in college, it had always been Steven.

After he had died, she used to cry every night. But little by little, the days between the bouts of tears lengthened. There had even been a few times when she'd suddenly realized she hadn't cried in almost a month, and then she would feel guilty.

But she cried now. For Steven. For what they'd had and lost. For the security he'd given her. For the confusion Johnnie had brought into her calm life.

She felt the bed dip, felt Johnnie's warmth against her back, felt his hand on her shoulder, turning her to him, coaxing her into his arms.

She didn't know why she went to him, but she did. She buried her face against his bare chest, his arms a comfort, not a threat, the steady rhythm of his heartbeat a reassurance.

He held her that way for a long time. Later, beneath her ear, she heard a low rumble followed by a deep laugh. "Ah, Maggie May," he said, hugging her to him. "You're not boring. Not boring at all."

Chapter 7

*H*er Volkswagen Beetle must have been on autopilot, because Maggie didn't even remember driving home. But then the little car had always had a mind of its own.

Safe in her own driveway, Maggie turned off the ignition and sat there while the engine rattled and wheezed. She let out the clutch, allowing the car to die a dignified death. Then she hurried to the safety of her house.

Maggie never locked her door in the daytime, but she locked it now before seeking the cool dark solace of her bedroom.

Her heart was beating too fast and her hands were shaking as she sat down at the oak dresser—a wedding present from Steven's mother. On the dresser top was a plain mahogany jewelry box. She opened it, searching through the contents until she found a gold band. Her wedding ring.

She slipped it on her finger, the metal cold but comforting. Something she could see and feel. A tangible reminder of Steven.

She'd put it away shortly after his death, not wanting to wear it as a symbol of grief for others to see. She'd wanted her grief to be private.

But now she needed to feel the ring on her finger. She needed to bring Steven closer. He was too far away. And in losing that feeling of nearness, she felt she'd somehow betrayed him.

Maybe if she had a cemetery to visit. But Steven had been buried in Ohio, in a plot owned by his family. There had been talk about leaving him in Hope, but Steven had never really adapted to the desert town the way Maggie had. All the while he'd lived there he'd been homesick for the rolling hills of Ohio. Not that he'd complained. It hadn't been in Steven to complain, not even at the end, when he'd been in so much physical discomfort. But Maggie had known.

At one point, she and Steven had discussed the possibility of returning home—he'd never quit calling Ohio home—but she'd talked him out of it.

When it came to Steven, Maggie felt guilty about a lot of things. About whether or not she'd handled his illness the way it should have been handled. Maybe if they'd gone to more doctors, more hospitals. And had it been selfish of her to keep him in a place that was alien to him so they could have a few more months together? To keep him in a land that was washed-out and flat, that was too open, too distant?

The desert hadn't been Steven. Steven had been green hills rolling down to meet quietly rushing streams. He had been crisp fall days, flannel shirts, and the Irish setters his mother raised. He'd never belonged in the desert, and it sometimes haunted her that he'd spent his last days there.

Quality, not quantity.

Who the hell had coined that phrase? Certainly not someone who had faced a life-and-death decision as she'd faced. She'd done whatever it had taken to keep Steven alive an extra week, an extra day.

His last two weeks had been spent in a hospital in El Paso where he'd been surrounded by his family. But it wasn't the same as being in Ohio.

During that time he never mentioned home except for one night, the night before he died. He'd awakened, confused and disoriented, talking about his old coonhound, about how they both loved to run through the woods.

Maggie hoped that's what they were doing now. Running through the woods.

How long had it been since she'd talked to Steven's mother? she wondered. She must call her. Tonight. It would be good to hear Marcella's voice, good to talk to her. And if Steven's younger brother, Elliot, was home from law school, Marcella would put him on the line and he would tease Maggie and ask when she was coming to visit. He'd ask if she'd been practicing her spiral throw. Elliot had always told her he'd never seen a girl who could throw a football so ungracefully.

Maggie recalled the first time she'd gone to Steven's house. She'd found herself caught up in a whirlwind. All the roughhousing, all the laughter at the dinner table, all the joking and teasing.

She'd loved it.

She missed it.

She'd wanted some of that sense of home and family for herself.

Even though she was content in Hope, there were times when, alone at night, listening to the quiet around her, she would think about Marcella and her warm home. And Maggie would think of the babies she'd never had.

Steven.

She missed him. She missed him so much. She missed the closeness. She missed the nights spent lying in bed, talking quietly in the dark. She missed his support, his gentle strength, his understanding.

He'd been her husband. He'd been her best friend. Her love.

She searched through the jewelry box until she found a gold chain. She slipped the ring on the chain, then hung the chain around her neck, letting it fall inside her shirt.

A reminder of what love and making love were supposed to be. She would wear it as a warning to herself. Like a cross worn against vampires.

Growing up, she'd had a friend who'd always fallen for the wrong guy. It there was a loser within a hundred-mile radius, Robin would somehow find him. At first Maggie had tried to make her see the guy for what he really was, pointing out all his faults, all the reasons she should have nothing to do with him. But it never worked. In fact, it only made things worse. It made Robin want him more than ever.

Now, after all those years, Maggie could sympathize with Robin. Now she could see that the situation had been out of her control. It was instinct, like birds flying south for the winter or like turtles crawling across freeways and interstate highways to return to their birthing ground.

Instinct was a powerful thing. But now that Maggie was aware of her problem and the reason for it, she was prepared. She could fight it. She had evolved enough to think with her brain, not her hormones.

It was fine and dandy for Maggie to tell herself she wouldn't think about Johnnie, but that night when she was asleep, her subconscious kicked in and trampled her evolution theory all to hell.

The next morning she woke up in a tangle of sheets and a heavy wanting deep in her body.

Maggie never dreamed in color; in fact, she rarely even remembered her dreams, but this time she'd dreamed in the most amazing Technicolor. And she remembered everything. Everything.

Her dreams had been so real that after waking up she carried their mood and tone and—heaven help her—their sensuality around with her for hours.

In one dream she and Johnnie had rolled around on the floor, ripping off each other's clothes. In another he made love to her in the middle of a desert, in broad daylight, his eyes never leaving hers, reflecting the brilliance of the sun.

Two days later she was still dreaming in color, but she'd seen no sign of Johnnie and she could only surmise, with a strange mixture of relief and regret, that he'd left town.

Maggie sat on the stage, legs dangling over the edge, waiting for the children to arrive for rehearsal. Her thoughts drifted from the problem at hand—where to find a piano player—to Johnnie. She felt a familiar gnawing fear, not for herself but for him. In Hope she felt as if he'd paced himself, that he'd been a little more in control than he was back there, in California. Back there was where he'd been when he'd almost died. Back there was where things moved too fast, where people got caught up in the craziness of life.

Stop, she told herself. She had to stop. This infatuation was juvenile, silly, embar—

The back door opened. A shaft of light spilled across the wooden floor, bringing with it Johnnie Irish.

She felt a slow drumroll deep in her stomach.

She watched as he strolled down the aisle toward her.

"I thought you'd left town," she told him, her voice relatively level, definitely at odds with the death grip she had on the edge of the stage. Under her palms she could feel the roughness where the wood had been sawed all those years ago.

"Yeah, well—" Hands braced behind him, he hoisted himself up beside her. "Thought I'd stick around." He glanced at her. "You don't mind, do you?"

She avoided his eyes. She couldn't look at him, not with what had happened at his apartment, not with the X-rated dreams she'd been having. Her gaze fell to his hands, to long fingers that were drawing lazy circles in the dust that had settled on the stage floor.

Nice hands. Beautifully shaped hands. Sensitive hands. Hands that had touched her breasts, touched her—

"Maggie?"

Her eyes lifted, then managed to stop short before making contact with his, locking on his mouth instead. A mouth that was a little full. A mouth that was soft. Warm. A mouth that had touched her intimately.

"Do you mind?" he asked again.

Yes.

No.

Yes.

She didn't know. He confused her. He made her do things she would normally never do.

Her hand flew to her chest, her fingers touching the outline of the ring where it lay beneath her T-shirt, against her heart. Her friend Robin had been Catholic and she used to say feverish Hail Marys. Maggie should have paid closer attention. She could use some of those prayers right now.

"Have you found someone else to play piano?" he asked.

"No. No, I haven't."

"Good."

Bad. *He* was bad. Bad for her.

He slid from the stage and walked to the piano. But of course he didn't really walk. Walk didn't describe the graceful yet sexy way he moved.

Yesterday Maggie had gotten her hair trimmed, and while she'd been at the beauty shop some of the girls had been talking about Johnnie. About how sexy he was. About how they'd like for him to—

Stop.

Johnnie sat down at the piano bench, his hair falling forward, fingers moving into place over the keys. Hands skimming pale ivory. A light touch. A sensual touch.

And then he began to play.

Something ghostly. Something dreamy. Something Maggie had never heard before.

Music had always been an important part of her life, yet she'd never had it create as vivid a picture as Johnnie was creating now.

It was as though she'd never heard music before. Haunting. Wistful. Mysterious. Tempting. It flowed around her, sensual, like a caress.

The music evoked images of a sheer floating gown made of fabric so light it could have been drifting cobwebs. It took her away to a dark garden, surrounded by moss-covered stones, where the sweet scent of jasmine lay heavy on the night air. She could feel dew-kissed grass beneath her bare feet, feel a damp breeze against her skin.

Enchantment.

When the music was over, when the last bittersweet notes drifted away to be absorbed by the ancient walls of the opera house, Maggie could only sit while the silence settled into the spaces around them, while the memory of the music echoed in her mind.

She couldn't say how much later it was that Johnnie slid around on the piano bench, his feet flat on the floor, hands clasped between his thighs. "You never did answer me. Mind if I stay?"

When she was little, she used to watch old black-and-white horror shows. One popular scene was of a sleeping girl who would suddenly awaken. Then, mesmerized, arms straight out, eyes closed, she would get out of bed and walk straight into the arms of a mysterious stranger. Somehow the stranger never seemed a threat, but rather a symbol of dark, seductive passion.

That's how she felt. As if this whole situation were totally out of her control. As if she'd been mesmerized.

And the final strains of the music kept echoing in her head.

Haunting. Wistful. Seductive.

Through a fog, she realized he was still waiting for an answer. "No," she said. "I don't mind."

He smiled, and she felt a corresponding vibration deep inside.

Then she had a reckless, totally out-of-character thought. Maybe they should just do it. Maybe that would get him out of her system. Maybe he was like Christmas. Maybe the anticipation was better than the real thing, and once it was over she would be able to get back to normal.

Her own thoughts shocked her. It wasn't in her to do such a thing. She was just making noises in the dark to cover up the seductive whispers.

He was still watching her, a faint smile playing about the corners of his sensual mouth. A smile she managed to return with a feeble one of her own.

Chapter 8

Not a creature of habit, Johnnie nonetheless began jogging. He wasn't exactly sure why. Maybe just for the hell of it. Or maybe it was because he knew Maggie thought he was undisciplined and he wanted her to see that he could toe the line if he felt like it. He just didn't feel like it very often. Whatever the reason, he decided to take up jogging.

He was the type of person who never walked if he could drive, never ran if he could crawl. Funny thing was, it didn't show. He didn't have a potbelly or sagging biceps. He didn't get out of breath if he dashed up a few flights of stairs.

It was purely genetic. He supposed his physical makeup was one thing he could thank his mother and unknown father for, if nothing else. He'd been blessed with a body that didn't seem to require much maintenance—at least outwardly. He could eat a lousy diet, stay out all night, do all the things he shouldn't, even go comatose, and it didn't show.

Jogging was something his doctor had been recommending for years, harping that it would help regulate his blood sugar, and reduce his need for insulin by making the insulin work better on muscles and fat cells. But exercise took structure, something Johnnie had never been very good at.

But now, possibly out of sheer boredom, he thought he may as well give it a try. Just for the hell of it.

He didn't own the right jogging threads, but that didn't matter. Shoes were the important thing, and he had good shoes. That was one thing he was careful about, his footwear. Feet could get infected. And infection could lead to amputation. Johnnie knew a diabetic who'd lost a toe, then a foot, because he hadn't worn the right shoes.

A good foundation. Very important.

The first day he took off decked out in a pair of jeans and a white T-shirt.

He made it a mile. A gasping, lung-stinging, side-aching mile. To celebrate his accomplishment, he almost jogged right into one of the local cantinas for a cold one. But at the last minute he changed his mind.

Back at his apartment he showered and changed, and decided he didn't feel a helluva lot better. In fact, he felt worse. Jogging was a waste of energy, a waste of time. A real pain in the ass. Tomorrow he'd sleep in.

But the next day he was up with the sun, ready to do it all again. Doc Underwood would have been proud. He made it a mile and a quarter, came home, and tested his blood sugar level. He even ran the old dipstick urine test.

Yep, he was going to turn into a regular hypochondriac if he didn't watch out.

Jogging in jeans was uncomfortable. They had a tendency to chafe, so he graduated to sweatpants. The sweatpants were hot, and after too much perspiration built up they had a tendency to want to go south, so he took the scissors to them, chopping them off just above the knee. Quite a look with his high tops.

He'd start out with a T-shirt, but when he got hot he'd peel it off and tuck it into the back waistband of his sweatshorts. He was actually contemplating the purchase of a headset when he saw what was happening. If he wasn't careful, he would turn into one of *them*. One of those obsessive yogurt-slurping, bean-sprout-growing health nuts. He shuddered. If he wasn't careful, he'd find himself reading food labels in order to *avoid* chemicals.

He didn't get the headset, but he didn't stop jogging either. Within two weeks he'd reached his goal of two miles. Which not only took him past the ballpark and past Harriet's and past the crazy lady who swept her dirt yard all day and chased him with her broom whenever he happened by, it also took him past Maggie's.

The first morning he caught her outside watering the catalpa tree. That made him feel good, seeing her watering the tree he'd given her. She looked up with eyes that weren't quite awake yet, her face mirroring total surprise, most likely at finding him up at such a time. Or possibly finding him involved in physical activity.

"Just getting in?" she asked sweetly.

He laughed. It occurred to him that she made him laugh quite a bit. "You're supposed to say good morning," he told her.

She made a face.

He continued on, feeling her eyes on his back as he went. Even though he'd gone almost one and a half miles, even though his lungs would normally be begging for him to quit, he didn't feel tired anymore. He felt buoyant. It was a little like the Van Morrison song. The one about jumping hedges. He didn't jump any hedges, but he sailed over a couple of tumbleweeds as he cut across a vacant lot.

Maggie watched until Johnnie was out of sight, still surprised at seeing him out so early. And jogging, of all things. It just didn't seem like a Johnnie Irish thing to do. Or course he hadn't looked the typical jogger, not with his dark sunglasses, bare chest, jagged sweatshorts, and white leather high tops.

He jogged by again the next day. And the next.

Even though she saw him every day at rehearsals, this was different. There were a lot of streets in Hope. He was deliberately jogging down hers, flashing a grin her way, a grin that said, "Look at me." He made her smile. And he made her look. And made her begin to watch for him every morning.

Saturday was laundry day. Maggie was carrying the last basket of dirty clothes to the car when she heard the *slap, slap* of Johnnie's sneakers against the pavement. This time he came up her driveway, stopping a few feet away.

"Laundry?"

With a rattle of metal, she slammed the flimsy Volkswagen lid closed and turned around.

Same dark glasses. A black cap, worn backward, the snapped band across his forehead, presumably to keep the hair away from his face.

Bare chest. Bare legs. Those high tops.

His chest was muscular, with rounded pectorals and glistening shoulders, with skin that was suntanned and smooth.

"Volkswagens are neat. Trunk in the front, that bubble body." He shook his head in what appeared to be amazed admiration. "Those crazy Germans. Notice how these cars look as strange today as they did twenty years ago?"

She smiled. "I never really thought about it, but you're right."

"Here, hang on to these a second, will you?" He whipped off his cap and glasses, handing them to her. He pulled out the cotton T-shirt that was tucked in his waistband and used it to wipe the sweat from his face, neck, and chest.

Bronze flexing muscles, dark armpit hair.

When he was done grooming himself, he slipped his arms into the armholes of the shirt, lifted the neck over his head, then tugged the shirt into place, his hair popping out all over. He finger-combed it back from his forehead, retrieved and replaced his cap, then the dark glasses. "Mind if I come along?"

"Come along?" she asked blankly.

"To the Laundromat."

"Why?"

He shrugged. "I like them."

"This isn't like the ones you have in California with bars and video games. It's just a place to wash and dry clothes. A hot, humid, linty Laundromat."

"That's the place." He started circling her car. "The last one of these I ever drove was purple with daisies painted all over it."

"Driven by a girl named Moonflower?"

He smiled. "How'd you guess? Volkswagens are pretty neat," he repeated. "Fun to drive."

Why didn't he come right out and ask her if he could drive it? He was just like a kid, with his broader-than-broad hints.

She made the offer he wanted to hear, and within a matter of seconds he was behind the wheel.

"You have to pull out the choke," she said from the passenger seat, "then push it back in the second the engine starts to kick over. Otherwise it'll flood."

He did as she instructed.

With the engine running, he reached for the radio. There was no radio. In fact, there was no radio, no heater, and not an awful lot of floorboard.

Instead of heading straight for the Laundromat, he took her on a tour of some of his old haunts, pointing out various points of interest.

"There's where the old pool hall used to be. And see that water tower? We used to climb up there on Fourth of July to watch the fireworks. Best seat in town."

"I'll bet."

They rattled and hummed around a few more corners. "There's the church I used to go to."

"You went to church?"

"Don't look so surprised. I went to church on Sunday, and Bible school every summer—loved those cookies and Kool-Aid. I know you won't believe this, but I even wanted to be a minister at one time."

"Oh. Come on."

"It's true. But then I got caught making out in the choir loft and decided I really wasn't cut out for holy leadership."

They stopped at a red light. "How about a Chinese fire drill?" he asked.

Was he serious? High school kids were the only ones she knew of who bailed out and ran around the car during red lights.

"They play a different version in California," he said.

"Oh?"

"They have sex during the red light."

"That must be most enjoyable. Especially the foreplay."

"I couldn't say. It's one of those things I've always wanted to try, but just never got around to. You know how that goes."

Tour apparently complete, they headed for the Laundromat. When they got there, the parking lot was empty. Even with the detour, they'd still managed to arrive early enough to beat the Saturday crowd.

Johnnie cut the engine, hung his cap and glasses on the rearview mirror, and pulled the trunk catch. With a metallic scrape, the hood popped up.

They both grabbed a basket and carried it inside, where the sickening sweet smell of fabric softener hung in the humid air, and the glare of fluorescent bulbs cast an unflattering light across the rows of yellow washers.

Maggie dug into her purse for change and immediately began feeding the machines. Johnnie helped himself, slipping the coins into the slots, then sliding the coin feed into place. "Just like Las Vegas." He grinned, thoroughly enjoying himself.

Water poured into the machines. Next came the laundry soap, followed by clothes and towels and sheets.

Everything was going smoothly. The machines were humming along, filling the air with the smell of soap.

That's when Johnnie began to strip.

One minute he was talking about a guy he knew who'd splashed bleach in his eyes, the next he was taking off his clothes, hardly pausing in his story.

He reached behind him, tugging his shirt over his head, the movement sending his rib cage and shoulder blades into relief. Shirt off, he lifted the lid on the white load, tossed in the shirt, and let the lid slam shut again.

Then he hooked his thumbs under the waistband of his sweatshorts and shucked them too.

At least he was wearing underwear.

But not the silky black bikinis she might have expected. These were baggy gray-and-orange-striped boxers with an elastic waistband that hung low around suntanned hips and a hard stomach.

On most men the baggy pants would have looked ridiculous, but on Johnnie they were cute. To be honest, they were more than cute. They were sexy. How could boxers be sexy?

With a flick of the wrist, he tossed the sweatshorts in another machine.

Not waiting to see what else might come off, Maggie plopped down in a plastic molded chair, picked up a tattered women's magazine, and started thumbing through it, nothing in the issue registering.

Johnnie's striptease must have been over, because from the corner of her eye she could see him lever himself onto the folding table, where he sat, legs swinging, fingers drumming. Three seconds later he jumped down and strode to the bulletin board, where a disgusting gray jockey strap hung by a thumbtack.

"Single white male wants to meet single white female," he read. "Must like cigar smoke, beer, and sex during televised football games."

"You're making that up."

"I am not." He pointed to a five-by-seven card. From the shade of yellow, she could only surmise that it had been there for some time.

"Says it right here."

He continued his perusal and she went back to her magazine.

"How about this one? Want to trade a horse for a moped or something of equal value."

Tiring of the bulletin board, he went over to check out the soft drink machine. He straightened and looked across the room to her. "I'm thirsty, aren't you?"

Which meant he didn't have any money. Of course he didn't have any money. Where would he put it?

"There's some more change in my purse," she told him.

She heard her purse's zipper slide open, heard him rummaging around inside. Then she heard him laugh.

She looked up.

"This is one of the goofiest driver's license photos I've ever seen," he said, laughing some more.

She jumped out of her chair and headed toward him. "Give me that."

"I'm not done," he said, still sizing up her photo. "What's that on your face?"

"Where?"

"There." He pointed to her picture.

"A zit."

"A zit? Were you on the rag or something?"

She made a swipe for her billfold. "Give me that."

He pulled his arm back.

She lunged.

He raised his arm high above his head, the billfold out of reach.

She jumped and stretched. No good. With both hands she shoved at his bare chest. "Creep."

He lowered his arm. "Okay, okay. I don't know what you're so mad about."

"You." She jerked the billfold from his hand.

"What did I do? You told me I could get some change from your purse."

"I didn't tell you you could snoop through my things. You're like a child." She thought a moment. "You *are* a child."

"So what if I am? I'd rather be a child than thirty-two going on a hundred."

Like you, were his unspoken words. She was about to retaliate when she realized they were fighting again. About nothing. So what if he was a child? What difference did that make to her? None. None at all.

"I don't act a hundred," she mumbled, digging out some change and trying to hand it to him.

He crossed his arms at his chest.

"Take it," she insisted, shaking it at him.

"I don't want it."

"You said you were thirsty."

"I'll drink water from the sink."

"Oh for Pete's sake. Now you're pouting. I can't believe it."

"There you go. When do you ever hear anybody under eighty say 'for Pete's sake'? And who the hell's Pete?"

"I can say whatever I want to say."

"And what do you want to say?"

"Boxer shorts are stupid. That's what I want to say."

"I'll take them off."

"Is that all you think about? Sex?"

"Who said anything about sex?"

She clicked her tongue and crossed to the soft drink machine, dropped in the change, and looked over the selection. There was one diet drink, an orange soda. She pushed the button. Following a series of thuds, the can rolled into the metal tray. She fished it out, pressing the cold can to his bare chest. "Don't be such a baby."

"You're mean, Maggie May." He took the can, popped the top, and offered her a drink.

She took a sip, then handed it back, a temporary cease-fire.

Behind them the machines kicked into their spin cycle.

Johnnie grinned. "Kind of like a climax, isn't it?"

Oh brother.

Chapter 9

*K*nock, knock, knock.

It wasn't an urgent knock, or an apologetic knock. In her sleep, Maggie wondered if it was a knock at all. Perhaps someone was playing the drums. Or maybe it was a metronome. Her music teacher used to keep a metronome on top of the piano to make sure her students kept in tempo. *Click, click, click.*

Knock, knock, knock.

She finally came awake to realize rather stupidly that someone was rapping on her front door. With her brain still sluggish, she turned her head to look at the digital clock next to the bed. The green numerals said 3:21 A.M. A strange time for a visitor.

Never having been one to wake up easily, and too sleepy to be alarmed, she threw back the covers and shuffled barefoot to the living room, where she flipped on the wall switch and opened the door a few inches.

Standing in the tungsten glow of the porch light, eyes squinted against the sudden brightness, was Johnnie. He was dressed all in black, not an unusual shade for him.

"Get on some dark clothes and come with me," he told her. "I need your help."

Just like that. No hello, sorry to wake you. No explanation.

She crossed her arms just below the picture of Tweety Bird that adorned the front of her sleep shirt, and leaned against the door-jamb. "For my own peace of mind, is this anything illegal?"

He blew air through his nose, as if the idea were totally preposterous. "Of course not."

"Anything that might put us on the front page of the *Hope Chronicle?*"

"I need help. When a person needs help, you're not supposed to ask questions. You just say sure."

It surprised her that he would think that way. Was that the kind of friend he would be? One who gave without question?

When she didn't immediately jump at the chance to go with him on his mysterious adventure, he dismissed her as a lost cause. "Forget it." He made a downward sweep with one hand, as if to erase his invitation. "I can handle it myself. I just thought you might like to come along. But forget it. Go back to bed with Tweety."

He was walking away when she called after him. He turned on the narrow sidewalk, head tilted to one side, dark eyebrows raised in question. Black hair, black clothes. A man looking for trouble. An outlaw. A man she was attracted to in spite of herself, in spite of her better judgment. A man who was self-destructive and irresponsible and totally wrong for her. A man who would walk out of her life without a flicker of remorse.

"Wait," she said. "I'll be right out."

He looked quite pleased with himself and she realized she'd played right into his hands. He smiled a creased, ornery smile. "I knew I could count on you."

He'd known all along that she would come. He was used to women following when he beckoned. But that wasn't why she was going, she told herself as she headed to the bedroom. Somebody had to keep an eye on him. Somebody had to make sure he stayed out of trouble.

She didn't own much black, but she managed to dig up a pair of knee-length, chopped-off black sweatpants that she'd accidentally washed with a load of white towels. Unsightly, but they would do. Along with that, she slipped on a Harley-Davidson T-shirt she'd gotten at the school's Christmas gag-gift exchange three years ago.

Before tonight it had never been worn. There was a first time for everything.

Outfit complete, she turned off the light and hurried through the dark house and out to the car, where Johnnie waited, fingers drumming impatiently on the steering wheel.

They turned north, driving through silent, sleeping streets, heading in what she soon realized was the direction of Harriet's house. When they were about a block away, Johnnie shut off the headlights, cut the engine, and let the car coast the final block, stopping just short of Harriet's driveway.

"Come on." He slid out of the car and went around to the trunk. Maggie got out more slowly, beginning to have serious doubts.

The night was moonless. The only thing keeping them from being lost in total darkness was a couple of yard lights down the block and the glow of stars overhead.

Johnnie opened the trunk, reached inside, then handed Maggie two shovels and a flashlight.

It didn't take a genius to see that they shouldn't be doing whatever it was they were doing. "Johnnie, I don't think this is a good idea." She spoke into the darkness in a hushed, strained voice. "I've changed my mind. I want to go home. I didn't know there would be digging involved. I thought we'd just toilet-paper a few houses, soap a few windows—"

"Hey, if you want to leave, leave. Nobody's stopping you." He turned his back to her and lifted something from the trunk. Something oblong. A tangy, bittersweet scent filled the air. The smell was familiar. Like marigolds. And the sweet smell of petunias.

Flowers?

He wasn't digging up bodies or burying bodies or looking for a route to China.

"Don't turn on the light yet." His voice was full of suppressed excitement, sounding like a little kid's on Christmas Eve.

"Flowers?" she asked.

"Won't Harriet get a kick out of them in the morning?"

"Maybe. If we don't scare her to death tonight."

"Her bedroom's at the back of the house. If we're careful, she'll never hear us."

Careful. Did he know the meaning of the word? "What about the police?" she hissed. "What if they drive by and see us?"

"Ever hear of anybody getting arrested for disturbing the dirt?"

"No, but—"

"Then come on."

It really was a lovely idea. And one that was so Johnnie. Where other people, herself included, might think of something they'd *like* to do, Johnnie carried it past the idea stage. He acted upon it.

They crossed the yard to the place where an empty flower bed ran from the front step to the left side of the house.

Watching him work, she got the feeling that he'd pulled this kind of job before. Like someone accustomed to lurking around in the dark, he deposited the flowers on the ground, took the flash-light from her, and quickly wrapped it in a T-shirt before turning it on. It cast just enough light for them to see what they were doing.

They began digging. And as they dug, it occurred to Maggie that she was having fun. An excitement tingled through her that was a little like the way she'd felt as a kid playing hide-and-seek. She could remember hiding, sure that she would be discovered, sure that the heavy *thud, thud* of her heart and the loud rasp of her breathing could be heard at least a half a block away. Sometimes the person would find her. Sometimes not. But there was always that excitement.

The ground wasn't packed hard and they finished breaking it up in a matter of minutes. Maggie was reaching for a flower when a hand touched her shoulder. She jumped and almost screamed.

"Make sure you get the rows straight," Johnnie whispered in her ear, his breath stirring the hair that had slipped from the band at the back of her neck. "Harriet likes straight rows. But then you probably know that. Isn't it some kind of teacher thing?"

"Shhh."

She wanted to laugh. She was *going* to laugh. The only thing that saved her was knowing it would ruin Johnnie's surprise if they were caught. She let out a strangled breath, drew in another for stabilization, and reached for a marigold.

With the two of them working, they were completely done in another ten minutes. Finished, they quickly grabbed everything and hurried for the car, running with knees bent, heads low. They put the shovels in the trunk, careful so the metal didn't clang, then tossed in the empty box. Leaving the trunk slightly ajar, they scrambled for the front seat.

"Wait to slam the door," he instructed.

The engine was running before they were barely settled. Headlights off, they moved silently down the street. Two blocks away, Johnnie threw the gearshift into park, jumped out, and shut the trunk, then hurried back to the driver's seat. Doors slammed, then they were off, headlights on, wheels moving over pavement.

Mission accomplished.

Maggie's heart was still thundering in her chest, and she hadn't yet caught her breath. She pulled in lungfuls of air. "Why do I always want to laugh at the worst possible moment?"

"Fear of *faux pas*. It's some kind of disease, I think."

"I laughed at a wedding once," Maggie confessed.

"A wedding? Major *faux pas*."

"The vocalist sounded like a country singer, yodeling through songs that were supposed to be tender and moving. I didn't even feel it coming, but all of a sudden I just burst out laughing."

"One time I was at a ground-breaking ceremony," Johnnie said, "and the guy backing the place couldn't get his shovel in the ground. There he was, all spruced up in a suit and tie. First he tried to scoop up a little dirt. Nothing happened. He may as well have been digging in cement. So he put one shoe to the shovel. Nothing. Then he jumped on it with both feet, pogo style. Great visual comedy. Everybody cracked up."

"How awful," she said, laughing herself.

"Not really. You had to know the guy. He was a jerk."

They were almost at Maggie's house when she realized that, even though dawn was another hour away, she didn't feel like going home.

"How about we get some coffee someplace and go watch the sun come up?" Johnnie suggested.

Maggie hadn't done that in years, not since she'd lived in Ohio. When she was first married, she and Steven used to get up early sometimes just to watch the sunrise. She would like to watch one again.

There was no place in Hope that was open all night, so they

swung by Maggie's, washed up a little, made a quick pot of coffee, poured it into a thermos, grabbed a couple of oranges, and headed for the edge of town where the sky was open and uncluttered.

They sat on a smooth, round rock still cool from the night, drinking coffee and eating orange slices.

It was like watching the curtain rise on the first act. A faint glow showed along the horizon. An occasional bird called from the distance, and a lizard scuttled across the ground, from cactus to cactus, eager to beat the heat of the day.

It turned out to be a beautiful sunrise. One of the most magnificent Maggie had ever seen. "How can such a sparse land have such a wonderful sunrise?" she wondered out loud.

"I always figured that every place is allowed so much color," Johnnie said. "So Texas gets the sky."

She looked over at him, expecting to see a wry twist to his lips, a hint of sarcasm that hadn't been apparent in his voice. It wasn't there. He was smiling, but it was a soft smile that would have been undetectable except for a gentling around his eyes and mouth. He was watching the dawn, one arm linked around his bent knee, the new light washing over his face, reflecting in his eyes, making his skin a perfection of sepia tones. A morning breeze kicked up, lifting his hair from his brow. He closed his eyes for a moment and tilted his head back ever so slightly. Maggie swallowed and turned her eyes back to the sky.

After the red and violet and pink burned to yellow, they gathered their things and left. Before taking Maggie home, Johnnie swung by Harriet's house. As they drove slowly past, Johnnie and Maggie slumped down in the seat, low-rider style. They spotted Harriet outside, watering her new flowers.

Johnnie and Maggie looked at each other and smiled a private smile, then they moved on down the street.

Back home, Maggie got out of the car, shut the door, then bent to look in the window. Johnnie was sitting with one arm draped over the steering wheel, his hair tousled, his eyes sleepy, his smile sexy. He looked her up and down. "Nice outfit."

She glanced down at the Harley shirt and lint-covered pants, made a face, then shrugged her shoulders. "Thanks." She meant thanks for the night, thanks for the sunrise.

He seemed to understand. "Have a good time?" he asked.

She could only reveal so much. "Yes. But I'm still waiting for Elvis."

"Aren't we all? See you at rehearsal this afternoon?"

"Yes."

He put the car in gear. She let go of the door and took two steps back.

"You're a good sport, Maggie May. It'll be hard to top last night, but I'll think about it and see what I come up with."

That meant they might go somewhere together again. The thought thrilled and scared her at the same time because she was mature enough to know that nothing could come of this.

He pulled away, leaving her with a sudden emptiness, the few hours until she'd see him again seeming to stretch out to infinity.

Free-falling. She was free-falling. And even though it was nice, she knew it would be most unpleasant when she hit bottom.

Chapter 10

*H*e'd been doing okay, at least in his opinion. Too okay. Maybe it was the moon, or maybe Maggie was right about Hope being too boring for him, but one evening Johnnie found himself climbing the walls.

If he were in California, he could find a million things to do. Briefly he thought about driving to El Paso to catch a plane for L.A., but he'd come to Hope to get away from his work and all the people. Two weeks ago Hope had looked pretty good.

It wasn't that he minded his own company. He'd just never been one to like being alone for an extended period of time. He needed noise. He needed crowds.

Instead of doing anything as desperate as a spur-of-the-moment flight to L.A., he headed out into the night, strolling down to one of the small, neighborhood taverns. The building was typical of Southwest Texas. It was a flat-roofed adobe with a courtyard that allowed the overflow and noise to spill outside. Inside, a band was playing—a Tex-Mex group complete with a steel guitar and accordion. Johnnie liked accordions.

For the first hour he sat in a dark corner of the courtyard, watching people, drinking diet cola and water. Being good.

But gradually the noise and music coaxed him inside. It was inevitable. Something cosmic. Something out of his control. Like a kid learning to ride a bike, heading straight for a wall. He could try to stop, try to turn, but the wall kept getting closer, sucking him in.

Within another hour he'd put away several beers, had danced several dances, and told a repertoire of jokes. He lost track of time, the way he sometimes did when he was enjoying himself. He wondered why he hadn't come to the tavern before. He'd been missing out, that was for sure. Good music, good beer, good people.

Sometime after midnight he joined the band. Even though he had a voice that sounded like a bullfrog, he got up and sang a number. Everybody laughed and applauded. It was what he'd missed, what he'd needed. His fix of crowd approval. And even though he probably wouldn't remember what song he'd sung tomorrow, it was great while it lasted. Great while it was happening.

Things were still going great when Phil Harmonic happened in, a fellow drifter drawn by the noise. Johnnie waved him over. Phil gave him a quick smile of relief. With his shopping bag clutched to him, he made his way through the crowd to take a seat on the barstool next to Johnnie's.

Phil was the kind of guy old ladies immediately needed to feed. The kind of person they plied with cookies and invited in for a bowl of hot soup.

Johnnie treated him to a couple of precooked hamburgers, a pickled egg, and a handful of beef jerky.

Phil ate everything but the egg.

"You know those things bounce if you leave 'em in vinegar long enough," Johnnie told him. "That's one of the only things I learned in school."

"It'll bounce?" Phil picked up the egg and examined it in amazement, turning it in his hand. Then he dropped it. Both men watched as it splat against the wooden floor.

"Guess not," Johnnie observed.

The egg must have reminded Phil of birds, because within a few seconds he was whipping out his sketch pad, eager to show Johnnie the drawings he'd done that day.

Their heads were bent over the bar, both of them admiring a nesting cliff swallow, Johnnie for the craftsmanship, Phil for the sheer beauty of nature, when a meaty hand with hairy knuckles and geometric rings reached between them and ripped the picture from the sketch pad.

Johnnie swiveled around to see a lumberjack of a man in a black leather vest and stained T-shirt waving Phil's picture above his head.

"Want it, Bird Man?" he taunted, mincing around while holding the ragged-edged paper between his fingers.

A circle quickly formed: people anticipating a diversion.

When had the crowd turned so rough, so seedy? Johnnie wondered.

Beside him, Phil slid off his barstool and lunged for the drawing. "Give it to me," he said, sounding close to tears.

The man laughed and held it higher, a good six inches beyond Phil's reach. "You're not gonna cry, are you, Bird Man?"

There was no thought. Only reaction. Johnnie let out a battle cry and dove for Phil's tormentor.

Johnnie had never been much of a fighter. Oh, he got *into* fights, but he was all emotion and not much skill. Within a fraction of a second, he was flying backward, crashing to the floor.

Had he gotten in a hit at all? Was that pain radiating from his knuckles? He hoped so.

He shoved himself to his feet, searching for his opponent.

What had started as an altercation between three men quickly turned into a classic barroom brawl. People were crawling all over one another. Chairs were flying. Glasses breaking. The band had stopped playing as the musicians scurried to protect their instruments.

Caught up in the spirit of it all, Johnnie jumped on a chair and shouted, "I can whip anybody's ass in this place!"

The door slammed open. In came the cops.

The fighting quickly dwindled to nothing. When everything cleared, there was no sign of the guy who'd started the fight. Phil had checked out too. The only thing left of him was a torn, footprint-smudged drawing in the middle of the floor.

Johnnie was allowed one phone call.

Which was a surprise, considering the jail was in Hope, Texas.

But then where else could someone go down on record as being arrested for "conduct unbefitting a gentleman"?

Bail had been set at two thousand dollars. He needed to post ten percent of that amount in order to get out. Or he could stay until his trial, which they told him could be anywhere from one day to a week. At first he thought, what the hell, he'd take the jail sentence. But then they tossed him in the can.

It turned out to be a cell he'd been in before. Over fifteen years ago. For a few seconds he felt time slip away. An overpowering feeling of futility swamped him.

Johnnie turned and wrapped his fingers around the cold metal bars of the cell door, shouting for the deputy. He'd changed his mind. He'd make that one phone call.

Ear to the receiver, Johnnie counted five rings. Then he heard a crash, followed by Maggie's mumbled hello.

He made it brief. The facts, ma'am, just the facts.

"I should leave you there," she said when he was done briefing her.

A wave of panic swept over him. "You can't," he choked out.

A pause. Then, "I'll be there as soon as I can."

After hanging up he was led back to his cell. "Where's Sheriff Cahill?" Johnnie asked as the metal door clicked shut.

"Got off at midnight."

One less thing for Johnnie to worry about. Not that he couldn't handle Cahill, he told himself. He just didn't feel like dealing with him at the moment.

While waiting to be sprung, Johnnie paced the cell, reading the graffiti that covered the walls. Somewhere in the mess was his name. He searched, but couldn't find it. Maybe it had faded. Or been covered up.

This is no different than an apartment. A small apartment. You got your bed with a mattress as thick as a shingle. In the corner is a sink and toilet. What's so bad about it? All the comforts of home.

Except the door was locked. Except that he had no control over the situation. Except the only way out depended upon somebody else. Except that he'd been here before and he was afraid he'd come full circle. Afraid that nothing in his life had really changed. That the years spent in California didn't count for anything. Maybe they'd never even happened. . . .

Maggie.

How long had it been since he'd called her? Hours? Days? Weeks?

Come on, Maggie. I can't stand this much longer. Come on. Maggie to the rescue. Here she comes, to save the day. That means that Maggie May is on her way.

He tried to shove his hands into his pockets, then remembered he didn't have any pockets, which was better than not having any hands. They'd taken his clothes and made him put on an outfit with no buttons or zippers, something like a doctor would wear to surgery.

Come on, Maggie.

A criminal. He'd been cuffed and tossed into the back of a patrol car, just like a criminal. Just like some felon. At the jail, he'd been stripped and given baby clothes, then fingerprinted.

Come on, Maggie.

He did some more reading. *Life's a bitch, then you die. Life's a bitch, then you die.* Over and over. It must have been written a hundred times. He discovered a particularly graphic account of a sexual encounter, complete with illustrations. He paced some more. He couldn't keep his feet still, or his hands still.

If he had a pen, he'd add his own stream of consciousness to the graffiti, but they'd made him empty his pockets, taking everything, even the lint.

Why didn't they let *him* have a pen? They let all the other people have pens. And knives. Some of the stuff had been carved into the wall. What kind of jail was it where they let them have knives? What kind of place were they running here? He'd have to get on them about that.

Come on, Maggie. Get your butt down here.

Footsteps.

Regulation soles hitting a cement floor. It was the same cop who'd locked him up. Kind of young. Kind of self-important. In his hands were Johnnie's clothes.

He unlocked the cell and tossed the clothes inside. "Get dressed and come on out. Your bail's been paid."

Thank you, Officer.

Johnnie played it cool until the cop was gone. Then he scrambled into his clothes. To hell with underwear. To hell with socks. Shirt, jeans, shoes—that was all he needed. Nothing illegal here.

He found Maggie standing near the counter in the same room where he'd been fingerprinted. Her hair was messy, a jacket had been thrown over her Tweety Bird nightshirt and a pair of jeans.

He wanted to drop to the floor and hug her feet, but then he caught the look in her eyes.

Uh-oh.

Without saying anything, she handed him a manila envelope. Inside, he knew he'd find his keys, wallet, and whatever else they'd dug out of his pockets.

He glanced up. She was staring at his black eye. Automatically his hand went to the swelled area. He winced, then gave her a sheepish smile. "Want to know what the other guy looked like?"

"Not really."

Pissed. She was really pissed. "Not a scratch," he said.

She wasn't listening. She was heading for the door.

He waved to the chief of police—couldn't let them know he'd almost lost it back there—then followed Maggie.

"Come on. Lighten up," he told her as he slid into the passenger seat of her car.

She started the engine and pulled away from the curb. "I should have left you in jail."

The thought made him feel sick.

"Do you know that Karen and I had to go through her kids' piggy banks to come up with enough money to get you out? Try to explain bail to an eight-year-old." She banged her open palm against the steering wheel. "I can't believe I did it. I can't believe I didn't leave you there."

"I couldn't have stayed," he said quietly.

"Maybe that's your problem. Maybe you've never had to face responsibility and the consequences of your own actions."

She had him all wrong. But it was useless to argue. He let out a defeated sigh and slid down in the seat, his knees braced against the dash, eyes closed.

Maggie glanced over at him. Beneath the flicker of the streetlights, his face looked pale and drawn, the bruise under his eye appearing even darker. When she'd seen it, she'd wanted to ask if he was okay, if he'd been hurt anywhere else, but she hadn't wanted to give him that satisfaction.

She was disappointed in him. Just when she'd begun to let down her guard, just when she'd begun to think that the things they said about him were lies, he went and did something like this, reaffirming her initial impression of a brat with no self-discipline.

When they reached his apartment, she got out of the car and went up with him. On the landing he paused to search through the manila envelope, finally pulling out a set of keys. He unlocked the door and swung it open. Inside, the lights had been left on.

She shut the door behind her, watching as Johnnie flung himself across the unmade bed.

From the reading she'd been doing on diabetes, she knew that his insulin level had most likely been drastically altered by alcohol and lack of sleep. If during the night it became too low, he could go into a coma. "Shouldn't you test your blood sugar level?"

He moaned, shifted to a sitting position, and rubbed his head, leaving his hair sticking up all over.

The test kit was on the counter. She picked it up and handed it to him.

His actions were automatic, the test something he could practically do in his sleep. And that was good, because judging from his appearance, sleep wasn't far off. With an efficiency of movement, he pricked his finger, smeared blood on the test strip, then inserted it into the readout machine.

Beep.

He let out a resigned sigh, then prepared a syringe. Before she could protest, he stuck the needle through the fabric of his pants, into his inner thigh. He pushed in the plunger, removed the needle, dropped it on the dresser, and sprawled back across the bed, one arm flung over his face.

"There's not enough room in here for you and your disapproval," he said clearly.

"Fine."

Before leaving, she went around the tiny apartment turning off lights, in the process stepping over food cartons, clothes, newspapers, and what looked like manuscripts.

He let out a puzzled laugh. "I don't know what it is about you," he said. "Why do I feel guilty as hell about going out for a few hours? About going to a tavern? Big deal."

"You were drinking. Diabetics shouldn't drink." She bent over and picked up some litter, throwing it into a paper bag near the kitchen counter. "And I think you're forgetting about the fight part, and the jail part."

"Are you so perfect?" he asked. "Don't you ever do anything against your better judgment?"

She took a look around her. "Yes."

His arm came away from his face. His cockiness was back. "What did you ever do that you knew you shouldn't?" he asked with disbelief. "Wear a green blouse instead of a yellow one? Flats instead of heels?"

Black eye. Blood on his shirt.

"You. You were against my better judgment."

He let his head fall back against the pillow and gave a surprised laugh, the way he did so often when he asked her a direct question that she answered with a direct answer.

"Night, Maggie."

She turned off the lamp and stood in the darkness, unmoving while her pupils adjusted.

He scared her. Scared her because he seemed predestined to go the way of so many other celebrities who'd gotten too much too fast. But it wasn't Hollywood that had made him who he was. She knew that now. No, she blamed it on a mother who had been totally lacking in maternal instinct. A mother who had been not only uncaring but cruel. Neglect was bad enough, but cruelty . . .

If Johnnie had been Maggie's child, she would have rocked him to sleep and told him bedtime stories. She would have loved him. . . .

The rhythm of his breathing changed, telling her he was asleep.

She went to stand at the window. The moon cast strange shadows on the landscape, cast dark, depressed shadows in her mind. What if she hadn't reminded him about his insulin? What if she'd dropped him off and he'd gone to bed and slipped into a coma? Nobody would have known.

Nights like this were commonplace for Johnnie. On the edge, not seeming to care if he lived or died.

She crossed her arms at her chest, pulled in a deep, shaky breath, and blinked her eyes against the sudden blurring of the moon and stars.

Yes, she felt sorry for whoever fell in love with him, because that person was in for a lot of pain. It would hurt to stand by and helplessly watch him destroy himself.

Chapter 11

hree days later Johnnie appeared in court, spent ten minutes before the judge, and ended up paying a three-hundred-dollar fine. His brief time in jail had spooked him, no question about it. But now that it was over, now that he was a free man, Johnnie could look back on his panic-filled phone call to Maggie with embarrassment. He'd flipped out over nothing.

Maybe it was a case of self-preservation, but he made it a point to shrug off the entire episode, to dismiss it from his mind—something he was good at doing.

With each passing day, the play took shape. Johnnie was amazed at how things were pulling together, considering what a mess it had been to begin with.

At first he'd had some trouble telling the kids apart, but little by little he became familiar with their names and individual personalities. There was Travis, a kid with red hair and an attitude to match. And Jackson, who was always stirring things up, never paying attention. Maggie was constantly having to drag him here or there. But when it came time to say his part, he always knew it, plus everybody else's.

And then there was little blond-haired Sara, the girl he'd noticed from the start. Turned out she belonged to a friend of Maggie's. Turned out Sara had robbed her piggy bank for his bail money. Shameful. No wonder the mother glared at him whenever she came to pick up her daughter.

Maggie explained that Karen didn't have anything against him personally. She hated all men. That was right after Karen grudgingly agreed to be his page-turner for the program. He could hardly wait.

A few evenings later Johnnie got the running bug again. This time, instead of going to a tavern, he opted for something safer. He hopped in his car to cruise the back roads.

In California he rarely communed with nature, but lately he'd discovered something compelling about the desert. Its sunrises and sunsets. They more than made up for the colorlessness of the day. It was ironic that the very dust that stung your skin and eyeballs was the same stuff that broke up the sun's rays into particles of diffused light.

How could he have forgotten what it felt like to watch the sky put on a light show? How could he have forgotten the ache it made in his chest, a pain that was part loneliness, part wonder?

The desert seemed to speak to him, so it was the instinctive place for him to go when he had trouble sleeping.

Once there, he'd watch the night sky. Sometimes a person could see more than one falling star at a time. It was rejuvenating. Standing beneath that vastness made him feel almost new, made him feel that the world wasn't such a bad place.

One night he was heading back to town when a red light flashed behind him and a siren let out a few short squawks. Johnnie's gaze automatically dropped to the speedometer. Forty-five.

He pulled to the side of the road, shut off the engine, and waited while the police car pulled up behind him, the glare from its headlights illuminating the interior of his rental car.

A door slammed.

Footsteps crunched across gravel.

"Out kinda late, aren't you?"

The voice, with its heavy southern drawl, was a voice out of the past. Brace Cahill.

He was older and heavier, but not much different from the way

Johnnie remembered him. The drawl, the Stetson, the beige uniform with pants he kept hitching up. The attitude. It was all there.

Cahill was the epitome of every small-town cop in every car-chasing B movie Johnnie had ever seen. The ultimate redneck. Every longhair's nightmare.

It would have been funny, except that this guy was real. He could put a person in jail, and he could put a person in prison.

"Been drinkin'?" Cahill asked.

"No."

"Driving kinda slow. Took that last corner kinda wide."

The years fell away. Suddenly Johnnie was seventeen. Suddenly he was a loser, an outcast, trying to make it in an adult world.

At seventeen Johnnie rarely spent any time at home, not even to sleep, but for some reason he'd stopped by one night and found Cahill in bed with his mother. Cahill was married and didn't like being caught in the act of adultery.

"Forget you seen me here, kid," he'd told Johnnie. Johnnie promised, not any more eager than Cahill to have his mother's sexual habits laughed about over coffee at the Hope Cafe. But the next day Johnnie was thrown in jail on a trumped-up charge.

A week later Cahill unlocked the jail cell door, saying, "Let's go for a little drive."

Johnnie was tough and mouthy, but he was still hardly more than a kid, and ingrained somewhere in his subconscious was a somewhat twisted respect for authority. Johnnie went with him.

He was put in the caged backseat of the squad car and driven to the edge of town. Once there, Cahill let him out, tossing a duffel bag after him.

"Start walkin'."

Johnnie stared at him.

Cahill's hands were on his hips. One hand shifted so his fingers were just touching his unsnapped holster.

There were all sorts of stories about Cahill, and whether Johnnie believed them or not, he did know that Cahill wasn't shy about using a gun. He wouldn't be afraid to fire it. And if he hit Johnnie, if he killed Johnnie, no one would ask any questions. If he were someone else, then maybe. But he was Johnnie Irish, and he didn't have a prayer.

So Johnnie turned and started walking, north away from Hope, all the while feeling Cahill's eyes boring into his back. It wasn't until he passed the billboard advertising the next gas station that Johnnie heard the police car's engine turn over, heard the tires squeal across the blacktop. But Cahill didn't head back to Hope. He followed Johnnie for almost a mile. Then he finally made a U-turn, spraying dust and gravel.

And so thanks to Cahill, Johnnie had left Hope behind.

And now here he was, back where he'd started. And things hadn't changed. He was still an outsider, a loser. And Cahill was still an ass with a badge.

Since there was no Fourth Amendment in Hope, Cahill had Johnnie stand along the road while he searched the car. In the glove compartment he found a used syringe. Drug paraphernalia.

Johnnie was forced to walk the center line, heel to toe, recite the alphabet, then close his eyes and put a finger to his nose. After that, he was forced to suffer the final humiliation. He was hauled downtown for a breath test and a strip search.

It was four in the morning by the time he'd convinced them that the syringe had been used for insulin.

Back at his apartment he checked his blood sugar, gave himself an injection, and fell into bed.

But he couldn't sleep. Things he hadn't thought about in years, things he thought he'd forgotten, kept flashing through his brain like scenes caught in the flash of a strobe.

Memories moved in and out.

Sleep beckoned, then shifted just beyond reach. Beckoned, then shifted away . . .

When Johnnie was little, about four or five, his mother would have men over and make him stay in the closet. She'd lock the door from the outside and tell him not to make a sound. If he did, she would beat him. Sometimes she'd forget that she'd put him in the closet at all. But Johnnie didn't always mind. Sometimes he preferred the closet.

Sleep drifted closer, reaching out to him. . . .

"Johnnie—"

Her voice came to him out of the darkness, making him jerk awake.

He scrambled up from the mattress that had been tossed into a corner. Sometimes, when she'd been gone all night, she'd come home and trip over him. That made her mad, and Johnnie always tried not to make her mad.

Now Johnnie the child stood watching her as she brushed her hair, watched as she sprayed perfume under her arms and between her legs. Once she'd made him drink some of her perfume. For days he'd tasted it every time he breathed.

He watched as she opened a tube of red lipstick and darkened her lips, like a smear of blood across her mouth.

"I want you to stay in the closet and don't make a sound." With a click of metal against metal, she capped the lipstick and put it on the edge of the dresser. Suddenly she was looming over him. She took his chin in one hand and squeezed, her nails jabbing into his cheeks as she examined his features, as if looking for someone else. Used to these inspections, he waited, wondering what was wrong with him, wondering what he had to change about himself so she would like him.

"Your mouth's too big," she told him with the voice of someone who would know such things. "And your eyes are too big."

It had to be true, because she was his mother. He squinted, trying to make his eyes smaller. He pressed his lips together.

She laughed. "What a funny person you are." She frowned. "You're too much like him."

She grabbed him by the arm and dragged him toward the mirrored dresser. "See how funny you look?" She leaned over and sniffed. "And you stink." She picked up a bottle, and before he could duck she'd sprayed him in the face with perfume. It burned his eyes and burned his throat.

He tried to pull away, but she had her fingers wrapped around his arm—mothers were strong. She pulled him toward her. He braced his bare feet against the gritty floor, skidding closer.

Her face was grim. "Never try to get away from me," she said through clenched teeth. Her breath smelled like the stuff she gave him to make him sleep.

With his free arm, he swung. He didn't mean to hit her, only push the sickening sweet perfume away. But his hand brushed her cheek. She jumped, knocking the dresser. The lipstick, in its gold metal holder, skittered across the floor.

She turned into the other person, the person who terrified him.

"Why, you little—" She grabbed him by both arms, her finger-nails digging into his flesh. "After all I've done for you, you un-grateful animal. That lipstick cost three dollars."

Flecks of foam formed at the corners of her mouth, white against the red of her lips. "Don't you know how much I've done for you?" she shrieked. "If it wasn't for you, I'd be married to some rich man right now. Don't you understand? If it wasn't for you, I'd be happy."

She hit him. Again and again. He didn't make a sound, didn't cry out because that made her even madder. Instead, he longed for the closet, longed for the darkness.

Remnants of long-ago dreams, long-ago nightmares, swirled around him, pulling him down, sucking him under.

Knowing they were dreams, Johnnie tried to kick them away, struggling to get to the surface, struggling to wake up.

He came awake with a jolt, sitting upright, his body drenched in a cold sweat. His heart was knocking against his rib cage, his breathing coming short and fast.

Jesus.

For a short time, Johnnie had been lulled into a false sense of security. He'd let himself forget just how much he hated this place.

He ran a trembling hand through his sweat-damp hair. He had to get the hell out of Hope.

Chapter 12

*H*e didn't show up.

It was three days before the actual play and Johnnie didn't show up for rehearsal.

Nothing. Not a phone call, not a note. Nothing.

Maggie's initial reaction was one of worry, so she phoned his apartment, only to have him answer and tell her he wasn't coming.

"Are you sick?" she asked.

"No. I'm just not coming." Then he hung up.

Hung up!

She knew it, she knew it, she knew it.

If she knew it, then why in the hell had she gone along with him? And what in the hell was she going to do now?

She swung her foot at the closest thing, which happened to be a metal folding chair. She stubbed her toe, the pain fueling her anger. She had enough presence of mind left to cuss in half-formed expletives while she hopped around on her uninjured foot.

Her anger was good for one thing. It took her sailing through an entire afternoon of rehearsal. She was superwoman. Super pissed woman, banging out notes on the piano and directing at the same time. By the time it was over, she must have burned up five thousand calories, and her anger was still at a full, rolling boil.

After the children had gone, she paced back and forth on the stage. "Stinking, self-centered, thoughtless, inconsiderate—" She was madder than she could ever remember being in her entire life. She was shaking, she was so mad. She was spitting mad.

Mad at Johnnie, but just as mad at herself. Because she'd known better. She'd known better than to count on him. She was a fool, a fool, a fool.

Three days before the play, the jerk deserts her!

Chaos.

It surrounded him like an aura. He carried it with him like some crazy crest. And he left it behind when he was gone, like a town in the wake of a tornado. He tore things up, then walked away whistling.

She should have known better. She *had* known better.

She continued to pace, back and forth on the stage. What was she going to do? Cancel the production?

The children had worked too hard for that.

Postpone it?

Fliers were already up, tickets printed and sold.

She didn't hear the back door open, but she knew someone was there because she saw a sliver of light appear and disappear as the door opened and closed. Then Johnnie was strolling toward her, as if nothing on earth was wrong, as if he hadn't just turned her life upside down.

She wanted to jump from the stage, grab him by the T-shirt, and shake him until his teeth rattled.

Her anger created a buzzing in her head, a haze over her eyes. Through it she saw his mouth moving. She managed to catch the gist of what he was telling her.

He was leaving town.

In a tiny part of her brain that was still able to reason, she recognized the fact that she was losing control, and never having been one to get mad very easily, she wasn't handling it well. Not well at all. But she didn't care.

"You bastard!" She pointed a shaking finger at him. "I knew you wouldn't stay! I knew we couldn't count on you!"

He had the gall to look taken aback, even hurt. How dare he! Why should *he* look hurt? He was the one doing the hurting!

But then she decided that she must have misread him, because he immediately bristled, gesturing angrily in the direction of downtown Hope. "I'm bored out of my mind here!" he shouted, his voice booming up to the rafters.

"Oh, poor baby," she said with saccharine sarcasm, a sarcasm she quickly dropped to allow her temper free rein. "You are the most selfish, self-centered, self—"

He flew at her. In four strides he was at the stage. Never pausing, he vaulted up beside her.

Even though she could feel his anger swirling around her, she didn't step back. She refused to give him the satisfaction. His eyes, only an arm's length away, cut into hers.

"Maybe if you'd loosen up a little," he said, "maybe if you weren't such a tight-kneed prude, things would be a little more interesting around here."

"Of all the—" With him, it always came down to sex. "Are you saying if we had sex you'd stay?"

His anger softened a little, was replaced by an equally unflattering smugness. "That depends."

"On what?"

"On whether or not you're a good lay."

She'd never slapped anybody in her life. Until now, it had always seemed an immature and overly emotional thing to do. She raised a hand and swung. Hard.

His reflexes were quick. He blocked, his fingers locking around her wrist. The impact of the deflected blow sent a jarring vibration all the way up her arm to her shoulder socket.

"That's something you'll never know," she said through gritted teeth. "Whether I'm good or not. I want to go down in history as being the only woman in America you haven't screwed."

He laughed, but there was no humor in the sound. He was still holding her wrist high in the air. He pulled her close, his body slamming against hers, almost knocking the wind out of her. His other hand pressed against her lower spine. If anyone were to come in, it would look as though they were performing some bizarre dance.

"You're a self-righteous hypocrite," he said, his voice soft, threatening. In his eyes she read unshakable determination.

She tried to jerk away, but he held her fast. Suddenly his leg was behind hers, pushing at the back of her knees, making her fold. Her wrist slipped free of his grip. Arms behind her, she caught herself as her bottom hit the polished floor.

He dropped to his knees beside her, moving to cover her with his body. Before he could make contact, she scrambled backward across the floor.

His hand lashed out, grabbing her ankle, dragging her back to him.

"Let go of me! I hate you!" she screamed.

He pulled her underneath him. He held her down with his weight, forcing her legs apart, insinuating himself between her thighs.

She raised a hand to hit him once more. He grabbed it, stopping her. Off balance, they rolled until she was on top, her legs splayed on either side of his hips, her heaving breasts crushed to his rapidly rising and falling chest.

And as Johnnie stared up at her, he could see that her anger and hate were gone. Now there was only fear.

His own anger dissolved. He let go of her arms, closed his eyes, and let his head drop to the floor.

"Go ahead, hit me," he said, suddenly weary of the whole thing.

"W-what?"

"Hit me. I won't stop you this time."

Now that his eyes were closed, all of his senses were focused on his painful erection, throbbing against his zipper, against her warmth. Even without his eyes closed, he could remember how she felt. All soft. And warm. And wet.

Her weight shifted. She shoved herself upright, causing her pelvis to press against him even more, giving him even more of a pleasurable pain.

He groaned, just managing to keep his hands from cupping her bottom and grinding her into him. He had to have release. He'd never been in this kind of situation, where he couldn't get release.

Then her weight was completely gone, but he was still in agony. He flung an arm over his face, waiting for his body to calm down, his breathing to quiet, his muscles to relax.

Finally he opened his eyes.

She was standing a few feet away, her arms crossed at her chest, one leg straight, one hip out, her face flushed, hair hanging down her neck, having come loose from the band at the back of her head.

"Why are you leaving?" she asked.

He had to give her credit for trying to put things back on track. But damned if he'd tell her about Cahill and what had happened last night. It was too degrading. He just wanted to forget about it. He just wanted to get the hell out of Hope as fast as he could. "I told you, I'm bored."

"When are you leaving?"

"Right away. I'm driving to El Paso, then catching a flight to California." He needed to get going. He'd stayed too long already. Now that their wrestling match was over, the claustrophobic feeling he'd been fighting all day was coming back.

"What would make you stay?"

He didn't answer.

"Sex. Would you stay for sex?"

He drew in a breath, almost choking. "What?"

"You heard me. What if I told you I'd have sex with you if you stayed?"

He let out his breath. "Then I'd say you were bluffing."

She frowned.

But she was right about one thing. He wanted her. He'd like to have her at least once before he left.

He shoved himself to his feet and faced her. He didn't understand it, but he suddenly had the urge to touch her, not in a sexual way, but a comforting way. Just for the sake of touching her.

"If we ever do make love," he said, silently moving toward her, "it will be because you want to, and I want to."

He did touch her then, a palm to the side of her blood-warm face. Surprisingly she didn't move away. She simply stared at him, lips parted. He couldn't resist. He kissed her. Not a soft, gentle kiss, but a possessive kiss, his tongue quickly outlining her lips before plunging inside to stroke the wetness of her mouth. Her breasts were pressed to his chest. He could feel the hardness of each nipple, feel himself rising again, straining against the seam of his jeans.

One hand came down to cup her bottom. He lifted her into him, making sure she could feel him. Then he pulled his mouth from hers. "I'll stay," he told her, staring into her wide amber eyes. "But not because of some bargain."

He couldn't help but feel a twinge of self-mockery. His present attitude toward sex was a little different from the one he'd had only a month ago. And he supposed he should give Maggie credit for that.

She was still watching him, still pressed to him, one hand gripping his shirt sleeve, her eyes full of confusion and a sort of bemused wonder.

He kissed her again. Quickly this time, before he was tempted to pull her to the floor and make love to her so she wouldn't forget him.

He could put up with Hope, Texas, for three more days. And three more nights. He would survive the nightmares. The tossing and turning and trying to forget. He would do it for Maggie.

Chapter 13

*J*ohnnie had been right about the bluffing. But Maggie had been desperate, desperate enough to offer him what she thought he wanted. Not that she approved of lying, but the situation had called for extreme tactics, no matter how out of character. How had he seen through her so quickly? Was she that transparent? Or was she really such a goody-two-shoes? Enough of one to make her offer ludicrous?

Probably, she admitted with a certain amount of hurt pride. She wasn't *that* old-fashioned.

It didn't matter. The important thing was that he'd stayed.

And now the day of the play was upon them. Barring any major catastrophe such as a missing piano player or sick lead actor, the event they had all been working toward would take place in a little over five hours.

Maggie had been in a really strange frame of mind over the last three days. Depressed and unfocused. Concentration seemed to take more energy than she had. If not for the help of Johnnie and Karen, the final rehearsals would have been total disasters.

What was her problem? PMS? She'd never been bothered with PMS before. Whatever the cause, Maggie was stressed-out. With each advancing minute, her nerves wound tighter and tighter. Even though she really couldn't spare the time, she tried lying across her bed, listening to the relaxation tape Karen had given her for her birthday, but the gentle sound of waves lapping against a shore failed to soothe her.

The cooling unit in the hallway kicked in, reminding her of the oppressiveness of the weather, the unbearable heat of the past few days. She hoped that by evening the temperature would drop enough to make the opera house bearable.

As curtain time approached, Maggie dressed for the play, deciding on a black sleeveless dress that seemed to be in keeping with her strange mood. Her hair she left down.

Then, just before leaving the house, she paused and removed the wedding band from around her neck.

When she arrived at the opera house, the first person she saw was Johnnie. He was wearing a black suit and black tie, his hair slicked back. He'd even shaved for the occasion. At the moment he was talking to a cluster of children, keeping them entertained while they waited for things to get under way.

He glanced up, saw Maggie, and flashed her a brilliant smile.

Her heart lurched. Something heavy landed in the pit of her stomach. He looked away, his attention drawn back to the kids.

It came to her then—a blinding realization. She finally understood the reason for her depression. Johnnie. In a few hours he would be gone. In a few hours he would no longer be a part of her life.

Standing in the wings, she heard the rustle of programs and the loud hum of people as the seats filled. Then it was time. The house lights dimmed. The audience fell to silence.

The evening she'd looked forward to all school year passed in a series of jerky, disjointed frames, like a movie reel fed through a crummy projector. One moment Maggie was aware of being in the middle of Act One, Scene Two, the next they were halfway through Act Two. She pulled herself together, only to drift again, only to have reality fade in and out of focus.

Johnnie, on the other hand, was cool and collected. Just another day in shantytown. Karen sat beside him turning the pages while he played beautifully, effortlessly. His music made the show complete, pulling everything together, adding just the right touch.

Act Three came and went just like the others, dissolving into the curtain call, then the standing ovation, the thundering applause reaching deafening proportions when Johnnie took his bow.

It was total confusion, a swell of noise and heat and bodies. People shook her hand. Mouths moved. Heads nodded.

"Wonderful production . . ."

". . . best you've ever done . . ."

". . . beautiful . . ."

"Funny . . ."

"Congratulations . . ."

"Great job . . .

Maggie was peripherally aware of some of the children jumping around on feet that seemed attached to springs. Others were quiet, totally wiped-out now that the weeks of hard work were over.

It was then that she spotted Sara, off by herself, crying. For a brief moment, Maggie's head cleared. All too familiar with the instant crash that could follow a long period of seemingly endless anticipation, Maggie went to her.

"At first I w-was sad a-about being in the play at all," Sara said with a series of shoulder-jerking sniffles. "Now I'm sad a-about it being over. W-what will I do tomorrow? I won't have the play to look forward to."

"I'm sure you'll be able to think of all sorts of things to do. How about swimming? Or playing outside? And didn't your mother say you were going on a vacation sometime soon?"

"Yeah. But it won't be the same."

"It will be a different kind of fun. And next year we'll do a different kind of play."

"But I won't be able to be Amelia ever again. I liked being Amelia."

"No, you won't be Amelia, but next year you can be somebody else, somebody brand-new, somebody you might like as well, but in a different way."

"I want to be Amelia."

Maggie sighed, realizing it would take time for her to adjust. A good night's sleep would probably do wonders.

"I don't want to play anybody else," Sara insisted. "It won't be the same."

Maggie stroked her soft hair. "Maybe not. But it might be even better. Did you ever think about that?"

"No." She wiped her tears with the back of one hand, gave Maggie a watery smile, then hurried off to find her mother in the crowd.

There was still the cast party to get through. Some of the mothers had set up tables of cookies and punch backstage and now, *en masse*, everyone moved that direction.

Maggie had been through this before, so the social graces came almost secondhand, yet she couldn't help but wonder if she was making any sense. She tried to focus on the discussion of the play, but just when she thought she was doing fine, her mind would wander and pretty soon she would find herself searching the room for Johnnie.

Finally the crowd began to thin, then dwindle to almost nothing. The Kool-Aid and cookies were cleared away.

Time to go.

Outside, the night air was welcoming and cool against Maggie's hot cheeks, but it did nothing to revive her brain. Time continued to proceed like a disjointed dream that didn't follow the rules of moving logically through time and space. She knew she should get in her car and leave, but still she lingered until there were only two cars left, Maggie's and Johnnie's.

Johnnie strolled across the lot, undoing his tie as he approached.

"Guess this is goodbye," she said when he reached her side. From nowhere, taking her completely by surprise, tears threatened. She swallowed and looked up at the orange glow of the streetlight. "What time are you leaving?" she asked.

"Before dawn."

She nodded. It was on the tip of her tongue to tell him to be careful. To watch his blood sugar and get his rest and eat right. But she caught herself. It wasn't her place to lecture him. And he wouldn't listen anyway. Tomorrow at this time he would be a thousand miles away. Once there, he would forget everything she'd ever told him. He'd forget her.

"You were great tonight," she said.

"So were you."

She shook her head. She'd been kidding herself all along. She could see that now. All along she'd told herself that Johnnie wasn't her type, while all along she'd been falling a little in love with him each day.

She would miss him terribly. Who would have thought that she, of all people—someone who had known a perfect love, someone who had shared quiet secrets with a gentle man, who had shared fear and pain and eventually death—would fall in love again, and with a man who couldn't be more wrong for her? A man who would never be a part of her life.

Time to go.

What now? Should she shake his hand? How ridiculously formal. She'd planted flowers in the middle of the night with this man. They had watched the sun come up together.

Johnnie spared her the immediate decision by asking, "Want to go for a ride?"

The car windows were down. Night wind blew through her hair.

"How about some tunes?" Johnnie slipped in a cassette. It fell into place with a click. Lazy, dreamy music floated around them, adding to the sense of unreality.

They turned off the highway, onto a dirt road, following so many twists and turns that Maggie was soon lost.

Twenty minutes later they stopped in the middle of nowhere—flat land blanketed by a huge sky.

Johnnie shut off the engine, leaving the key turned to auxiliary so the music continued to wrap around them.

She stared straight ahead, through the windshield. The landscape was stark. There were no hills, no buildings. Only a few dark shadows cast by tumbleweeds and small piñon trees broke the light of the stars and half-moon.

Johnnie got out of the car and slammed the door, the sound echoing through the stillness. Once outside, he took off his jacket and tossed it in the open window, onto the backseat. Maggie could just make out the black of his suspenders against the white of his shirt.

She got out of the car and joined him, levering herself up onto the hood. It felt warm against the backs of her bare legs.

"You know why they call them dog days?" he asked, his head tilted back as he stared up at the sky.

Hardly a moment went by that he didn't surprise her with some small revelation into his character. "Because it's so hot?" she asked.

"Because of Sirius, the Dog Star. You can't see it now, because in July and August it rises and sets with the sun. But that's where they get the dog day thing."

"I didn't know that."

"Now you do."

She couldn't see his face, but she heard the smile in his voice. She heard the brush of his starched shirt as he moved.

Layer by layer, day by day, she had come to see a little more of him. She thought of them together, as a couple. Impossible. Oil and water. "We're so different," she said, voicing her thoughts.

"Not so different," he said.

She made a small sound of protest and looked up at the sky. So vast. So many stars . . .

"Ever camp out?" he asked.

"When I was little and in Girl Scouts, we used to go camping. What about you?"

"Not the conventional way."

"What does that mean?"

"Not with a tent and a sleeping bag."

"Then it wasn't camping. What did you do? Sleep on the ground?" For some reason, a picture of Phil flashed through her mind.

Johnnie made a small, let's-drop-it sound, along with a shrug of his shoulders.

She was quiet for a few moments, thinking about those nights under the stars. "Sometimes we'd sit around the campfire and play a game called True Believer," she told him. "Each person was supposed to reveal something she wanted in life. Want to play?"

"Nah."

"Oh, come on."

"What am I supposed to say?" he asked. "Give you some beauty-contestant answer like 'I want to see an end to world hunger'?"

"It has to be personal. A personal dream."

"Like group therapy."

"Like getting to know each other." This wasn't working, she decided. "Forget it."

"No, I'll do it," he said, not sounding like he really wanted to at all. "I'll even start."

"Okay." She waited, eager and curious to know what kind of dream Johnnie harbored deep within his heart.

"Meeting an alien has always been a personal dream of mine," he said. "That and spotting a UFO."

He wouldn't even play along. She supposed that was just as much of a revelation as anything.

"How about you? What do *you* want?"

Soul-searching came easier for her, but then it did for most women. "I once read an article about a lady who won the lottery," she said. "The reporter asked her what she planned to do with the money and she told him she might buy some new windows. I'd like to be like that woman. Content. Satisfied to quietly view the world through new windows."

"That's nice, I guess, but don't you want to be a part of what you see?"

"Not a big part."

"So you don't want anything."

"I didn't say that. I said I'd like to not want anything."

"How about marriage? Think you'll ever get married again?"

"I don't know. Right now it doesn't seem likely. I'm used to living alone. I like it."

There was a period of companionable silence. Then he asked, "Want to know what I want right now?"

"What?"

"To touch you."

Her breath caught.

"What do *you* want?" he asked.

He'd turned her game around, a game that was suddenly no

longer a game. "I guess we aren't so different, then," she whispered, her hands braced on the car. "I want you to touch me."

Johnnie turned, his hip pressing against her knee. With a hand braced on either side of her, he leaned closer. "I think I'm going to miss you."

Where had that come from? he wondered. Not that it wasn't true, but he hadn't intended to reveal his feelings. He *would* miss her. The way she made him laugh. The way *she* laughed. The way she was always surprising him with her bluntness, her honesty. And it came to him that he trusted her, and he hadn't trusted very many people in his life.

"You'll forget me," she said.

There she was, getting right to the point. If he was honest with himself, he probably *would* eventually forget her. But now, right now . . . he wanted her.

He threaded his fingers through her hair, his fingertips skimming her scalp, the soft strands of hair sliding over his wrists. "I think the line is, *don't* forget me."

She laughed, a burst of surprise. "You'll forget me," she repeated, almost as if to make it so, to remind herself that nothing here was permanent.

"I'm not sure," he said slowly. He didn't want to miss her.

In the moonglow he could see her face turned to his. He knew an invitation when he saw one.

Their mouths touched. Soft. Warm. Her lips opened under his, her hands moved over his arms, his shoulders, his back. She shifted, adjusting her body to his, welcoming his hips between her legs.

This was a Maggie he didn't know, a Maggie who was new to him. He tore his mouth from hers, gulping in air. "Maggie—wait. Let's get something straight. This isn't some sort of payment, is it?" Where had this nobility come from? A month ago he would have taken her any way he could have gotten her. "This isn't because I stayed, is it?" he asked.

Slightly trembling fingers touched his lips. How could the touch of her fingers against his mouth turn him on so much? How could such a gesture be so sexy?

"I want you," she said.

Thank God for Maggie's bluntness.

He wanted to touch her everywhere, he wanted to feel her breasts in his palm and in his mouth, but damn if her dress wasn't zipped in back. And things were moving way too fast. His senses were overloaded with his sudden and intense need for her.

His tongue filled the warmth of her mouth the way he wanted to fill her body, moving with a suggestive motion. She moaned, her hands tugging his shirt free of his waistband to slip beneath the tail, palms to bare skin.

Through her dress he caressed her breasts. Frustrated by the double layer of fabric, he moved down.

The night was hot and she wasn't wearing hose. Her legs were bare and smooth, the muscles tight. He traced a path from calf to knee, to the taut tendons of her inner thighs. Her panties were high-cut. He slid one finger below the elastic leg opening, following it from her hip, across her pelvis, and down, briefly touching the warmth between her legs.

A quick, indrawn breath, held in expectation.

He retraced his path, back and forth. Every time his hand returned to the warmth between her legs her breath caught.

He slipped his hand down the front of her silk panties, his palm cupping her while his fingers explored her soft folds, parting her, delving deep inside. "This is where I want to be," he whispered hoarsely, his voice not sounding like his at all. He stroked her.

Her hands were at the waistband of his pants, unfastening the hook, pulling down the zipper across an erection that strained against the unfamiliar clothing, touching him through the fabric of his jockey shorts. He felt himself harden even more.

For the past month he'd been living like a monk and he wasn't sure how much more of this he could take. But Maggie didn't seem at all interested in slow either. She pushed his underwear out of the way. Then she was holding him, her breathing coming in short, warm puffs against his neck. He heard her shoes hit the ground, then felt her legs wrap around him.

With his fingers he pushed the narrow crotch of her underwear to the side. She lifted herself to him and he filled her.

"Maggie . . . wait—"

Sweat had broken out on his whole body. His heart was pounding in his head. "I know I've kidded you about this, but are you on the pill?"

She stilled. "No."

"Are you using any kind of birth control?"

An embarrassed pause. "N-no."

He took a deep, shuddering breath, then withdrew. With blood still pounding in his ears, he reached in the open window of the car, fumbled for his billfold, dug out a condom, and turned back to Maggie. With shaking hands he tore open the pack.

Amazingly she took it from him. Her forehead against his chest, she put it on him, her small hands unrolling the latex until it covered him completely. He tilted his head back, sucking in air through his teeth. With his hands he felt his way back to her, shoving up her dress to her waist. "These . . . have got to go." Linking his fingers under the waistband, he stripped off her panties, tossed them in the car, then pulled her to him. He tested her, making sure she was still ready.

He'd wanted to love her slowly, touch her everywhere, taste her, savor her. But attraction, too long ignored, had culminated into a desperate, almost frenzied last-minute need to know each other in the most intimate way.

Within a heartbeat he was inside her. He moved with long, deep strokes, hoping to compensate for the almost total lack of foreplay. And then all thought vanished and it was just the movement, the incredible feel of their joined bodies meeting again and again. Shudder followed shudder. Then blessed release.

When it was over, his legs were shaking, and Maggie's legs, still draped around him, were shaking too. Her limp arms were around his waist, her head against his chest. Their clothes were damp and clinging as their chests rose and fell, both of them gulping for air.

When he came back to earth, he pushed her hair back from her face. "Maggie?"

"Mmm?"

"You okay?"

She nodded.

"This is just frustrating as hell, doing it here on a car."

But it had been great. He couldn't remember when he'd ever had such an experience. Maybe never. But then again, maybe it was because he'd gone without sex for so long. Whatever the reason, he wanted to experience the last ten minutes all over again. "Let's go somewhere else. Somewhere with a bed."

She nodded.

He slowly withdrew and took care of business. Then he found her shoes and helped her slip them on before she walked around the car to get in the passenger side.

His apartment was closer than her house, so he headed that direction. On the way, he kept thinking about the fact that she wasn't wearing underwear. He was hard before they got to his place.

Inside his apartment, Maggie kicked off her shoes, then stood waiting in the middle of the combined living room/bedroom. He hadn't bothered with a light, but the soft glow of a nearby street-lamp penetrated the drawn curtains, casting shadows and creating a subdued glow.

She'd done it. *They'd* done it. And they were about to do it again. So there really wasn't much sense in having second thoughts, she reasoned. Don't think, she told herself, while a blinding sexual awareness thrummed through her veins.

She watched as he toed off his shoes, at the same time slipping his arms free of his suspenders. He tossed his shirt aside, then came to stand in front of her, toe-to-toe. Reaching behind her, he unzipped her dress, pulling it down her shoulders to her waist, to finally let it fall to the floor. She stepped free so that she stood before him in only her lacy black bra. Then he reached behind her and undid the clasp, freeing her breasts.

She hadn't tried to cover herself before, but she did so now, arms crossed at her chest.

"Don't," he said.

She let her arms fall to her sides. "I don't have much in the breast department," she whispered.

He laughed—a wonderful sound of denial that she almost thanked him for. "They're beautiful," he whispered. With both hands he caressed their sloping tops, then the roundness underneath, sliding his fingers under the creases where breast met rib cage. "Perfect."

Don't be tender, don't be gentle, she thought in a final, panic-filled attempt to save herself from this man. Knowing that she would rather live with the guilt of uncommitted pleasure than the pain of a tender farewell, she suddenly wanted their encounter to be sex and nothing more.

Sex and nothing more, she told herself, distantly aware of the irony of her new viewpoint.

He bent his head and took the tip of one breast in his mouth, pulling and sucking until she felt a corresponding pull deep within her. She touched him, her hands on either side of his head, her fingers threaded through his hair. Wanting, wanting.

"Just sex," she gasped out, in hopes that her words would define their relationship.

His head came up. His lips were wet, his eyes passion-drugged. "Don't get weird on me."

"I'm being honest."

He walked her backward and pressed her down on the bed. "What if I want more from you?"

"You can't have more. And you don't want more."

He quickly rid himself of the rest of his clothes, put on a condom, and joined her, his naked length and weight pressing against her, chest to naked chest, thigh to naked thigh. With his knee he urged her legs apart and entered her. After achieving full penetration, he stopped and held himself perfectly still, the sound of their breathing filling the space around them.

With arms braced on either side of her head, his eyes locked with hers, he said, "This is just sex. Is this what you had in mind?"

"Yes."

He was watching her, waiting. Except for the pulse beating in his neck, except for his rising and falling chest, she would think him totally unaffected.

"Could you maybe move . . . a little?" she suggested.

"Like this?"

He lifted his hips, stroking her once very deeply. There was a hint of a smile to his mouth, but the perspiration on his forehead and the tension in his shoulder muscles gave him away. He wasn't as unaffected as he pretended.

Then he went back to waiting, unmoving. Not kissing her, not holding her.

Hot tears gathered behind her eyes. "Why are you doing this?"

"Why did you want to make me feel like I'm nothing to you but a roll? Chicks do that to me. They just want to be able to say they've slept with me. I thought you were different. I *know* you're different."

She hadn't thought about him, how her words would make him feel. She'd only been trying to save herself. "I'm sorry. That's not what I meant. I meant that I know you're leaving. I know I won't see you again. That this is just for tonight."

The weight of him pressed against her as he lowered himself, gathering her to him, kissing her tears, then her mouth. "Let's start over," he whispered.

She tightened her legs around him, a sob escaping her.

He shushed her, stroking her hair, placing soft kisses on her eyelids, her cheek, her throat. Too tender. Too sweet.

"Tell me I can have as much of you as I want," he whispered. "For tonight."

"Yes."

Then he withdrew, ignoring her protest. "I want to touch you, and hold you, and taste you," he whispered, his mouth moving over hers, then down her chin, her throat, her breast. His hand moved between her legs. Her breath caught as his finger stroked, sending waves of fire through her. She arched against his hand.

He slid down, kissing the valley between her ribs, then her navel, her abdomen, and lower.

"You can't," she whispered, drawing her knees together.

"I want you to remember me." He waited.

She opened for him. "I'll remember you."

Hands cupping her bottom, he lifted her to him, his tongue stroking her. "Swear?"

"I swear!"

She was lost. Her fingers dug into his hair as she arched against him.

Inside she felt coiling heat. A drowning.

A waterfall. She was crashing over the water's edge. She stiffened and cried his name.

Suddenly he was inside her, catching her, filling her, holding her tightly. Then he shuddered against her, his face buried against her neck, his breathing a harsh rasp in her ear.

• • •

They couldn't stop. Maybe they were making up for the last month. For Maggie, maybe the last few years.

Half an hour later they were in the shower, the bathroom lit by the soft glow of candlelight. Johnnie washed her with soap-slick hands, moving them over her breasts and her buttocks and between her legs. He turned her around, so her back was to his chest. He held her like that while he washed her again, over and over and over.

They just managed to make it out of the shower. Maggie was ready to sink to the floor, but Johnnie sat on a nearby chair. Hands on her waist, he pulled her to him. She covered him slowly. And as she did, his eyes closed. He leaned his head back against the wall. "Oh, Maggie," he said in a tortured, breathless voice. "You amaze me."

Later they moved to the bed, both exhausted. She curled up against his chest, his arm around her, and fell instantly asleep.

She had no idea how long she'd slept when she felt him jerk, like someone waking from those first moments of sleep.

"I fell asleep," he said.

She stroked the satiny skin of his chest. "That's okay. You need to sleep."

"No." His voice held strain. "I have to take you home."

So, that's the way it was. Now that the sex was over, it was time for them to go their separate ways. Just what she'd wanted.

She found her bra in the middle of the floor. Mechanically she put it on. Then she stepped into her dress.

Hot tears came from nowhere, clogging her throat, almost blinding her eyes. She grabbed her shoes and ran for the door.

"Maggie, wait!"

She heard him searching for clothes, heard him stumble. Then she was out the door, pounding barefoot down the metal fire escape, barefoot across the sidewalk as she hurried through the darkness for home.

She'd gone two blocks when a car approached, then slowed as it got even with her.

"What the hell's the matter with you?" Johnnie shouted from the car.

"Nothing. I like a nice brisk walk."

"Get in and I'll give you a ride home."

She kept up her speed walking, eyes straight ahead while the car coasted along beside her. "Don't need one."

"Come on. You're not wearing any underwear."

She stopped.

He stopped.

The window was rolled down. His neck was craned so he could see her across the passenger side. In his hand was her black underwear. She grabbed it and tossed it back in his face. "Go to hell."

In the house behind her, lights came on.

"You're drawing a crowd," he warned. "Come on, Maggie. Get in."

Defeated, she jerked open the door and plopped down in the bucket seat. As he pulled away, she grabbed the panties, stuffed her feet into them, and pulled them up under her dress.

When she was done, she sat looking straight ahead, her arms crossed at her waist, fighting the grief-laden hysteria that was building in her. Filling her, choking her, smothering her. She couldn't breathe. She felt dizzy. She pulled in a short, tight breath, alarmed and embarrassed at the sob that suddenly escaped.

She pressed a hand to her mouth.

"Are you crying?"

His voice came out of the darkness. And in her private agony, she thought she detected dread, and maybe a little disgust, in his tone.

"No."

She managed to say the word without exhaling or inhaling. With hardly any sound at all. So far, so good. She had to get home, get home, get home. He had to drive faster.

"You said you wanted it," he said.

"I know." Good control. Nothing telltale there.

She'd heard of people crying like a dam had burst. Now she had firsthand knowledge of what it felt like. She was sitting there, thinking she was going to make it home in one piece, when without warning she fell apart.

She began to sob, and once she started, she couldn't stop. She'd lost control. Of everything. Her emotions. Her life. Everything.

The car slammed to a stop. The gearshift was thrown into park, the engine cut.

"Jeez, Maggie."

Raw, confused emotions tore at her throat, clawed at her chest. He reached for her.

As surely as the sun rose and set, she knew if he touched her she would shatter and there would be nothing of Maggie left. "Leave me alone!" She shoved his hands away.

He recoiled as if she'd struck him. And he didn't try to touch her again.

By the time they turned onto her street, her crying had slowed to an occasional quiet sniffle.

He swung into her driveway, the headlights falling on a black Jeep with Ohio plates.

"Who's that?" he asked.

She'd been scrunched up on her side of the car, head down. Now she looked up. "Elliot," she said to herself.

"Who's Elliot?"

"A friend."

Johnnie watched as the driver's door opened and a guy stepped out. Joe college. Fraternity jock.

Healthy.

Healthy, wealthy, and wise.

Without a word, Maggie got out of the car and slammed the door.

A half hour ago she'd had Johnnie all undone. Now she'd forgotten he even existed.

Johnnie watched as she ran to Elliot and threw herself into his arms, watched as the man held her, comforted her.

Chapter 14

$\mathcal{T}$wo days later Maggie stood in the front yard, her back to the catalpa tree, watching as Elliot swung his duffel bag into the Jeep.

He's changed, she thought, not for the first time. He was more adult now than young man. What was he? Twenty-three? No, twenty-four. Maggie had been married for two years by that age.

Elliot turned and reached for her, pulling her into his arms, up against the solidity of his chest. He'd often hugged her when Steven was alive, but she sensed that this was different. It may have been her imagination, but this time he seemed to hold her a little tighter, a little longer. And did he touch her hair? Just ever so lightly? Did he hesitate ever so briefly as he let her go? Did he almost kiss her?

Elliot was the younger brother she'd always wanted. She'd never intended for their relationship to be anything else. Never dreamed he would want it to be more.

Maybe she was wrong.

She hoped she was wrong.

She didn't want to lose him too.

"You'll think about it?" Elliot asked, the morning breeze lifting his sandy hair from his forehead.

Watching him, she felt a wave of affection rush through her.

"You'll think about coming back to Ohio?"

Arms crossed at her waist, she nodded.

"I don't like the idea of your living here alone. With no family nearby." His blue eyes were watchful.

Blue eyes.

Except for Johnnie's being shot with black, their eyes were the same color, yet totally different. The difference wasn't shading, but how they viewed the world. Elliot had grown up surrounded by people who supported him, approved of him. His eyes were open and trusting. Johnnie's, when he wasn't laughing, were cautious, suspicious, vulnerable.

"Get some sleep," Elliot said.

They'd been up late both nights he'd stayed with her, talking and reminiscing. Thankfully he hadn't asked anything about Johnnie, or about the way she'd looked the night he'd arrived. She couldn't discuss Johnnie with Elliot. Their relationship would be too hard to explain, especially when she didn't understand it herself. Especially when it wasn't a relationship at all.

But each night, long after Elliot had gone to sleep on the couch, Maggie had stayed awake, thinking about Johnnie. It was too late for regrets, but whenever she played the scene back in her mind, particularly those last few minutes in his car, she saw something she'd been too upset to see at the time. She'd hurt him.

I never meant to hurt you.

That's what she would like for him to know. But being a realist, she knew he'd probably already dismissed the incident from his mind. After all, she was forgettable.

She should have found reassurance in the fact that he wasn't thinking about her the way she was thinking about him. He'd come to Hope to pull himself together, not fall apart. But she didn't feel reassured. Instead she felt a dazed hopelessness that burned in her chest and throat.

"If you decide to leave Hope," Elliot said, "we could have you out of here in a day."

He wasn't exaggerating. She could well imagine the whole Mayfield clan, all the aunts, uncles, and cousins, converging on her house to sweep her and her belongings away. They would take her back to Marcella's, a place that was secure and safe.

"If I decide to leave, you'll be the first to know," she told him.

He grinned and nodded, suddenly seeming the teenager she'd once known, someone familiar. At the same time she felt a loss, knowing he would never be that teenager again. She felt the sudden, unexpected urge to cry and she steeled herself. It was only lack of sleep that was making her emotions especially raw, she told herself.

Her answer apparently satisfied him, convincing him it was just a matter of time before she came to her senses and started packing.

He swung himself into the Jeep and slammed the door. For a moment she envied his youth, his optimism.

"Drive carefully," she told him.

He started the engine, then leaned out the open window, resting an arm on the door frame. His face was serious once more. "I hope you aren't staying here thinking of somehow hanging on to that last year with Steven. He wouldn't like that, you know."

The depth of his astuteness amazed her. And the truth of his analysis took her totally by surprise. He was right. In retrospect, she could see it was exactly what she'd been doing. Hanging on to Steven. At first anyway. Then little by little, the town of Hope had grown on her. Little by little, she'd begun to feel a part of it.

Then Johnnie had come along. He'd made her forget that she was a widow, made her forget that she wasn't the kind of person who had sex without commitment.

Elliot's gaze scanned the flat street with its lawns, most of them burned from the dry, scorching heat and lack of rain. Except for a few diehards, the people on her block had given up trying to keep their lawns green.

"It's so flat here," Elliot said, "so *brown*. Don't you miss the green hills? Don't you miss trees that change color and lose their leaves?"

Yes, but trees sometimes block the sun.

Not for the first time, she found herself defending Hope. "There's so much sky here."

He squinted and looked up, then shook his head.

He didn't understand. He didn't understand that as pretty as Ohio was, Maggie had grown accustomed to being able to see from horizon to horizon. In Ohio there wouldn't be enough sky for her anymore. In Ohio her eyes would keep searching for a distant horizon that wasn't there.

. . .

Sherman relaxed in the den of Johnnie's Hollywood Hills home while Johnnie played host. From the kitchen came the sound and smell of popping corn. As soon as Sherman got a whiff, a familiar buzz of excitement ran through him. The feeling was just the same today as it had been thirty years ago when he'd stepped into his first theater.

Except for one thing.

He took off his cap, ran a hand through his thinning hair, then replaced his cap, adjusting it so it felt just right.

Going bald.

It was something that preyed on his mind. He had dreams—nightmares—about it. He didn't want people calling him chromedome behind his back, but in another year or so he'd have a monk's ring around his head. And everybody knew how stupid that looked.

Of course there were implants, but he'd seen some that looked like a checked cornfield, little tufts of hair planted in perfect rows no matter what angle you eyed them from. Farmers used to check corn using string as a guide. Sherman didn't know anybody who checked corn anymore—it was rather a lost art—but he was damn sure he didn't want a checked field on top of his head. But he didn't want people calling him chromedome either.

What he really didn't want was to get old.

Yesterday the kid behind the counter at the 7-Eleven had called him sir, like he was some old man.

"Don't you hate it when people call you sir?" Sherman shouted over his shoulder, in the direction of the kitchen, where the sound of popping corn had faded.

Johnnie strode into the den, handed Sherman an overflowing bowl, then plopped down on the couch, resting his popcorn on his propped-up legs, bare feet on the coffee table. "What I hate is when people call me asshole."

Sherman laughed, glad to have Johnnie back, glad to see he was getting to be his old self again. Those first few weeks after his return from Texas had been touch and go. Johnnie had been moody and distant, and Sherman had wondered if taking some time off had really been the thing for him to do.

130

Physically he looked good. Better than he'd looked in years. But mentally . . .

After Johnnie had come back, Sherman would sometimes catch him staring into space, his brow furrowed, eyes reflective.

Maybe it was the new movie he'd just signed up to make, but in the last few days Johnnie seemed more together, and Sherman could only hope that the bad spell was over.

Johnnie picked up the remote control, clicked on the VCR, and started the tape Sherman had given him a week ago. An old Charlie Chaplin flick. When someone from a film company's archives told Sherman he'd come across some never-before-seen Chaplin, Sherman had managed to finagle a copy for Johnnie. So far Sherman had seen the tape of short takes five times. There was no telling how many times Johnnie had seen it.

They watched in silence for a few minutes, then Johnnie said, "It feels good to be back in California."

Did he mean it? With Johnnie you could never be sure. He could be trying to convince himself. He hadn't said anything about his trip, and Sherman could only speculate as to what had gone on out there.

"All those songs written about going home—" Johnnie tossed a handful of popcorn in his mouth. "Bunch of shit," he said with his mouth full. He swallowed. "Going back messes up your head . . . throws you into some kind of time warp. Sometimes, when I was in Hopeless, it didn't seem like any time had passed at all. I kept thinking about things I'd completely forgotten. Weird things about my mother. Things I didn't need or want to remember."

Johnnie never talked much about his childhood. During interviews, whenever background questions came up, Johnnie would say that his parents were dead and he didn't have any brothers or sisters. If the interviewer insisted on probing deeper, Johnnie would simply get up and walk out. End of interview.

"Sometimes we're better off forgetting things," Sherman said. "I remember this time in grade school when my pants fell down in front of the whole class. I'd completely forgotten about it until my ten-year high school reunion. Some girl just had to bring it up."

Johnnie laughed, then apologized, then laughed some more.

"I guess it *was* funny," Sherman said, "but not to me. I was never much into taking off my clothes in front of people."

"You should have gotten a double to do the moon shot," Johnnie said.

Sherman laughed. "Maybe so."

Johnnie took a drink of diet cola, then examined the can, his expression growing reflective. "When my mother found out I had diabetes, she cried," he said out of the blue, making Sherman wonder just how much Johnnie's trip had unlocked, making him wonder again if it had done more damage than good.

"I thought she was crying for me, but it turned out she was thinking about how much my diabetes would cost, and how it would disrupt her life."

"She wasn't sympathetic at all?" Sherman recalled the time he'd been told that his daughter Cicely had a heart murmur. It had scared the hell out of him. For about a year he'd treated her as if she were made of glass. And even now he still got up several times during the night to check on her.

"Remember the movie *Whatever Happened to Baby Jane?* When the bedridden old chick gets really sick and suddenly the nutty sister is falling all over herself trying to be nice? My mother was like that. For a few days. Then she got pissed. Really pissed, because I'd screwed things up."

"That's not normal," Sherman said.

"I know that now. But I didn't know it then."

Johnnie's story made Sherman feel a little ill, but it didn't surprise him. Through the years Sherman had been able to piece things together, enough to gather that Johnnie'd had it pretty rough as a kid. Sherman also suspected that his mother had very possibly been insane.

Johnnie's feet dropped to the floor and he sat up straighter, his attention on the TV. "This is the good part." He pointed, directing Sherman's gaze to the set, just the way he'd done all the other times they'd watched the tape.

It was classic Chaplin, one that may have been a little too risqué for the time. Ol' Charlie was flirting with a girl, his eyebrows bouncing up and down, his smile not innocent in the least. Then he fell to his knees, hands clasped together, begging for much more than a kiss. It was a great scene.

"Did I tell you I met somebody in Hope?" Johnnie asked.

"No." More revelations.

"Name's Maggie."

The news was delivered in a very nonchalant way. A studied nonchalance.

"Maggie. Nice name." Sherman would like to see Johnnie meet someone and settle down. Sherman's wife, Judy, was always saying that if Johnnie ever met the right girl, he'd probably make a halfway decent father and husband. Sherman had his doubts, but he'd still like to see Johnnie give it a try.

"Did I mention that she hates my guts?" Johnnie asked.

That surprised Sherman. Johnnie never had any trouble with women. He could always get anybody he wanted.

"Maybe she's just acting like she hates you. Women do that sometimes. It's a little game they play. And anyway, I always say that a negative reaction is better than no reaction at all. At least she knows you're alive."

Johnnie took a swig of cola, then rested the can on his bent knee. "We're polar opposites, that's the problem. But there's this attraction. . . ." He shook his head while keeping his gaze riveted on the television. "Have you ever stood near the edge of someplace really high, like a mountaintop or a tall building, and felt some unknown force trying to pull you to the edge? That's how it is when she's around. I know I'm gonna die if I take one more step, but I don't care."

The Chaplin tape ended. Chaplin hadn't gotten the girl either.

Sherman took off his cap. "What do you think?" He lowered his head enough to give Johnnie a good view of his thinning hair. "Implants, toupee, or should I just shave the whole damn thing?"

Johnnie was quiet a moment. "You know what I think would look great?"

"What?" Sherman asked, hopeful.

"A tattoo. One giant tattoo."

Sherman slapped the cap back on his head. "You're a lot of help."

Johnnie laughed.

It was good to have him back.

Chapter 15

There were a lot of things that could throw a person's system out of sync. Like depression. Or sleep deprivation. Or too little food. Too much exercise.

After Steven's death, Maggie had missed a couple of periods. She'd begun to hope that she was pregnant, but when she'd finally gone to the doctor, she found out she wasn't. Her condition was blamed on nerves, stress, depression, and lack of sleep. Her doctor gave her some tranquilizers and sent her home. One day of drugs and she decided she didn't like living in a fog, so she dumped the rest of the pills down the toilet.

So when she missed her period she didn't give it much thought. Instead she concentrated on getting ready for the new school season, which would soon be upon them.

It was sometime during the first week of classes that Maggie realized she'd missed another period. Shortly after that, the headaches started. She woke up with one, and went to bed with one. Then she began having trouble with her stomach. One minute she would be starving, the next she would throw up the food she'd just eaten. And sometimes she was so tired she couldn't make it through the day without lying down for a nap.

Was something wrong with her? A lot of illnesses started with headaches and fatigue. Of course there was another possibility, but it was too unthinkable. . . .

A few days later Maggie was in her classroom gathering up her things to go home when a wave of exhaustion and dizziness brought her sinking into the nearest empty seat. She rested her head on her crossed arms—just for a few minutes.

She was concentrating on her breathing when a tap at the door made her aware of her surroundings. Footsteps sounded on the floor, followed by Karen's concerned voice. "Maggie, are you okay?"

Maggie tried to lift her head, but couldn't. If she did, she might throw up. "Tired," she mumbled.

Karen's hand touched her shoulder. "Are you sick?"

Maggie nodded. "I think I have the flu." So her friend wouldn't be overly worried, Maggie lifted her head and forced herself to sit up straighter, taking deep, steady breaths, hoping to keep the dizziness at bay.

Karen pressed a cool hand to Maggie's forehead. "You don't feel hot."

Karen dragged a chair close to Maggie's and sat down, inspecting her with a critical eye. "But you look awful."

Maggie managed a weak smile. "Thanks. I feel awful."

Karen questioned her, and Maggie ended up listing her symptoms.

Her friend sat there, arms crossed, a thoughtful frown on her face. "Maggie, is there a chance you could be pregnant?"

Maggie's heart slammed against her rib cage. Her stomach lurched. "No. I don't think so. No." It wasn't possible. "I can't be pregnant. Anyway, being pregnant doesn't make you feel like you're dying."

Karen laughed. "I threw up for six months when I was pregnant with Timothy. And I was chronically tired. I couldn't go to the grocery store without having to take a nap in the parking lot before heading home."

"I can't be," Maggie whispered.

The fear she'd kept under control surfaced, along with a now wavering denial. She stared at her friend, then away, down at the names carved in the desk in front of her. "We used birth control," she whispered.

"Nothing but abstinence is a hundred percent."

"Question fifteen on the sex education exam, I believe," Maggie said with self-mockery. She looked up at Karen. "This can't be happening."

Karen couldn't give her any words of encouragement. She simply pressed her lips together and shook her head, her expression one of total sympathy.

"Come on," she said, getting to her feet and slinging her purse over her shoulder. "I'll give you a ride. And I'll treat you to a home pregnancy test on the way."

Maggie tried to answer but instead found herself making a dash for the back door. She made it just in time to throw up.

Pink meant positive.

Maggie stared at the pink ring in the bottom of the test tube, then slowly dumped the contents down the drain. Then she walked into the bedroom and sank down on the bed.

She spent the following week in a daze, unable to think straight about the most mundane things. Getting dressed. Eating. Brushing her teeth. Brushing her hair.

A baby.

She couldn't have a baby. She was single. She was a *widow*, living in a small town where everybody knew everybody.

She could lose her job. If that happened, she wouldn't be able to support a child. But she could get another job. In another town. Away from Hope.

Where? Ohio?

No. How could she possibly explain a pregnancy to Marcella and Elliot? But they would find out eventually.

Maybe.

Maybe not.

There was adoption. There was abortion.

Abortion. Oh God, no.

Then adoption.

Could she carry a baby for nine months, only to give it up, give it away to a smiling, "Kodak moment" couple who would adore and cherish her child?

Nobody would love my baby as much as I would.

She could keep her baby. Couldn't she? But that would be a

selfish, purely emotional decision. She was thinking only of herself, not the baby. A child should have a father. A child should have security.

And what about Johnnie? Should she tell him about the baby?

Maybe, if circumstances had been different. Maybe, if they'd had some kind of relationship, if they'd been a couple. The way things were, telling him would only make a bad situation worse. He would only think she was trying to trap him into marriage or child support. No, she was in this by herself.

What am I going to do?

Days passed without her awareness. She was sick. She was exhausted. She didn't know what to do or where to turn. She'd never felt more alone. If it hadn't been for Karen . . . But Karen couldn't make up Maggie's mind for her. It was something she had to decide for herself, by herself.

A baby.

One moment Maggie would think that she couldn't possibly have a baby, and the next she would start daydreaming about white wicker bassinets and tiny booties.

A baby.

She couldn't have a baby.

A baby.

Would it be fair to the child? To grow up without a father? To grow up bearing the weight of her mother's mistake?

If things got too rough in Hope, they could always move. They could go somewhere far away where nobody knew them. And Maggie would love her child more than anything—that had to count for something.

Maggie went to visit Karen. "I'm keeping the baby," she announced.

Tears gathered in her friend's eyes. At the sight of them, Maggie started to cry too.

"I'm so glad," Karen said, jumping up from the couch to give Maggie a hug. "You've always wanted a child. Maybe this is a fulfillment. I've always said you'd make a great mother."

Maggie nodded, blinked, and sniffled, certain she'd made the right decision. "I will, won't I?"

But a few minutes later, after they were done blowing their

noses and drying their tears, Maggie began to worry again. "When I think about the responsibility of bringing a new life into the world, when I think about going through it all by myself, it overwhelms me. It scares me so much."

"It's scary, even when you're married," Karen said. "And you can't depend on a husband anyway. Take it from me." She thought a moment. "What about the father? Are you going to tell him?"

Maggie shook her head.

"You know, I actually think you're lucky. No guy. What could be better? And I'll be here. Hey, I'll even go to Lamaze classes with you." Karen was warming to the idea. "I still have all my maternity clothes. The dresses would be too short for you, but the tops would fit. And baby clothes. I have a closet full of baby clothes. And a high chair and a playpen."

"You'd really go to Lamaze classes with me?"

"I'd love to."

Maggie's brief bout of excitement faded. "What about school? What will I tell my students? I'll probably lose my job. I'll end up trying to raise a baby on welfare and food stamps." The picture was bleak.

"Who says anybody has to know? I knew a teacher who timed her pregnancies so she'd have her babies in the summer. She'd go through most of the school year without anybody even knowing she was pregnant."

"I'll probably get huge."

"You're tall. You won't show for at least another couple of months. That will get you into the second quarter. And anyway, I don't think they can fire you unless they can prove you've done something wrong at school."

"Karen, this is Hope, Texas."

Karen waved her hand. "Yeah, but it's the nineties."

Shortly after Thanksgiving, everything blew up. It hadn't been Maggie's figure that had given her away—she hardly showed. And she'd always worn fairly baggy clothes, so no one was suspicious when she left everything with a waistline hanging in her closet.

Maybe it was the way she turned green during school lunch. Or her mad dashes to the bathroom. Or maybe someone who worked for Maggie's gynecologist in the nearby town of Little Burgundy knew someone in Hope. Whatever the reason, news of Maggie's pregnancy was all over town. The air was buzzing with gossip.

Whenever Maggie stepped into a room, conversation dropped to nothing. People would cast a variety of glances her direction, ranging from embarrassed to sly. Some of the men would stare unblinkingly at her, as if waiting for some kind of invitation. She was no longer the unapproachable widow. She was a fallen woman.

Complaints were sent to the school superintendent and the school board. Parents wanted Maggie fired.

Petitions were left in prominent places like the post office and grocery store. The final humiliation came when the *Hope Chronicle* began printing letters to the editor written by outraged parents, all concerning Maggie and the bad influence she was having on the town's youth. The school board finally agreed to call a special open session to discuss what to do with their pregnant, unmarried teacher.

As the day of the meeting drew near, people continued to argue back and forth.

"What she does on her own time shouldn't concern the school."

"But she teaches sex education."

"Goes to show it can happen to anybody."

"Who's the father?"

"She won't say."

"Bet it's that fella who stayed at her house those couple of days last summer."

"Bet it's Johnnie Irish. Not even a saint could say no to him."

For two weeks running, Maggie's pregnancy was the main topic of conversation at the Hope Cafe, the gas station, the pool hall, the post office, and the Laundromat. And even though people argued about whether she should stay or go, everyone agreed that there hadn't been such an uproar in Hope since the day of the Johnnie Irish parade.

Chapter 16

Johnnie stood staring at the strings of colored lights, his shoulders hunched against the cold December night. He was surprised to find the outside of Harriet's house decorated for Christmas. The lawn even had a plastic snowman, and the roof, Santa and his reindeer.

He knocked and waited.

He felt like hell. He was dog tired. His head hurt, his eyes burned, his muscles were crying out for sleep. He really should start paying closer attention to his doctor, he decided. Or Sherman, who'd been on his case more than usual lately. Hell, even Edith, the woman who shoveled out his house once a week, had been after him to get his act together.

His excuse was the same one he always used. He was between movies. And when he was between movies the days were long and the nights were longer. It was easy to fall into his old restless habits of prowling all night, sleeping all day. Under those conditions it was hard, if not impossible, to keep his insulin regulated.

He kept telling himself that he had to get a grip on the situation. Every night he'd say that this was it. Tomorrow would be different. Tomorrow he'd get up early and start jogging again. Tomorrow he'd go to bed at a decent time. But then tomorrow would come and somebody would invite him to a party and all his well-intended plans would be forgotten.

Then the Christmas cards from Harriet had come. The first one had been cheerful and breezy. A friendly chat about her cat and the neighbor kids. The second card had been a rambling, incoherent mess. She'd wrapped up by saying she missed her husband. And that it was cold in Hope. That's what had really gotten to him. The cold business. Put a lump right in his throat.

And so here he was, back in ol' Hopeless, standing on Harry's front porch.

The door opened, fanning the scent of Christmas his way.

It was one of her good days. He could tell by the brightness of her eyes and the straight set of her shoulders.

"Johnnie!" she said in delight and surprise. "You're the last person I expected to find on my front step."

No kidding. So much for charging in and saving Harry's Christmas, he thought wryly.

He'd expected to find her sitting at home while the season passed unnoticed. But here she was, not appearing depressed at all, looking full of the Christmas spirit, looking the picture of health. There was no sign of the person who'd written the Christmas card in shaky penmanship and broken sentences. Quite the opposite. Judging from the expression on her face, he'd say she was wondering what the hell she was going to do with her uninvited guest.

It had always been his way to do things without much forethought or afterthought. But lately he'd been questioning some of his choices. And after they'd been made, he sometimes regretted them. Back in California it had seemed right to come and see Harriet. Now it seemed all wrong.

But it was too late. Harriet was urging him inside, one hand on his arm. Once he was settled at the kitchen table, she put a cup of coffee in front of him. "How long are you staying?" she asked.

He took a sip of coffee. "Just passing through."

She gave him one of her you-can't-fool-*me* looks. "Johnnie, nobody just passes through Hope."

He smiled at her sharpness, glad that she seemed so much her old self, alarmed that she'd seen through him so easily. "It was a little out of my way," he told her, "but not much."

And now that he was back, he could admit to himself that it wasn't just Harriet who had brought him to Hope. For the last few months he'd been feeling fairly pleased with himself at being able to put Maggie Mayfield out of his mind. Now he realized she'd been with him all along. Now that the sting of her after-great-sex rejection had dulled, at least somewhat, he wanted to see her. He wouldn't mind some more of that great sex.

Conversation rambled.

He and Harriet discussed the local residents, with the exception of the one person he really wanted news of. Harriet asked about his work. He told her about the projects he was considering, one of them being a dramatic role, something he'd never tried before.

While they sat talking and drinking coffee, he couldn't help but notice the way Harriet kept glancing up at the wall clock. He was about to ask if she was expecting a beau when the doorbell chimed. Harriet wisked off her apron, tossed it over a chairback, and hurried to answer the door.

"Johnnie's here."

Harriet's loudly whispered words stole the breath from Maggie's lungs. For an instant she experienced total body-freezing panic. When she could finally move, her initial instinct was to run. But common sense took over. With her heart beating madly in her ears, she stepped inside the overly warm house and shut the door behind her.

While the blood continued to roar through Maggie's head, Harriet fussed around her, taking her jacket and giving her a pat on the arm. "Why don't you go in and visit with him?" she said. "I'll wait here for the others."

Maggie didn't move. She didn't want to be alone with Johnnie. But wouldn't it be worse to wait until the house was full of people? It would be just like him to bring up their night together. The local gas station was conducting a paternity pool called "Who's the Father?" Last she'd heard it was Johnnie 36, Elliot 29. She didn't want to give them more fuel for gossip.

Her fingers shook as they skimmed the front of her black velvet dress. It was gathered above her breasts, falling in a straight line to her knees, and even though she was almost five months along, she hardly showed, partly because her morning sickness had only just subsided.

There was no way he could tell. Not unless he touched her, and she wouldn't let him touch her.

She put an ice-cold hand to her burning cheek, looked down once more to assure herself that there was nothing to give her condition away. Then, taking a deep breath, she crossed the living room and stepped into the kitchen.

He was leaning against the wall, arms crossed at his chest in a sort of bad-boy, vagrant pose, denim-clad legs crossed at the ankles. The only incongruous thing about the scene was the cup of coffee he held in one hand.

It was strange to see him in winter clothes, to see him wearing a baggy gray sweater instead of a black T-shirt. The suntan she remembered was gone, replaced by his more customary pallor, a pallor that reflected his life-style of too many parties and too little sleep and served as a reminder of how wrong he was for her.

"Hello, Johnnie."

Through the roaring in her ears, her voice sounded almost normal. She congratulated herself.

"Maggie."

Those two syllables were all it took for her to tell that his voice was the same. Deep. Bluesy. With just the merest hint of what had to be theatrically crafted longing, enough to almost make her think he'd missed her.

She was trying to make sense of his presence in Hope, a presence that would bring more speculation, that would most likely have people rushing out to change their selection in the gas station pool. For someone accustomed to a simple life, she found it all too overwhelming, too complicated.

"What are you doing here?" she asked bluntly.

He put down his coffee cup on the table and took a step toward her. She took a step back. And she kept going until she bumped into the counter, until she couldn't go any farther.

He smiled, but there was an intensity in his eyes that made her knees want to buckle. "Maybe I've missed you. Maybe I came back to see you."

She laughed at his obvious joke, but her laugh sounded brittle even to herself. "I don't think so."

He took another step. And another. He was within touching range and she had nowhere left to go. "Tell me the truth," he said in a low voice that was meant just for her. "Don't you ever think about that night last summer?"

She swallowed. He wouldn't believe her if she said no, so she didn't say anything.

"Sometimes I lie awake at night," he whispered, "aching for you."

She could almost hear Karen translating for her. *He misses the sex, not you.* But wasn't that what Maggie had wanted? Just sex?

Before he could take that last step she put a hand to his chest, to hold him back. "What happened last summer was a mistake."

"How did I know you'd say that?"

He stepped closer, pushing against her hand. She could feel the indentation where rib met rib, muscle met muscle. She could feel his heart beating under her palm. Her arm bent and she was trapped against the counter, the length of his warm body pressed to hers. Memory, triggered by his scent and by his touch, rushed through her, making her weak. She drew a trembling breath and closed her eyes.

His hand touched the side of her face.

"Don't," she whispered.

His fingers skimmed the column of her throat.

Her breath caught. "Don't."

He touched her breast.

"Maggie—"

Her name came softly, breathlessly, with a hint of question. Then his hand moved down, across her rib cage . . . to the soft contour of her stomach.

His hand stopped.

Her eyes opened. In his she read comprehension, puzzlement, and shock.

His brows drew together. Both of his hands, fingers spread wide, cupped her abdomen. "A baby?" he asked, his voice full of wonder and awe and confusion.

"Yes."

He was quiet. She could almost see the gears turning in his head. "Whose baby?"

Her throat was dry. She swallowed again, but it didn't do any good.

"Who's the guy?"

"Guy?"

"You know. Hubby."

He doesn't know.

She didn't answer. She couldn't answer.

"Is it Elliot?"

He released her and took a couple of steps back. "Mr. Jock. Mr. Silver Spoon. Mr. Both Feet on the Ground. Bet that's who it is, isn't it?"

Forgive me, Elliot.

"Why shouldn't I marry somebody like him?" she demanded, lifting her chin a little higher.

He raked the fingers of both hands through his hair, seeming oddly shaken. He cast his eyes around the kitchen, looking everywhere but at her, his gaze finally settling on the cake on the counter behind a tray of glasses. A baby shower cake decorated with pink rattles and blue booties, and CONGRATULATIONS MAGGIE.

The party had been Karen's idea, a baby shower in honor of Maggie's recent victory in the Maggie Mayfield versus irate parents controversy. Maggie had won by a landslide, proving that it took only a few highbrows to stir up trouble. And proving that Hope wasn't as heartless as Johnnie claimed.

How ironic for him to show up now. But then he'd always had a habit of appearing at the most disturbing times. As if he had some kind of built-in radar.

He seemed to be trying to put it together, to grasp it all, when the doorbell rang. Harriet's footsteps could be heard crossing to the door. Then came the sound of laughter and feminine voices.

"I've gotta go," he said, suddenly looking trapped and eager to be gone. "It's been nice." Moving like someone who'd had one too many drinks, he reached the kitchen door. "Tell Harry I said good-bye. I'll give her a call later. When she's not busy." And then he was gone.

Johnnie was ready to open the car door when a shout from behind had him looking over his shoulder. Maggie was hurrying toward him. Hands braced on the door frame, he tilted his head back and took a deep, stabilizing breath. Above him, stars swam in and out of focus.

"Are you okay?" she asked. "I thought maybe . . ."

"I needed a Lifesaver?"

"Maybe."

More together now, he straightened away from the car and faced her. He realized, with the same unfamiliar sense of loss he'd felt in the house, that she was somebody he didn't know anymore. She was different from the Maggie he remembered. Pregnant, she was fragile and untouchable. In profile she looked so delicate, as if the child growing inside her was sapping her of her strength, her vitality. Fear for her crept through him.

"You okay?" he asked, hoping her answer would dull his panic-filled worry. "I mean with the baby?"

"Fine."

"You better go inside. It's cold out here."

"It feels good. Now that I'm pregnant, I'm always too warm."

For a split second back in the house, he'd been afraid that she was going to say the baby was his. Women did that. Always trying to slap him with a paternity suit. And so he'd hedged. But then when he found out what was really going on, for some inexplicable reason he'd felt stunned. Hurt.

As he watched her, it came to him that he'd had it wrong. All along he'd thought he could come back to Hope anytime and everything would be the same, that Maggie would be the same. And it came to him that, yes, there had been the sex thing between them, but it had been more than that. He'd come to think of her as his friend.

He was going to miss her.

Along with his discovery came a surprisingly selfless thought. He wanted her to be happy, with the blond-haired jock or whomever. "You'll make a great mom," he told her.

He could see that his words surprised her. No, he supposed he didn't say nice things all that often. He'd have to work on it.

He forced himself to smile. Then he held out his hand, remembering the game they'd once played all those months ago. "Rock, scissors, paper?" he asked. "For old time's sake?"

She tilted her head to one side and smiled a little tremulously. "Sure."

"One, two, three—"

She was rock. He was scissors.

That's the way it would always be with them, he decided. He might be famous, but Maggie'd had him beat right from the beginning. Unlike him, she had her act together. She knew where she'd been and where she was going.

"You always win, don't you?" he asked.

Something too much like sadness flitted across her features, and that bothered him. "Not always," she said.

Curtain call. This was it. Show was over. Time to go.

He smiled. "Have a nice one."

"You too."

He was getting into the car when she quietly spoke his name. He straightened and faced her.

"I rented *Canadian Geeks*."

She'd seen it? The thought pleased him and scared him at the same time. What had she thought of his first flop? Had she liked it?

"You were very funny. I loved the snowshoe scene."

"That's me." He put a hand to his chest, to the heart she was breaking. "Mr. Funny Man."

Then he turned away for the last time.

Late that night he pulled into the parking lot of the El Paso airport. He got a good deal on a ticket. Nobody traveled on Christmas Eve.

Chapter 17

*I*n January Maggie and Karen started Lamaze classes. At first Maggie wondered if it was worth the trouble, since they had to drive forty-five miles each way to attend, but the classes ended up being fun. She was relieved to find out that she wasn't the only single mother there, although she couldn't help but experience a certain amount of discontentment and longing at seeing husbands and wives together.

But all in all it was nice to be around other pregnant women who were in about the same stage of pregnancy as she was. And it helped to become familiar with the mysteries of childbirth. That somewhat calmed her fears, of which she had many. It was interesting, too, seeing how various people faced prepared childbirth.

There was one poor father who had earned the name Fainter. He couldn't watch a film without slinking from his chair in a dead faint. The first time it happened, Maggie thought he'd fallen asleep. But then, right during the episiotomy, he slithered to the ground, just like someone in a cartoon, his pregnant wife barely managing to keep his head from cracking against the floor.

After that, people waited to see how long it would take for him to go down. Cruel but entertaining.

"It just goes to show you how helpful men are," Karen said later as she guided her battered yellow car onto the straight, flat, two-lane road that led back to Hope. "The last thing I'd want in the delivery room is a husband who's going to need medical attention."

Maggie agreed. "But I did feel sorry for him. He was trying so hard."

"Only because he wanted something in return. That's the way guys think."

Maggie could see where this was leading. Karen was getting primed for her who-needs-a-man spiel. It was too bad her ex-husband had done such a number on her. "You can't tell me that all guys are selfish," Maggie argued.

"All straight guys. I know for a fact that all straight guys don't care about families, or about love, or about whether or not your mother just died, or whether you have to go into the hospital for a heart transplant. All a guy cares about is where he's going to stick it next. Nope," she said with a toss of her blond head, "the only person a woman can depend on is another woman."

"What about Timothy? In a few years he'll be an adult. Will he be one of the men you hate?"

"It's totally different if you're related. He'll treat me okay, and his sister okay, but his girlfriend? His wife? Forget it."

Maggie sighed, her eyes focused on the scenery. Flat bare land dotted with an occasional tumbleweed, twisted tree, and yucca, plus an occasional dirt road that seemed to lead nowhere.

"Got a joke for you," Karen announced, veering to avoid a roadkill. "Why does it take longer to make a male snowman than a female?"

Maggie moaned. "Why?"

"Because when it's finished, you have to hollow out the head, then add a raging sex drive."

"Cute." Actually less crude than most of her jokes.

"I've got another one. Why did the man cross the road?"

Maggie asked the obligatory *why*?

"To get to the blonde on the other side."

It was no use, Maggie decided. Karen would hate men for the rest of her life.

• • •

That night Maggie gathered up her courage and called Steven's mother to tell her about the baby. Even though she knew the news wasn't something Marcella would be overjoyed to hear, Maggie was still hurt by Marcella's reaction.

"I can't talk now," she told Maggie. "I'll call you later."

Realizing that Marcella had no intention of calling back, Maggie hung up, her sense of abandonment complete. It was devastating to have someone you'd always cared for turn away. But Maggie couldn't let it get her down. For her baby, she had to be strong.

Later, as she lay in bed, something woke her. She put a hand to the taut roundness of her stomach, feeling a small, walnut-sized bump. A foot? A hand? A knee?

What a marvel, a wondrous gift it all was, she thought, lying there in the darkness with her baby, feeling a bittersweet, unconditional love for the life she carried inside her.

She would take care of this child, she swore with a fierce protectiveness she'd never felt toward any other human being. She would love this child like no child had ever been loved.

Hand shaking, his entire body drenched with sweat, Johnnie pressed the gun to his head, the metal barrel cold against his temple. He clenched his eyes shut, every muscle in his body drawn tight.

Then a calm came over him, a blessed, numbing calm.

He pulled the trigger.

The sound of the gun blast echoed in the tiny room. Darkness fell.

"*Cut*. Print."

That was it. The wrap-up of the final scene of Johnnie's first dramatic role. *The Big Goodbye* had always been one of his favorite books, and when the screenplay came along, Johnnie had jumped at the chance to play Harley Strange.

It was a career risk, switching from comedy to drama. It was even more of a risk to do a film that didn't have the traditional happy ending.

But Johnnie had reached a financial point where he could take that risk. And this time around, there would be no test-screening audience to reject the shocker ending. The director wasn't going for broad appeal. He wanted to tell the best story he could tell, happy or sad.

It used to be that Johnnie made a movie with the audience in mind. But while he was making *The Big Goodbye* he kept thinking about Maggie. What would she think of this scene or that scene? He knew it wasn't healthy to dwell on her, but when did he ever do anything that was?

Hot and tired, but feeling more satisfied than he'd felt in some time, Johnnie headed for his trailer.

"Wrap-up party at seven," someone shouted.

Johnnie waved and nodded.

They'd been in Mexico three months and everybody would be glad to get home. He should avoid the party, but he was expected to be there. Parties always had all the wrong things, though, and he knew his body needed sleep and a balanced meal. If he kept on the way he was, with his diabetes out of control, he could end up blind, or dead. He wished it mattered more to him, he really did.

Inside his trailer, he sprawled out on the couch, too tired to bother peeling off his black leather pants and shredded white shirt. And anyway, he'd like to hang on to the character of Harley a little longer. He was going to miss him.

His eyes were almost closed when he spotted the stack of mail Sherman had sent how many days ago? It was still on the frayed lawn chair where he'd tossed it.

Without much interest, Johnnie sifted through the stack, pushing envelopes around, searching for anything that looked halfway interesting.

A lot of it was fan mail, some from kids, judging from the handwriting. A lot from women, judging by the sharp smell of perfume that had managed to cling to the envelopes even after a couple of weeks of lying around.

He uncovered a letter from Harriet.

A letter from Hope.

His hand hesitated. Then he picked it up and opened it.

No cause for alarm. It was full of the usual stuff like weather.

It rained today. Afterward there was a double rainbow. I love to listen to the rain.

Everything is green for a change, or as green as it gets here.

My poor kitty is getting old just like me. She had to be put on a special diet. Hope that keeps her from getting kidney infections. Don't like shoving those tiny pills down her throat. And it's hard for me to remember if I gave her one or not.

She went on to tell him who was getting married. And who was getting divorced. Who had died. And who hadn't. She ended her letter by saying,

The gossip has died down, and the people in town seem to have accepted Maggie Mayfield's pregnancy. A lot of them have even stood up for her on occasion. I do admire that girl and the way she's hung in there, single mother and all. But even with the town's support, she still says she might move after the baby comes.

Love, Harriet

Chapter 18

*S*he was in labor.

Or at least Maggie thought she was in labor. The pains she'd felt really couldn't be called pains, but rather sensations. Three so far. And since the baby wasn't due for another two weeks, Maggie wondered if she wasn't experiencing what Lillian, her Lamaze instructor, had called false labor.

While waiting to monitor the next twinge, she went over the baby's things, something she found herself doing several times a day.

Since her house was so small, she'd arranged a nursery in the corner of her bedroom. Karen had loaned her a bassinet, a changing table, and a wind-up swing. Maggie had told her she wouldn't need the swing, that she planned to rock her baby when it cried and hold her baby when it needed attention. Karen had just smiled a knowing smile and left the wind-up swing anyway.

Maggie ran a hand across the soft, tiny clothes. Stacks of white gowns, pastel sleepers and nighties. There were more diapers—both cloth and disposable—than anyone could possibly need, but again Karen had insisted. There was baby powder and baby soap and baby lotion and baby everything.

She was ready. She felt she'd done everything and read everything she could to prepare. Her one legitimate worry dealt with the chances of Johnnie's diabetes being passed on to her child, but a talk with her doctor had been somewhat reassuring. He explained that, since there was no diabetes on Maggie's side, the chance of her baby developing the disease was minimal. But just in case, they would monitor the child's blood.

Maggie was refolding the last baby gown when she felt another of the sensations. She checked her watch. Fifteen minutes after the last one.

There was nothing to worry about, she told herself. Everything was arranged. At the first sign of labor, Maggie was to call Karen, who could be at her house within ten minutes. From there they would drive the forty-five miles to the hospital in Little Burgundy.

Since it was Sunday, Maggie put a call through to Karen's home.

No answer.

Nothing to worry about. She was probably outside or making a quick run to the store. They had lots of time, all kinds of time. If they got to the hospital too early, Dr. Richards would just send her home anyway.

Nothing to worry about.

To pass the time, Maggie decided to lie down on the bed and practice her Lamaze breathing. Not that she really put much faith in it. It didn't seem very likely that a breathing technique could lessen a person's pain. But she'd try anything as long as it wasn't harmful.

Lying on her back, she relaxed her body the way she'd been taught to do. Then she closed her eyes, took a deep cleansing breath, and began her abdominal sleep breathing.

But she couldn't give it her full concentration. One thought kept going through her head. *This is it.*

At first the idea that her pregnancy would eventually lead to a baby hadn't seemed quite real, a tomorrow that would never come. But as her due date loomed nearer, as her body became swollen and heavy, her bladder crowded, and legs cramped, it began to seem more believable. And along with that reality came a real fear of childbirth.

She had once told Johnnie that she had a low tolerance for pain. He'd thought she was kidding, but it was true. She was a terrible coward.

And no matter what they said in Lamaze class, she knew that childbirth hurt. Karen had been kind enough to tell her that women had the babies because they were superior to men. That if men had to give birth, the pain would be too much for them. They wouldn't be able to live through it. Maggie could have done quite well without that bit of useful information.

And then there had been the expression on Dr. Richards' face as he'd measured her pelvis. He'd frowned, remeasured, then frowned again.

Too narrow, she'd thought. My hips are too narrow.

They'd have to do a cesarean. She couldn't possibly go through surgery. Maybe if they knocked her out, but they wouldn't. Women were *conscious* when they cut them open. Who could possibly survive something like that? She couldn't. She knew she couldn't.

She moved on to practice her steady-rate chest breathing, then her accelerated-decelerated breathing, then the no-push technique.

She was just finishing when she felt another contraction, this one seeming a little stronger than the others. She checked her watch. Sixteen minutes. No problem. But that didn't keep her from grabbing the phone to try Karen again.

This time Timothy answered.

"Timmy," Maggie gasped in relief, not realizing until that moment how nervous she'd really been, "get your mom for me, sweetheart."

With the bland voice of a typically unenthusiastic teenager, he said, "Mom can't come to the phone. She's in the bathroom throwing up."

Maggie gripped the receiver with both hands. "Throwing up?"

"Yeah, she thinks she might have the flu. Want me to give her a message?"

Tell her she can't have the flu because I'm having my baby. "She's really, *really* sick?"

"She's had her head in the toilet for the last two hours."

She was sick.

After hanging up, Maggie sat on the edge of the bed, staring into space. She had control of the situation, she told herself. She would drive herself to the hospital. No problem.

She got to her feet and headed for the door.

Her overnight case. She almost forgot it.

She went back to the bedroom.

Her clothes—should she change? No, shorts and a man's T-shirt were okay. Shoes. She needed shoes. She wiggled her feet into a pair of sneakers. Was that a knock at the door? Or her heart hammering?

She looked around the corner in time to see the front door swing wide open. To see Johnnie standing in the opening.

She felt a thud deep in her stomach that had nothing to do with labor.

Before she was aware of conscious thought, she caught herself thinking that she would like to see him look really rested sometime, really healthy.

He knows, was her next thought. Oh God. *He knows.*

He closed the door behind him. "Hi, Maggie May."

"How is it that you always show up at the most unexpected times?" she asked.

"Nice to see you too."

"Sometimes I think you must live right next door."

"Now, that's a thought."

"An alarming one."

"Did you happen to think that I might not be able to stay away?"

"From Hopeless?"

He was scrutinizing her, from her hair, which Maggie could feel slipping from the clasp at the back of her head, to her breasts, which weren't flat anymore, to her stomach, legs, shoes, then back to her stomach.

As if on cue, her body chose that moment to have a contraction that actually felt like something she'd expect a contraction to feel like. She forced herself to breathe shallowly while at the same time keeping her face passive. When the contraction ended, she noticed he was still staring at her stomach. "Is something wrong?" she asked.

"You're so . . . so—" He made a gesture with one hand.

"Big?" she asked.

He nodded.

"That's because I'm having a baby."

"I know, but . . . my God, Maggie. Are you having twins? Or triplets?"

She braced both hands against her lower back, a classic maternity pose, making her stomach stick out more than ever. "I'm not *that* big."

His eyes left her stomach and came back to hers. "You told me you were married."

"*You* told me I was married," she reminded him, her heart rate increasing. *He knows.*

"Yeah. Right." He braced one hand against his waist, rubbing the back of his neck with the other. "I can't believe that you, of all people . . ."

"What?"

"Having a baby. By yourself."

"I believe 'unwed mother' is the phrase you're looking for. But I prefer 'single parent.' "

"In Hope it will always be unwed mother. You know why? Because nothing changes in Hope. In another twenty or thirty years, it will *still* be unwed mother."

What did he want? Surely, even if he knew the child was his, he wouldn't want to claim it. No unmarried man wanted to be saddled with a child. Especially a nightlife-loving bachelor like Johnnie.

"Hope thrives on gossip," he said.

"We're old news now. Besides, it's not your concern."

"Why do you always do that?"

"What?"

"Push me away."

His question threw her. Was that how he saw what she considered strictly self-defense?

"What about the father? What does he say about this?"

Was he trying to trap her? "He has nothing to do with it. It's my body, my baby."

"You surprise me, Maggie. You've always seemed so conventional."

"Don't you mean boring?"

He flinched. Right on target.

"Who *is* the father, by the way?" he asked.

She didn't answer.

"Maggie, maybe it's slipped your mind, but we made love last summer."

"Sex. We had sex," she said, desperate to call a spade a spade.

"Whatever you want to call it."

"And you used a condom." Lots of them.

He was thoughtful a moment. "So, you slept—I mean had sex —with someone else besides me."

She put a finger to her chin and looked toward the ceiling. "Let's see, there was that baseball team traveling through town . . . and then there was—"

"Maggie—"

Why the sudden interest in her sexual habits? "Weren't you the one who always said I should loosen up?" she asked. "Not take sex so seriously? That it was just entertainment?"

"At first I may have said that. But give a guy credit. People change."

"Not that fast."

She thought of the way he'd hurt her, about the way he'd harped about wanting more than just sex from her. Shortly before he'd practically tossed her out of his apartment.

"Let's cut the bull," he said. "I want to know if the baby's mine. I have a right to know."

She struggled to hide her alarm. She'd read about unwed fathers who'd taken the mother of their child to court in order to gain custody. Johnnie would be able to afford the best lawyers. There would be no way she could compete with him.

Lying had never been her strong point. But then she'd never had a child at stake.

She knew she had to make this good, had to be convincing. She looked him in the eye, then spoke very clearly. "The baby isn't yours."

Was it the light that suddenly made his face seem paler? Surely relief made him draw a shaky breath, made him look up at the ceiling, then back at her.

"Elliot?" he asked, his voice strained, as if he struggled for control.

Her mother had always warned her that one lie led to another. Maggie closed her eyes and nodded.

A thoughtful silence.

"I hope you had a better time with Elliot that you did with me," he told her in a harsh voice, a voice that didn't sound at all like the easygoing Johnnie she knew.

Her eyes flew open.

"Of course you must have"—he glanced down at her stomach —"since you obviously didn't even think of birth control."

Such bitterness. Why was he so bitter? She didn't understand. Another pain hit her, this one much stronger and much closer than the last. She turned so he couldn't see it in her face.

"Was it good? Was *he* good?"

She didn't need this. Not on top of all she'd already been through. She'd been helping him, letting him off the hook, keeping him free, the way he wanted. Why was he lashing out at her? "Please go," she whispered, suddenly feeling weak and drained.

"Was it good?"

"Yes," she shouted, desperate for him to be gone. "It was wonderful. He was wonderful! The best! Now *get out!*"

"So good that you didn't even think about protection? So good that you didn't even think about the responsibility of bringing a new life into the world? Didn't anybody ever tell you where babies come from?"

"Get out! Get out! Get out!"

She started shoving him toward the door, and even though she wasn't exerting much strength, he moved in the direction she pushed.

"Of course with me you didn't think of it either," he reminded her, his voice heavy with sarcasm. "I guess you just get turned on and all your common sense deserts you. I was just a little more thoughtful than Elliot, huh?"

For him, of all people, to attack her, to turn so condescending, was more than she could stand. "You hypocrite! You talk about the people here. You're the last person I'd expect to condemn me for doing what I'm doing. Do you know how hard it's been to stand up to this town? Do you have any idea what I've had to put up with? How hard it was for me to make the decision I made and hope it was the right one?"

The regret she read in his face couldn't soften the hurt he'd already inflicted.

"Maggie, I'm sorry—"

"If you want to do something for me, get out." She flung open the door. "Go away and don't come back. Don't ever come back." A sob escaped her. She pressed the back of her hand to her mouth.

"Maggie, don't. You're going to hurt yourself."

"Get out!"

"Okay, okay." He staggered backward, through the opening.

She didn't hesitate. As soon as he was across the threshold, she slammed the door, sliding the bolt into place. When it was locked, she slowly lowered herself into the nearest chair.

She would wait until he was gone, then she would drive herself to the hospital.

A few minutes later she managed to calm herself enough to put in a call to her doctor. When he found out how close her labor pains were, he told her to come right away.

She hung up, grabbed her overnight case, and headed outside.

She couldn't believe it. Johnnie hadn't left. In fact, he was wandering around the yard like someone lost, or someone looking to buy. She headed straight for her Volkswagen. "You'll have to move your car," she said, tossing her overnight case into the back-seat, then easing herself into the cramped space behind the wheel.

Johnnie followed her, leaning in the window. "You shouldn't be driving. Why don't you let me give you a ride wherever you need to go?"

"No thanks. Just move your car." She pulled out the choke, put in the clutch, pumped the gas, and turned the ignition key. The engine whined, but wouldn't turn over. She gave it a rest, then tried again. The same repetitious grinding sound, followed by a suspicious gas smell. Her eyes flew to the choke. All the way out. She'd flooded the engine.

"I'll give you a ride," he said.

"No thanks." She shoved in the choke button. "I'll just sit here a little while. Then it'll start."

Another pain hit her. She doubled over, leaning her forehead against the steering wheel.

She forced herself to breathe shallowly, thinking all the while that if she could just make it back into the house she'd call a cab. Why hadn't she done that in the first place?

Her face was still hidden by her arm when she heard the door beside her open. Peripherally she was aware of him crouching down beside her. "Maggie?"

That was her undoing. The concern and worry in his voice. "I'm having my baby," she said in a wobbly voice. Then she started crying.

Everything after that was a blur. He asked her if she could walk, and when she nodded, he helped her from the car, settling her in the passenger side of his.

"The hospital's in Little Burgundy," she told him as he backed the car out of the driveway.

"That's forty-five miles!"

"I wanted my baby delivered by a gynecologist. He's the closest one."

"What if you have it before we get there?" Cool, calm Johnnie. Sweating bullets. Who would have thought?

"Don't worry," she said. "First babies usually take some time." She didn't add that she knew a woman who'd given birth in her car thirty minutes after realizing she was in labor—a story Maggie didn't like to think about.

In an attempt to distract herself, she tried to take in the scenery, what scenery there was, but it was hard. And Johnnie was no help. Instead of talking nonstop the way he normally would have done, he was silent, his white-knuckled hands gripping the steering wheel, his eyes focused on the two lanes in front of them.

At one point, Maggie noticed that the car seemed more lived in than a rental.

"It's mine," he told her when she asked. "I drove it to Mexico, where we just finished a movie. Sometimes I get tired of flying. And believe it or not, sometimes I like to be in control."

A half hour and three labor pains later they pulled up to the hospital. Johnnie helped her from the car, then retrieved her case from the backseat.

"Thanks," she said, trying to take the case from him.

He refused to let go. "I can't believe you were going to drive yourself, and in that excuse of a car."

"I thought you liked my VW."

"That's back when I was a foolish kid."

"When was that? Five minutes ago?"

"Something like that."

She started toward the double doors.

He followed.

She stopped. "What are you doing?"

"Coming with you."

"No. No, you can't."

"Wanna bet?"

She couldn't stand there arguing with him. He ended up following her inside. He helped her check in, causing a stir at registration when he was recognized. For a minute everyone completely forgot about her as they oohed and ahhed over Johnnie. Finally he had to direct their attention back to Maggie.

Suddenly they couldn't attend to her quickly enough. Before she knew it, she was put in a wheelchair and whisked upstairs to delivery, where she instantly became a nonperson as a nurse gave her a faded gown, prepped her, then finished their brief encounter with an enema.

After being so intimate with a total stranger, Maggie was relieved to see Dr. Richards's familiar face.

"Four centimeters dilated," he told her after a quick examination. He snapped off the rubber gloves and dropped them into a metal waste container. "I'll send in your friend before he wears out the hallway floor."

As soon as the doctor left, Maggie felt another contraction building. She focused on a bright pink stork dangling from the ceiling. Now that she was safe in the hospital, the pain didn't seem as severe. Maybe she wasn't such a sissy, after all. Maybe all those other women were the sissies.

Then Johnnie was there, in the room with her. His hair was sticking up in places, as if he'd nervously run his fingers through it several times.

"Well?" he asked.

"Everything seems to be going just the way it should." She was relieved to find that she sounded much calmer than she felt.

He let out his breath, then went to look out the window. The warm glow of late evening filtered in, bathing his face in soft light. It made her think of the night they'd planted Harriet's flowers. "Seen any sunrises lately?" she asked.

"Not since Hope."

He could do such special things. The flowers for Harriet. The sunrise. The way he made people laugh. The beautiful, haunting music he'd played that day in the opera house. Why couldn't he see that he was special?

"That song you played last summer. What was it?"

He continued to stare out the window. "I don't remember."

"In the opera house. You'd come by to see if we still needed you to play piano for us. You sat down and played a song. It was beautiful. I'd never heard it before."

He shrugged and turned back to her. Half his face was in shadow, half in light. "I don't know. Sometimes I make things up just for the hell of it, but later on I can never remember them. I never play the same thing twice."

The song had come from him? "You couldn't play it again?" The thought made her sad.

"No."

"But it was so beautiful." And now it was lost.

"Some songs are meant to be played once. Do you ever hear music and think it's one of the greatest songs you've ever heard, so you listen to it again and again? And pretty soon it isn't so great anymore. Pretty soon you're bored with it."

His words summed up his whole philosophy of existence. There was no stability in him. As soon as the new wore off, he moved on, looking for something fresh, something different.

"I like to listen to old songs," she told him. "There's beauty in familiarity, in knowing exactly what note comes next, in the anticipation of that note."

He smiled. "You would."

It struck her that his smile was full of self-mockery. She suddenly felt like a young child compared to him—someone who had seen and done too much. What did a person do when he'd heard all the songs there were to hear?

Her thoughts were interrupted by a contraction. She focused on the stork, using her accelerated-decelerated breathing. When it was over she was sweating, her heart beating rapidly, her mind filled with a strange combination of depression and eerie fear. She didn't want Johnnie to leave. She was afraid.

"Bad?" he asked.

"I have a confession to make," she said breathlessly.

He waited.

"I'm scared."

"I didn't think you were scared of anything." He looked a little scared himself.

"When I was little, I had a neighbor. She was this sweet, frail woman. Her religion didn't allow her to go to the hospital. Well, she got pregnant, and in the middle of the summer, on one of the hottest days of the year, she went into labor. I was outside playing, and I could hear her screaming a block away. I ran to my room and covered my ears, but I could still hear her. It went on and on for hours. They both died. The mother and the baby."

"Maggie—" He wrapped her hand in his. "That's not going to happen to you."

"Oh, I know it's silly, but it's something I can't seem to help."

Another contraction, more intense, lasting longer.

She squeezed Johnnie's hand, focused on the stork, and did her breathing. When it was over, it occurred to her that they were a little like the couples she had envied at Lamaze classes.

Chapter 19

*P*ain.

She was wrapped in it. Smothered by it.

They hadn't told her it would hurt so much.

Liars. They were all liars. Her Lamaze instructor, the writers of all the childbirth books she'd read. Liars. They'd called it discomfort. A more accurate description would have been the most agonizing pain a person could ever experience, multiplied by a million. No, not pain. It couldn't even be classified as pain. It was beyond that, in a realm all its own.

Never again would she complain about something as trivial as a headache or a backache.

The contractions were nothing like Lillian had perkily promised. Where were the valleys? Where were the moments of respite? For Maggie it was one never-ending peak. There were moments when the contractions lessened, but the pain was so severe that to cut it in half meant nothing.

For her, labor was like being an unwilling passenger on a runaway train, hurtling forward into a writhing pit of agony. A few times she tried to get up, feeling the need to escape, to get away and leave her pain behind. Whenever that happened, gentle hands would push her back down.

Nothing helped. Not the accelerated-decelerated breathing she'd given up long ago, or the shot of Demerol that was supposed to "take off the edge." The edge! It was still there, sharp and raw.

Labor was something not many women talked about, and now she knew why. They wanted to forget it. In her ignorance she hadn't realized there was such torture in the world.

"I didn't know it would hurt this much," she gasped to Johnnie, who was hovering at the perimeter of her private nightmare. Through a glaze of pain, she read his expression, his total helplessness, and she almost regretted her confession.

She was thinking about how dry her lips were when a cool, damp cloth touched them, then brushed across her brow.

As she concentrated on the feel of the cloth, as she wondered how he had known of her need, the pain intensified, driving out all thought, leaving nothing but body-racking agony. As much as she hated it, she knew she must focus on the pain, meet the pain. Otherwise, if she turned her back, it would win.

Maybe something was wrong. Maybe that's why it hurt so much.

Her body was soaked with perspiration. The green hospital gown stuck to her skin. There seemed to be a haze over her eyes, disconnecting her from the rest of the room, the rest of the world. She was alone. There was no today, no tomorrow. Nothing but pain.

But Johnnie was there, she reminded herself.

"I don't want to scream," she told him.

"Maggie—"

He leaned closer. With his fingers he eased her damp, tangled hair from her neck and smoothed it back from her temple. "It's okay to scream. We can scream together if you want. I'm one helluva screamer."

She would put that away to appreciate later. Later she would laugh. If she lived. She rolled her head from side to side. "Something's wrong. I know something's wrong."

"Nothing's *wrong*," he said, his voice fiercely determined.

But the fear was there, regardless.

Miraculously her next contraction eased more than the others. She seemed to be heading for Lillian's promised valley. Instantly she fell into an exhausted sleep.

This time when the pain returned she wasn't ready, wasn't braced for it. It took her by surprise, ripping her in two.

She screamed.

"Can't you give her something?"

Was that Johnnie? It didn't sound like him. Johnnie was too cool to ever sound rattled. To sound so scared. *Don't be scared*, she wanted to tell him. *I'm scared enough for both of us*.

Dr. Richards's voice drifted to her through a red fog. "We've given her all the Demerol we can. Too much sedation slows the labor, slows the dilation of the cervix. She's seven centimeters. Only three to go."

Only.

Time had taken on a strange quality. One moment Maggie was surprised at how much time had passed, the next she was wondering how it could move so slowly.

Nurses, who before had been chatting about the movie of the week they'd been watching in the lounge, now spoke in hushed whispers. *"What a shame."*

"Too bad."

What was too bad? What was a shame?

Dr. Richards spoke to her, his voice cutting through the wall of pain. "I was hoping that your pelvic bones would shift enough to accommodate the baby, but that isn't happening. Maggie, I'm sorry, but it looks as though we're going to have to do a cesarean."

No.

"Maggie, are you listening?"

"Yes." *No.*

"We have to do a C-section. I've already contacted an anesthesiologist, Dr. Martinez. He's one of the best."

An anesthesiologist? "He'll . . . put me to . . . sleep?" She hated the pitiful way her voice sounded.

"He'll give you a spinal. As soon as it's done you won't feel anything. I promise."

"No."

"I won't let anything happen to you or your baby."

He wasn't listening. He didn't realize she would die of shock. "I can't do it. I can't be conscious."

"You can."

I can't.

167

Her gaze reached beyond the doctor, locking on Johnnie. He moved closer.

"You'll come with me, won't you?" she asked.

His face paled. "Maggie, I don't think . . ."

She reached for his hand, squeezing it as another contraction pulled her down into the pit. *"Please."*

When the intensity of the contraction eased, Dr. Richards drew Johnnie aside. Whispered words drifted to her, enough for her to know they were discussing the possibility of Johnnie's presence in the delivery room.

Then Johnnie was there. Dr. Richards had given his okay. "I have to put on scrubs," Johnnie told her. "But I'll be right back."

She nodded. It wasn't until he touched her cheek that she realized she was crying.

"I'm afraid," she confessed in a wobbly voice.

"It's okay to be afraid. I'm afraid all the time."

She choked out a sound of disbelief. "What are you afraid of?"

"Everything." A thoughtful pause. "You. You scare the hell out of me."

Something else she would save for later.

The metal bed rails were locked into position.

"Meet you in the delivery room," Johnnie said.

She mouthed the word *bye.* Then she was wheeled down the hallway, toward surgery.

The lights in the room were blinding, the temperature so frigid that she began to tremble immediately. She was lifted to a cold, hard operating table.

And then Johnnie was there, taking a seat at the head of the table.

After an IV line was started, she was rolled to her side and told to curl into a ball for the spinal. The movement was almost more than she could bear. She moaned. Then, instantly ashamed, she bit her lip.

"While I insert the needle," Dr. Martinez said in a heavily accented voice, "you must not move."

She never even felt the needle. What was a needle inserted into her spine compared to what she'd already suffered? A mere pinprick.

Suddenly she was blessed with total cessation of pain. She let out her breath. Her muscles relaxed. She allowed herself to bask in the lack of sensation for a few moments before fear filtered in once more.

From nearby came the clink of metal—tools being laid out. The doctor and nurses were discussing blood and IVs.

"Maggie," Johnnie whispered, drawing her attention to him. "Don't think about what's happening. Just look at me."

She ran a tongue across her dry lips. "Talk to me," she said through tight vocal cords. "Tell me . . . about the movie you just . . . finished."

He told her how the story opened with a drifter pulling into a gas station along a two-lane highway. "A shack in the middle of no-man's-land. One rusty pump, a battered metal sign banging in the wind. Tumbleweeds rolling across the highway, piling up on the wooden porch in front of the roadside shack's only door."

She could see the place he described. She'd driven past such lonely spots.

"The guy goes inside, expecting to find it run by some ancient old-timer."

Maggie listened intently.

"Instead, he finds a guy in his early thirties."

"Your character," she said.

"Problem is, he's too sensitive for his own good. He was always getting hurt, so he moved to the desert to get away from life. The story is about the people who pass through his world, about how he unknowingly changes their lives. How he gives them advice and guidance, but he can't help himself." Johnnie sighed. "Sounds boring, I know."

"It sounds wonderful."

"What's your character's name?"

"Harley."

"Harley. I like that."

It was time.

"If you start to feel dizzy, put your head between your legs," the doctor told Johnnie. "And if you feel like you're going to faint, get down on the floor before it happens. We can't take care of two people at the same time."

"I'm not going to faint. I never faint."

Another liar. He and Lillian should get together. But Maggie kept her mouth shut. She needed him.

She closed her eyes. The overhead light created a red glow behind her lids. Since she couldn't see, her other senses kicked in, becoming stronger. She was aware of every muttered comment. Beside her, the nurses were talking about vacations and somebody's new hairstyle. Normal things. Reassuring things. A confirmation that nobody thought this was all that serious, a confirmation that life would go on, would be normal again. Soon this would be behind her, and she would be talking about vacations and hairstyles.

To her left, underscoring the whole event, was the steady beep of the heart-rate monitor. Just like in the movies. Just like real life.

Dr. Richards asked for scissors.

Dr. Martinez bent over, explaining that the IV contained a slight sedative. "You might feel a little drunk."

"The baby?"

"It won't hurt the baby."

One of the nurses patted her arm. Then she heard the sound of metal sliding across metal.

Clip, clip, clip.

She was being cut open, just like a length of fabric.

Her eyes flew open. Directly in front of her face was a green sheet, held up by a metal bracket—a screen so she couldn't see what was happening on the other side. But her imagination filled in all the blanks.

Above the green sheet, she could see Dr. Richards leaning over her, his hands bloody.

She squeezed her eyes shut, but the horrible image stayed in her mind.

Beep, beep, beep.

"Blood pressure's dropping. Heart rate erratic."

"Good Lord." Dr. Richards's normally cool voice was edged with panic.

Sounds of scrambling feet.

"Talk to her."

Even with her eyes tightly closed, Maggie knew it was Johnnie's hand that stroked her hair back from her forehead. And even though his hand shook, it brought her comfort.

"Maggie, remember the day of the Hope parade? I can still see you, leaning against the fender of that big Cadillac while the sun beat down, baking everything. Can you feel that sun, Maggie?"

Through the chill of the operating room, Maggie thought she detected a bit of warmth falling on her face. "Yes," she whispered.

"Stabilizing."

"You were wearing a red dress. I can see you getting behind the wheel of Clara's big ol' Caddy and laying rubber when you pulled onto the highway. The air was bone-dry. It lifted your hair straight out, then whipped it around your face. Can you feel that wind, Maggie?"

She *could* almost feel it.

"Forceps." Dr. Richards.

"You weren't wearing any makeup, and you didn't want to impress me. In fact, you didn't give a damn what I thought."

How had he known that?

"You want to know what I thought?"

He had her complete attention.

"Have you ever felt the breeze that comes off the ocean?"

"I've . . . never seen the ocean."

"Never seen the ocean? When you get out of here, I'll take you and your baby to the ocean. It's the cleanest air you'll ever breathe because it's filtered by traveling miles and miles over nothing but water. Anyway, I had that same feeling when I met you. It was like standing next to the ocean."

"Really?"

"Really."

From somewhere beyond the wall of their conversation came a small choking sound, followed by a tiny squall, then a louder one.

At exactly 3:39 A.M. Alexandra Marie Mayfield was born.

"A girl."

In Johnnie's voice was wonder. And Maggie had always thought that nothing could amaze him, that he'd seen it all.

Maggie opened her eyes to see Dr. Richards holding a squalling, trembling, red-faced baby.

Her baby.

A *girl.*

She hadn't a thought for anyone but her baby. Gone was the

171

irrational fear that had plagued her. Gone was the memory of the pain. What pain?

"She's beautiful," Maggie said, her heart full of such exquisite tenderness that tears filled her eyes. She'd never dreamed it could be like this. Never. She'd never dreamed there was such love in the world.

Maggie was still admiring her beautiful, beautiful baby when the nurse whisked the child away to be washed and weighed.

"Seven pounds twelve ounces. Twenty-one inches long."

"Quite a catch," Johnnie commented. "What are you going to name her?"

"Alexandra."

"Nobody should have to go through life with a name that has more than three syllables."

"I'll call her Alex."

"Just as long as her middle name isn't Trebek."

The nurse handed the bundled baby to Maggie, securing Alex in the crook of Maggie's arm. "Isn't she beautiful?" Maggie asked dreamily.

"Beautiful."

The voice beside her was Johnnie's, but he sounded totally wiped-out. She turned her head. He *looked* totally wiped-out. Above the green surgical mask, his eyes were bloodshot. A sweat-stained scrub cap was pulled down over hair that lay in shaggy strands around his neck.

"You better check your blood sugar," she told him. "Then get some rest."

"I can hang on a little longer."

His gaze was drawn from her, riveting to the doctor. His eyes widened. "What the hell's that?"

"A stapler. We use it instead of sutures."

Maggie let out a cry of alarm just as Johnnie clattered to the floor.

Chapter 20

*I*ncessant crying filled the tiny hospital room, echoing off the walls.

"You're holding her too tight," Johnnie said.

Maggie shifted the baby in her arms, but little Alex continued to scream bloody murder. "She's not crying because of the way I'm holding her. She's crying because she's hungry."

"Then feed her."

"I can't. My milk hasn't come in."

"Give her here. Maybe I can get her to stop."

"How? Has your milk come in?"

Johnnie laughed while carefully lifting the screaming bundle from Maggie's arms.

"Your mother thinks she's a comedian," he confided to the baby. He tucked her in the crook of one arm and picked up the pacifier with his free hand. "Think she'll fall for this?" He put the pacifier to his chest in the nursing position and stuck the rubber end in the baby's mouth.

The screaming stopped, but Alex continued to make throaty hums of discontentment, like an angry bee. He jounced her up and down as he paced the room. Then he started singing a nonsense song in a high-pitched voice—the kind of voice babies responded to so well. The song made no sense whatsoever. He was obviously making it up as he went. After the serenade, he told Alex some of the dumbest jokes Maggie had ever heard.

"Oh brother," she said after one exceptional bomb. "Karen's man-hater jokes are better than that."

Insulted eyes looked up at her above a now sleeping baby. "You don't expect me to tell her dirty ones, do you?"

Karen called several times. She still sounded wiped-out from the bug that had spread through her whole family.

"This place is like an infirmary," she told Maggie. "Buckets by every bed. I'm dying to see Alex, but there's no way I'm coming until we're all well. I wouldn't want to give a newborn what I've got."

"I understand," Maggie said. "And thanks."

"God, I'm sorry I let you down."

"You didn't let me down."

"I promised I'd be there for you."

"It's *okay*."

Seven days after Alex's birth Johnnie drove mother and baby home from the hospital. It seemed only right.

Three nurses walked them to patient loading and unloading. Maggie knew better than to think it might be little Alex who brought them out. As they said their goodbyes, all three women kept their eyes fixed on Johnnie. Obviously used to such open adoration, he flashed them a nonchalant grin and a wave.

"It'll be quiet around there with the little terror gone," Johnnie said as he pulled away from the curb.

He was talking about Alex. Sweet Alex.

At first Maggie had been maternally blind to her child's temper. But as the days passed she'd begun to realize that Alex didn't cry like the other babies in the nursery. She screamed. And if she didn't get what she wanted, she kept on screaming.

At the moment she was awake and quiet, a rare combination. As the miles ticked away, Maggie gradually relaxed.

She began to think they might make it all the way home without an eruption. But just about the time they passed a billboard advertising the Hope Cafe, Alex began exercising her lungs.

"Going to be an opera star," Johnnie shouted over the noise.

"Or a marathon runner."

"Or a clam diver."

Alex was hungry. Again. Even though Maggie hadn't minded breast-feeding her in front of the doctor and nurses, she didn't feel comfortable about doing it in front of Johnnie. She popped the pacifier into Alex's screaming mouth and hoped she could hang on for another twenty miles.

By the time they pulled into the driveway, Maggie's ears were ringing and her nerves were strung tight. While Maggie eased herself from the car, Johnnie rescued the squalling baby from the infant seat. For a split second, the screams changed from furious to expectant, then a questioning pause. As soon as she realized Johnnie wasn't serving lunch, her cries became furious again.

He handed her to Maggie. "You've got the goods."

Maggie carried her to the house, to the bedroom, undoing her blouse as she went.

For the first time in her life, Maggie wasn't flat. Her milk had come in with a vengeance and her breasts were swollen and hard and painful. Alex tried to nurse, but something was wrong. Madder than ever, she let go of the nipple, then tried again. Her face, which was already red, turned even redder. She screamed, arms pumping, legs pushing at Maggie's tender stomach.

Maggie was too tense and upset for her milk to come down.

Again she tried to get Alex to nurse, but it was the same thing all over.

This wasn't the way Maggie had imagined motherhood. She'd imagined herself breast-feeding her quiet baby while a gentle, sepia light poured in and blessed silence surrounded them.

She didn't blame Alex, she blamed herself. Even though she'd read all the books she could find, even though she'd bounced other people's kids on her knee and given them horsey rides, she didn't know anything about babies. She didn't know anything about being a mother.

• • •

By the time Johnnie got the car unloaded, Alex was still squalling. He could hear her through two closed doors. Hell, he could hear her from the driveway.

He rapped on the bedroom door, then opened it, the squalls making his head hurt.

Maggie was lying on the bed, Alex beside her.

They were both crying.

Maggie, with a tissue pressed to her mouth. Alex, with her legs and arms pumping in tight, angry circles.

"I don't know anything about babies," Maggie told him in a shuddering, broken voice.

But Johnnie understood that she had what was important, the one thing essential to motherhood—unconditional love for her child. What difference did it make if she couldn't always get the diaper on right, or that she sometimes held Alex a little too tight?

"You fed her and she's still crying? Maybe she needs to be changed."

"She hasn't been fed." Maggie closed her eyes and took a trembling breath. "I tried, but"—she hit at her chest with a tissue-clutching hand—"my milk won't come down."

"Won't come down?" What the hell did that mean? First it wouldn't come *in*, then it wouldn't come *down*.

"I'm too nervous. My stomach is in knots. My baby's hungry and I can't feed her."

Her explanation left Johnnie feeling baffled and totally out of his element, but he tried not to let panic overtake him. It wouldn't do for them both to lose it.

"She's not going to starve," he reasoned. "If you have to, you can give her some of the formula the hospital sent along."

"I don't want to give her formula. If I'd wanted to give her formula, I wouldn't be breast-feeding."

Johnnie took in the dark circles under Maggie's eyes, the exhaustion in her every gesture. He found it unnerving, the way she was watching him, waiting for him to come up with some magic solution.

Back at the hospital, he'd gotten a kick out of holding Alex, but that was because he'd known he could yell for a nurse anytime and two or three would come running. This was a different story.

There wasn't anybody he could call. It was just him and Maggie. And Maggie was falling apart.

Keep it light. Wasn't that what he always told himself whenever he was nervous, when things got wild? Don't sweat the little things. No need to panic. Everything's under control.

He crossed the room and picked up the screaming Alex. "Your mom needs a little R&R," he told her. He tried to get her to take the pacifier, but she wasn't falling for it this time. She was hungry and pissed.

He put her down in the bassinet. "How about some tunes?" He turned the crank on the circus mobile dangling above her head. "Ah, the long version of 'Rockabye Baby.' One of my all-time favorites."

He was rewarded by a watery chuckle from the bed behind him.

Alex was still crying, but her cries weren't as frantic. He tried the pacifier again, and this time she sucked on it, her unfocused navy-blue eyes wide, her face bright red.

"And they say today's music makes kids wild," Johnnie said, sitting down on the bed next to Maggie. "Why don't you close your eyes and rest a minute?"

Surprisingly she complied, but that just went to show how tired she was. He stroked the hair back from her face, letting the auburn locks spill through his fingers. Then he rubbed her back and shoulders. As he did, he could feel her relaxing, feel the tension leaving her taut muscles.

A few minutes later a groggy-voiced Maggie said she was ready to feed Alex.

Johnnie retrieved the baby from the bassinet and carried her to her mother. As he put her down, he could see that Maggie's milk had come down, all right. The front of her blouse was soaked.

She hadn't yet fed Alex in front of him. Maybe she was too tired to think about what she was doing, or maybe she was finally getting used to him. Whatever the reason, this time, lying on her side with Alex next to her, Maggie undid her blouse and the panel of her nursing bra, then brought the baby to her breast. As soon as a nipple grazed Alex's cheek, the baby turned her face and latched on hungrily, sucking so hard she choked, let go, gasped, then started all over. The worst hunger pangs satisfied, her nursing finally fell into a contented rhythm. Her eyes drifted closed, her small fist resting against the white fullness of Maggie's breast.

Johnnie stood there, committing the moment to memory.

Never in his life had he thought of himself as a family man. In fact, he found it totally impossible to imagine himself as a father. It just wasn't in him. But at that moment he felt a yearning he'd never felt before. At that moment he wanted a family. He wanted Maggie and he wanted Alex. He wanted to be a part of their lives. He wanted them to be a part of his.

Shaken by his own reaction, he lay down on the bed, careful not to disturb them.

It hadn't been anything like he'd expected, witnessing Alex's birth. He hadn't wanted to go into the delivery room. He'd been scared as hell, but Maggie had been lying there, her skin transparent, eyes shadowed, body racked with pain, begging him to stay with her. And he'd known, if it was the last mature decision he made in his life, that he couldn't tell her no, no matter how scared he was.

Now he wouldn't trade the experience for anything. It had been amazing. After his fear for Maggie had abated, after he'd known she was going to be okay, the magic had happened. He'd realized he was witnessing something profound. Something that the cynic in him had never expected, not in a million years.

A miracle.

It was quiet in the bedroom except for slow, steady breathing. He thought Maggie and Alex were both asleep when Maggie's voice drifted to him through the feeling of peace that had settled around the room.

"Johnnie?"

"Mmm?"

"Thanks."

He turned and pressed his lips lightly against her hair. She smelled like sweet baby and milk and Maggie.

Even though she'd said she needed to lose ten pounds, even though she said her breasts were too big, and her incision too ugly, he thought she'd never looked more beautiful. "No problem," he told her.

She smiled and let her eyes drift shut.

He could get used to this.

The realization came to him as a pain, a terrible ache, a terrible fear that made his heart race in panic. He'd told her she scared him, but at the time even he hadn't fully understood the extent of those words.

He was afraid of her. Afraid of loving her.

What was happening? What was he doing here? Johnnie Irish, somebody who never completed a relationship. Somebody who always cut out before the third act was over.

He didn't know.

He only knew it felt right. He only knew that the restlessness that screamed through him whenever he stopped running, or stopped making noise, was gone.

Chapter 21

*J*ohnnie didn't sleep much that night. The couch was too short, not made for a lot of tossing and turning and belly sleeping. But the couch wasn't really what kept him in no more than a light doze. He was afraid if he fell into a deep, REM sleep, he'd dream. And if he dreamed, there was a chance he'd wake up screaming louder than Alex.

How would he explain that one?

Don't worry. Whenever I'm in Hope I have dreams about my old lady chasing me with a bottle of perfume.

Ooh. Scary. It might impress Maggie even more than the barroom brawl.

The next morning he was up early, searching through Maggie's cupboards. Old Mother Hubbard didn't have anything on her.

"You have a piss-poor stash of food," he informed Maggie, shoving a can of mushroom soup aside to reveal an almost empty shelf.

"Alex wasn't due for two weeks," Maggie said. "I was taken by surprise."

So Johnnie went shopping, returning an hour and a half later with a trunk load of supplies.

Bending at the knees, Johnnie put the last of the grocery bags on the kitchen table. "Guess what I picked up?" He pulled out a tabloid. "Get this. 'Johnnie Irish secretly married to small-town schoolmarm.' " He laughed in ornery delight. "Schoolmarm! Think that's you?"

"I'm no marm," Maggie protested from her chair in the adjoining living room, a sleeping baby at her breast.

"Maggie Marm."

"Stop it," she said, trying to hide a smile. She shifted the baby and adjusted her clothes.

Tossing the paper aside, Johnnie went back to his groceries. He pulled out fresh broccoli. "Cancer fighter," he announced.

And apples. "Pectin. Gotta have your pectin."

Strawberries and green beans and whole-grain bread. Two *gallons* of milk.

"I read where nursing mothers are supposed to drink lots of milk," he said, opening the refrigerator and stopping the door with his knee.

Johnnie was enjoying himself. He'd played a family man in a couple of movies and had gotten a big kick out of it. It was a little like playing house.

"Sorry," Maggie said. "I can't get too excited about milk."

"I think I could maybe grow to like it." He glanced at her breasts, then away as he dug back into the sack. Breast-feeding was fascinating.

"Breast milk has a lot of sugar," she told him, looking down at Alex, touching her curled fingers.

"Sweet? I didn't know that." A thoughtful pause. "I'd like to try it sometime."

"It wouldn't be good for you."

"That's never stopped me before."

He didn't miss the color in her cheeks as she walked past him to put the sleeping Alex in bed. When she returned, Johnnie was waiting. He came up behind her and wrapped his arms around her, her back to his chest, the curve of her ear against his lips. At that moment her right breast released a stream of milk, soaking the front of her shirt.

Johnnie lay a palm against the spreading wetness. His lips curved into a smile. "Now I know what to do when your milk won't come down."

● ● ●

That night Johnnie fixed supper: grilled chicken, baked pota-
toes, green beans, and of course milk to drink.

"My doctor would be proud of me," he said, taking a bite of
green beans.

"I don't imagine that you're normally a model patient."

He wagged his fork at her. "You're damn sarcastic, you know
that?" His tone was serious, but Maggie could see the teasing laughter in his eyes.

"You bring that out in me."

"More milk? More chicken?"

She put up a hand and shook her head.

"A nursing mother is supposed to take in eight hundred more
calories than usual."

"Where do you get all this information?"

"While you've been doing all that snoozing, I've been doing my
homework, reading your baby books."

Alex chose that particular moment to wake up.

Seemingly without conscious thought, Johnnie scooted back
his chair and went to retrieve her. Maggie could hear him talking,
and Alex responding by quieting. He returned with the baby
tucked under one arm, sucking madly on her pacifier. He sat down
and resumed his meal, seeming perfectly at ease with a baby in one
hand and a fork in the other.

That evening, whenever the phone rang, Johnnie jumped up to
answer it, giving the caller the Maggie and Alex report. Difficult
birth. Okay now. C-section. Seven pounds twelve ounces, twenty-
one inches long. Beautiful. Lots of hair. Ten toes. Ten fingers.
Smiles.

He sounded like a proud father.

Maggie was in a deep sleep when something woke her. Expecting to hear Alex's hungry wail, she waited, listening. From the
living room came singing—a husky male voice maintained at
barely above a whisper. She checked the bedside clock: 5:30 A.M.

Careful of her healing stomach, Maggie slipped from the bed,
bare feet meeting cool floor. She moved quietly across the room,
stopping when she reached the doorway.

182

In the center of the living room, illuminated by a beam of light that poured from the kitchen, was Johnnie. Shirtless and barefoot, he had his back to her, his head bent, a baby blanket dangling over one denim-clad hip as his feet shifted silently from side to side. In his arms was Alex.

He was singing in barely above a whisper, his voice coming out deeper than usual, seeming to reverberate in the small room. And even though the tune was slightly flat, Maggie caught enough of the words to recognize the song. "Blue Suede Shoes." And a fairly decent imitation of Elvis.

Beneath the cadence of his voice, she could hear Alex humming her angry-bee hum as she sucked greedily on the pacifier.

The scene was funny, sweet, and oh so endearing. The contrast between the nuttiness of the song and the tenderness of the moment moved her as nothing else could.

After a time, Johnnie's voice faded to silence. His back still to Maggie, Johnnie continued to hold Alex, watching her, talking to her in a soft voice.

"Your daddy doesn't know what he's missing," he whispered to the baby he cradled in his strong, protective arms.

Maggie's breath caught—a constriction of pain in her throat. Somehow she managed to step quietly into the bedroom. Once there, she leaned against the wall, eyes closed.

How had this happened?

While still in the hospital, she'd struggled with herself, realizing deep down that she would have to tell Johnnie the truth about Alex, but she'd put it off, waiting for the right time, the right words.

Who was she fooling? She'd been scared. She was scared now.

What they'd shared had been so special, a moment of wonder in what had been a rocky relationship at best. If it could be called a relationship at all. She'd wanted to hang on to that shared magic a while longer. She hadn't wanted to ruin it.

But now, if she could go back, if she could tell Johnnie the truth from the very beginning, she would. She'd never meant to deceive him. At the time it had seemed the right thing to do for all three of them.

From the living room came a couple of whimpers, followed by Alex's classic scream as she grew dissatisfied with the pacifier.

Under cover of the noise, Maggie got back in bed and pretended to be asleep. The cries grew nearer. A hand touched her shoulder. Warm, reassuring in the darkness.

"Maggie? Don't get up," he whispered when she rolled to face him. He nestled Alex beside her on the bed. "She's changed, she's dry, and she's hungry." Then he left them alone, mother and daughter.

Maggie undid the tie on the front of her gown. How was he going to react when she told him? He would be hurt.

And he would hate her.

By the time she'd fed Alex and put her down to sleep, the sun was coming up. Maggie slipped into her housecoat, then went to find Johnnie.

He was sitting on the couch in the living room, checking his blood sugar with a test strip and readout meter.

This was it. After today nothing between them would be the same.

They had started out as enemies. She had hated his life of excess, hated the way he had ruined the parade. How trivial that sounded now. But then he had smiled at her and made her laugh. He had been there when she'd needed him. Somehow he had become her friend. Despite his self-destructive ways, in spite of her better judgment, she had come to care for him. She had come to love him.

But love wasn't always a beginning.

He looked up at her and smiled. The first time she'd come face-to-face with his good looks, she'd noticed how his smile had seemed more a shield than an open door. Now it was the other way around. But soon, very soon, that would all change.

"What do you know?" he said. "I should get a sticker for good behavior. My blood sugar looks fairly decent for a change. I won't need as much insulin today. You must be good for me, Maggie May."

I'm not good for you. I'm not good for you at all.

With deft, deliberate movements that were as second nature to him as brushing his teeth, he filled the syringe with insulin, flicked it down, then put the bottle on the coffee table. She watched as he stuck the needle straight into the fleshy part of his arm, then pushed the plunger.

184

I want to tell you that there was no one else. Just you. But she couldn't seem to make herself say the words.

Tell him. Go on. Tell him now.

From a few feet away, the phone rang. Maggie jumped, then picked up the receiver, relieved at the interruption. The call was from the owner of Harriet's old house, the woman frantically explaining that Harriet had shown up there, thinking the place was still hers.

"I'll go get her," Johnnie said as soon as Maggie hung up. He jumped to his feet, pulled on socks and sneakers, grabbed a shirt, and headed for the door.

Johnnie remembered Harriet's old place from meetings they'd had there when he was in high school. It was a big stucco house with a huge wraparound porch. When he was a kid, it had seemed like a mansion. He remembered wondering if she was rich. Now it seemed like a house. A big, homey house.

The new owners let him in, their faces anxious.

"She would never hurt anybody," Johnnie said.

The woman tugged at the belt on her robe. "It was just so startling to find her in the kitchen when I came downstairs this morning."

They led Johnnie through the house to the rear door. "She's in the backyard," the husband said.

Johnnie found Harriet on a bench in the garden next to the pond, a slice of bread in one hand.

He sat down beside her, took a piece of the offered bread, and tossed a few crumbs into the pond. Giant goldfish surfaced, eating the bread in single swallows.

"Harold put in this pond, you know," Harriet told him. "The fish were just tiny when we got them." She showed him their size with her finger and thumb. "If you're looking for Harold, he left just a while ago, but he'll be back pretty soon." She smiled, her head tilted to one side. "Some married couples like to go their own ways, but Harold and I . . . we do everything together. I worry about that sometimes. About what I'll do when he's gone. But it doesn't do you a bit of good to worry about what hasn't happened."

He hurt for her. It wasn't right that her home had been sold so her jerk of a son could get his hands on her money. Harriet belonged here, with her goldfish and flowers.

185

Johnnie blamed himself. He should have kept in touch, he should have taken care of her. So many things he should have done.

But it wasn't too late. The new owners might sell. He'd have to work on them. But would Harry accept the house from him? Probably not. But if she thought it came from her son . . .

"Maggie had a baby girl," he said, hoping to coax her back to the present.

"A girl . . . I always wanted a girl. I had two boys. Two sweet baby boys. Harold cried when they were born. Some people say men shouldn't cry. That it's a sign of weakness. You know what I think? I think it's a sign of character."

When the bread crumbs were gone, Johnnie got to his feet. "What do you say we go get some breakfast someplace?" he asked. "My treat."

"Waffles? I love waffles."

"Sounds good." He helped her up, alarmed by the frailness of her bones.

They ended up eating in a corner booth of the Hope Cafe. By the time they were finished, Harriet seemed a little more aware of what was going on, enough for Johnnie to take her back to her house.

"Sometimes I get confused," she told Johnnie as he helped her up the walk that led to her front door.

"Everybody gets confused now and then."

She stopped and looked at him. Unlike before, her eyes were now clear. "You were always so sensitive," she told him. "Too sensitive for your own good."

He gave her what felt like a crooked, aw-shucks sort of smile.

"I remember the first time I saw you with your long hair and frayed denim jacket, you scared me to death. But then I looked closer. I don't think many people look close enough to see behind the armor you wear. If they did, they'd find a vulnerable, sweet man."

"Sweet's not a word people normally use to describe me," he said, smiling down at her.

She squeezed his arm. "You've got a lot of ghosts in you. The secret is to let them go. You have to quit hiding from yourself. Sure, sometimes you get hurt, but getting hurt is okay. It just proves you're alive."

She looked over her shoulder, toward the door. "I had the most beautiful flowers there last summer," she said, nodding toward the area where Johnnie and Maggie had done their midnight planting.

He usually never thought about what was going to happen in a month, or two months, but he suddenly found himself thinking that they would have to plant flowers for Harriet again. Maybe watch the sun come up too.

"I just came out one morning and they were there," Harriet said.

"That so?"

Her face became serious. "You're special. Don't ever let anybody tell you different."

Time meshed, the way it sometimes did in Hope. A mingling of the old and the new. Harriet's words were the same ones she'd spoken to him years ago.

"I have to go in now and feed my kitty," she said, taking the steps one at a time. "If it wasn't for my kitty . . ." She opened the door and shuffled into the house. "Here, kitty, kitty, kitty . . ."

Before going back to Maggie's, Johnnie stopped at the gas station. He filled the tank, then went inside to pay.

On the chipped and faded counter, next to the cash register, was a propped-up piece of cardboard, lettered in black Magic Marker: WHO'S THE DADDY? ELLIOT OR JOHNNIE?

Next to the sign was a slotted coffee can and paper to write down wagers.

"What the hell's that?" Johnnie demanded.

The old geezer behind the counter shoved himself up out of his rusty metal chair. "Just some friendly betting. Care to put in your two cents? Odds are running two to one in the brother-in-law's favor."

"That's the dumbest thing I've ever heard. Do you know who I am?"

"Sure I do." The man sucked on his false teeth. "That should give you a little inside advantage." He laughed, coughed, caught his breath, then continued. "At first I thought it had to be the brother-in-law. He spent two nights in a row at her place. Just about"—he made an elaborate show of looking at the ceiling, face screwed up in deep thought—"about nine months ago. Far as I know, you never stayed the night until two days ago."

Johnnie ground his teeth and emitted a low growl.

"But now I have some inside information of my own." The man reached into the top pocket of his bib overalls. With two fingers he pulled out a piece of paper, slowly unfolded it, then paused for effect.

Hell, the guy belonged onstage. He was putting on one helluva performance.

"Maggie's checked out some interesting library books over the past few months."

"It's against the law for libraries to give out that information."

"I never heard of such a thing. Free world."

Sure. This was Hope.

"Let's see." The man adjusted his smudged glasses, tilted his head, and read: *"Diabetes and Your Unborn Child.* That was special-ordered through interlibrary loan. Came all the way from Oregon, I believe. Then there was *Diabetes in the Family: The Risks of Passing It On to Your Child. Pregnancy and Diabetes: Everything You Need to Know."* The man removed his glasses. "Now, I was talking to the sheriff, and he says you're a diabetic."

She'd lied to him.

For a few seconds, that thought filled every corner of Johnnie's mind. There was room for nothing else. Then, little by little, other emotions filtered in. Shock. Confusion. The hurt Harry had spoken of.

"What do you say?" the man asked. "We could close the pool right now." He dug around in a drawer and came out with a stub of a pencil. "Better put it in writing, so nobody thinks I rigged the thing."

Johnnie had always respected his elders, at least the ones who couldn't get around unaided, but this guy was pissing him off.

"Go to hell," Johnnie said.

The man threw down the pencil and pulled himself up straighter. "Listen here, Mr. Hotshot. We're just having a little fun, that's all. I don't believe in doing things in secret. Would you rather we slunk around, whispering in corners?"

188

Johnnie slapped a twenty on the counter. "That's for gas." He grabbed the sign from the counter and headed out the door.

The wind was hot, rippling his shirt, whipping his hair about his face, rolling a tumbleweed across the highway that led away from Hope. Away from Maggie. Away from Alex. It was the same highway he'd taken sixteen years ago, when he'd left Hope with no plans of ever coming back. He should have stuck to that decision. God, how he wished he had.

Once in the car, his initial instinct was to drive and keep on driving. He put the car in gear and stepped on the gas pedal. He'd gone about a mile when he pulled to the side of the road, gravel flying as he skidded to a stop.

He slammed a fist against the steering wheel. Damn her.

He was running away, the way he always ran away.

He knew that the thing to do was to go back and face her, confront her. But he was afraid. Afraid he might break down, and it was important that she didn't know how much she'd hurt him, how much she was still hurting him. He didn't want to give her that kind of power or satisfaction.

He turned the car around. Fifteen minutes. That's all it would take. He could maintain for fifteen minutes.

He didn't knock, although he felt like it. Strangers knocked. When he stepped into her house, Maggie looked glad to see him. But then, as he stood with his back to the door, watching while the pain of her betrayal squeezed his heart tighter and tighter, her smile of greeting faded.

"Johnnie? Is it Harriet? Is she okay?"

"She's fine. At least for now." He lifted the cardboard sign he was carrying, holding it up so she could read it.

She laughed a little nervously. "Hope's way of dealing with its unwed mother. At first it bothered me, but then I actually felt relieved that it was so out in the open."

"Did you bet?"

"What?"

"Did you bet on the father?"

"Of course not."

"If you had, who would you have bet on? Elliot?" He paused. "Or me?"

Her eyes rounded in alarm. At being caught. The last thing he wanted was an emotional scene. He was no good in an adult role, but this had to be played out.

"I believe in getting things out in the open too," he said. "The odds are two to one in Elliot's favor. But the *gentleman* who runs the gas station was kind enough to give me some inside information. He had a list of the library books you've checked out over the past few months."

She put a hand to her mouth. Her alarm, her silence, told him everything he needed to know.

"I'm sorry," she whispered, letting her hand fall limply to her side. "I was going to tell you."

"Sure you were." He laughed his old sarcastic laugh. After all these years, his acting was finally paying off. Here he was, standing in front of her, remaining cool, when all he really wanted to do was cry.

"What were you thinking when I came along and helped deliver my own baby? You must have really gotten a kick out of that. You must have really thought I was a fool."

She shook her head, her eyes swimming with tears. *"No.* When I first found out I was pregnant, I didn't tell you because I didn't think you'd care." Her eyes grew confused, her cruel words trailed off, as if she only just realized what she'd said.

"No." He put a hand to his chest. "I don't care about anything." He took a deep, stabilizing breath. He wouldn't fall apart. Not in front of her. "You know what I'd really like? I'd like sometime in my life to meet someone who didn't automatically think the worst of me. Someone who has at least a small amount of faith. But that'll never happen."

His voice broke on the last word. He prayed she didn't notice. He had to get away. Had to move fast. He had his hand on the doorknob when he stopped and looked in the direction of the bedroom.

Alex.

Oh God. Alex. He could picture her lying on her stomach, knees drawn up, bottom in the air, sucking her fingers.

Not just Maggie's child, but his. *His.*

"Will you be back? Will we ever see you again?"

She was his child too. That thought gave him strength.

He looked at Maggie for the last time. "The next person you'll be hearing from will be my lawyer."

Her face paled. She looked stricken. She reached behind her for a chair, then slowly lowered herself into it. "You wouldn't. You can't."

Her terror was almost his undoing. Before he could weaken, he jerked open the door and left, his long strides taking him away.

He drove north out of Hope, then west, across New Mexico, toward California.

He'd known it wouldn't last. What had he expected? A different ending? For them to have spent the rest of their lives together? For Maggie to marry him, for Christ's sake?

He'd spent the last week in a dreamworld. What an idiot. He wasn't the marrying kind. And he sure as hell wasn't the type who'd make a good father. What did he know about being a father? Nothing.

He had no reason to be mad at Maggie. What they'd had was just sex. No commitment. Hadn't she played by his rules? He had been the one, not Maggie, who had tried to turn things around, who had insisted on "one more time, with feeling."

No, family life wasn't for him. He'd go nuts living some Ozzie and Harriet existence. Chained to a lawn mower and a station wagon with wood trim. Vacations spent checking out places like Carhenge and the South Dakota Corn Palace. Wearing baggy shorts, sandals with black nylon socks, and a go-to-hell hat complete with fishing tackle.

No way.

A close call.

For a few days he'd been taken in, brainwashed. He'd forgotten who he was and where he'd come from. But now he was on track again. Now he had his head on straight.

The headlights illuminated a road sign. *Welcome to Arizona, the Grand Canyon State.*

Somewhere along the way he'd lost two hundred miles. Highway hypnosis. It was a handy thing when a guy had a lot of road to cover.

• • •

He made good time, but as he moved through the darkness Maggie's stricken face haunted him. Long after midnight he pulled up to a roadside tavern. Outside, next to the tavern door, was a pay phone where he put in a call.

As soon as Maggie answered, he could tell she'd been crying. He spoke into the stale mouthpiece. "Forget what I said about a lawyer. I didn't mean it. I won't try to take Alex from you."

A semi roared by, downshifting as it approached a curve in the road.

Johnnie swallowed, closed his eyes, and leaned his forehead against the glass of the booth. "I got to thinking. A kid would really cramp my style."

"Johnnie, where are you?"

Your daddy didn't want you. "But when she gets older, don't tell her I said that, okay? I want you to promise."

"I promise."

"Tell her I'm dead." He thought a moment. "And tell her I was the first person to make her laugh."

"Johnnie, where are you?"

"On my way home."

He hung up. Then he left the phone booth and headed for the bar.

Chapter 22

The only way Maggie knew Johnnie was alive was through the newspapers. He was back to working hard and playing even harder. The very thing she had feared had happened: She was going to spend the rest of her life waiting for him to self-destruct.

Two weeks after Johnnie's departure from Hope, Maggie heard that he'd ended up in another alcohol-induced diabetic coma. She immediately tried to get in touch with him, but it wasn't possible. His whereabouts were being kept a secret.

As soon as she got news of his release, she put in a call to his home, only to get his answering machine.

I can't come to the phone right now, because I'm either (a) feeding my pit bull, (b) having sex, (c) cutting my toenails, (d) trying to understand the appeal of Claymation. Leave your name and number and I'll get back to you.

She hung up.

She stared at the phone.

She got up and walked around.

She sat down and dialed again. This time she left a message.

"Johnnie, it's Maggie. I heard you were in the hospital, and I just wanted to make sure you were okay." She took a deep, trembling breath. "Alex is fine. Getting fatter every day." She paused, thinking of a million things she wanted to say. *I'm worried about you. I love you. I miss you. I'm sorry.* "Call me." She hung up.

He never called back. And she didn't try to call him again.

That night she dreamed the catalpa tree died.

On an afternoon in mid-May, Maggie was getting Alex out of the Volkswagen when a car pulled into the driveway, stopping behind them. Maggie turned around.

Elliot and Marcella.

At first the meeting was tense and awkward. But then Marcella started to cry, and Maggie started to cry. And then Alex, who was still strapped in her car seat, started to cry.

The women hugged. Then Maggie hugged Elliot while Marcella coo-cooed the baby, at the same time rescuing her from the seat.

"Isn't she just a doll?" Marcella said, holding Alex at face level. "Those blue eyes. That dark, curly hair. Will her eyes stay blue, do you think?"

"They haven't changed at all yet."

"Then they'll stay blue." Marcella fell into baby talk as she jounced Alex up and down. "Yes, they will. They'll stay blue."

Maggie smiled. She'd missed Marcella.

Elliot was less enthused over Maggie's child. He said hello and touched her fist, kind of a baby/grown-up soul shake. Then they all poured into the house, talking at once. Elliot about graduating from law school, Marcella about people Maggie knew in Ohio, and Maggie about Alex and all her stages of development. A remarkable child. A genius of a child.

"She needs to be changed," Maggie said, her arms out to take the baby from Marcella. "I'll just be a minute."

"Oh, let me," Marcella said, still holding the child. "Just point the way."

Maggie directed and Marcella hurried off down the hallway, baby-talking all the way, with Alex enthralled and answering nonstop.

"I hope we didn't come at a bad time," Elliot said, dropping into a chair and crossing his ankle over his knee. "Mom's been

194

depressed ever since . . . well, ever since she found out about the baby. I think she felt like she'd lost a son *and* a daughter. I couldn't let her go on the way she was. I was home for a visit and suggested we come down to see you."

"I'm glad you did."

He smiled, a little sadly, it seemed. Then he stared at her in a curious, slightly puzzled way. "You look different."

She lifted her arms, then let them drop back to her sides. "I've put on a little weight." Not to mention her new bra size.

"No, it's not that. Something in your eyes. I don't know. Motherhood, maybe."

"Maybe."

There was something different about Elliot too. As if he'd removed himself to a safe distance. Things between them weren't the same.

That evening Maggie and Marcella sat on the porch talking while Elliot was inside, keeping a nervous eye on Alex.

"I'm sorry I wasn't here for you when you needed me," Marcella said. "I never thought of myself as someone who would let emotions take over, but when I found out you were pregnant, I couldn't handle it. Then Elliot and I had a good talk. He's so logical, I know he'll make a wonderful lawyer. He told me I was being selfish, that I couldn't expect you to spend the rest of your life mourning my son."

"That doesn't mean I've forgotten him. Or will ever forget him. He was a very special person. I loved him very much."

"I know. But it's time to look to the future, to a new beginning. I guess what I'm saying is I want you to come back to Ohio with us," Marcella said. "I want to be a grandmother to Alexandra."

Alex needed a family. If not a father, then a grandmother. Maggie had been close to both her grandmothers, and she knew how important that kind of relationship was in a child's life. But to leave Hope . . . To leave Harriet, and Karen, and all the people who had stuck by her through her pregnancy . . .

"What is there here for you?" Marcella asked.

"I have my job. And the children's theater. My friends."

"Think of Alexandra. What will it be like for her when she gets older? I used to live in a small town. I know how people talk. In the city nobody knows you. You would simply be a widow with a child."

"Maybe that's why I like it here. Everybody knows me. I don't have to explain anything or hide anything. I'm through with lies."

"Then tell people the truth, if you feel you should. You know I've never been bothered by what people think. I just want things to be easy for you both. I just want you nearby. Texas is too far away."

Maggie was proud of what she had accomplished on her own, but she longed for the support of family. Marcella was right. It would be a fresh start. A whole new beginning. But when she thought about actually packing and leaving . . .

She couldn't make a decision yet. She was contracted to teach another year. Maybe after that . . .

The next day Marcella and Elliot left to go back to Ohio. Maggie begged them to stay another day, but Marcella said she didn't want to wear out their welcome. They'd be back, and maybe next time they'd stay longer. Maybe the next time Maggie would leave with them.

After they had gone, the house seemed empty and Maggie spent more time holding Alex, knowing she was spoiling her terribly.

June rolled around.

Soon it was time to begin another play. Once again Maggie was involved in tryouts and then daily rehearsals. Once again she wondered how they would ever pull it off, and if the children would ever learn their parts.

Sometimes at night Maggie would sit rocking Alex, and she would find it hard to believe that a year had passed since last summer. Sometimes it seemed only yesterday that Johnnie had banged his ear against the piano keys and made the children collapse on the floor. At other times it seemed years and years ago. A lifetime ago.

Before she knew it, the play was over.

People were full of compliments, telling her she was amazing to have pulled it off with a four-month-old baby to care for. But Karen had helped, and Harriet, not to mention the children, who were wonderful about keeping Alex entertained.

School started, and Maggie returned to teaching. It tore her up to leave Alex with a sitter, especially when she was changing so fast. Harriet offered to baby-sit, but Maggie didn't think it was a good idea. She was thankful that she didn't have to give specific reasons. Harriet had immediately agreed, admitting that her mind was going, and her health along with it.

To make up for the hours she wasn't with Alex, Maggie spent evenings playing and talking with her baby. And after Alex fell asleep, Maggie would stand next to her crib and watch her.

Time passed.

Alex grew and changed at a remarkable rate. Every stage of her development was documented in a baby book and on film. Every stage was treasured. Alex sitting up, Alex's first tooth, Alex standing, Alex's first step. Alex's first birthday.

Her birthday party was quite a celebration, with helium balloons and a clown cake. Alex was crazy about clowns. Like mother, like daughter.

Elliot and Marcella came for the occasion. While they were visiting Hope, Elliot took Maggie out to dinner, just the two of them.

Later, after Elliot had stopped the car in the driveway and turned off the engine, he asked Maggie to marry him.

Stunned, Maggie stared through the windshield. Light shone through the house windows, making her home look like a child's drawing.

"I've gotten a position at a well-established law firm where I have a good chance of eventually becoming a partner."

He was offering her security.

"I've been crazy about you for years. Ever since Steven brought you home and we played football. Remember when you tackled me?"

She smiled at the memory. So long ago . . . She'd been a child then. So had Steven. So had Elliot.

"You caught me off guard. I couldn't believe a girl had knocked me down. Me, the big high school jock."

Was he offering love?

"You don't have to answer me now. Let it soak in. Get used to the idea."

They were friends. Good friends. Wasn't that a strong foundation for a marriage? Until recently, until Johnnie, she'd been able to talk to him about almost anything. Could it be that way again?

She turned to him. Elliot. Sweet, good Elliot. "I need time to think about it," she said.

Within her field of vision was the catalpa tree. Growing green and tall.

Two weeks after Alex's birthday, Harriet died of a heart attack. Maggie tried to get in touch with Johnnie, but every time she called she got his answering machine. She hated to be so impersonal, hated for him to get the news through a recording, but she was forced to leave a message.

Chapter 23

The Hope Methodist Church's original structure dated back to 1890. Over the years it had been updated like most old buildings. The wood-burning stove had been replaced by electric heat, the outhouse by indoor plumbing. In the early 1960s a room had been added to accommodate the growing number of churchgoers.

Maggie was seated near the center of the original section, in a pew coated with layer upon layer of varnish. It looked as if half the town had turned out for Harriet's funeral. Some of the elderly women had complained loudly over the fact that the service was closed casket. To them, viewing the body was the high point. It was why they came. But a closed casket was what Harriet had wanted. Many times Maggie had heard her say that she didn't want anybody staring at her when she was dead, leaning over and saying how natural she looked and what a wonderful job the undertaker had done. If she'd wanted to be stared at, she would have joined the circus.

The church was filling fast. All the pew space was occupied and people were taking seats in the overflow room where folding chairs had been lined up, ten rows deep.

Maggie made a couple of surreptitious scans of the crowd, but could see no sign of Johnnie. Another conspicuous absence was Harriet's son, but that didn't surprise anybody. A bigger surprise would have been if he'd shown up.

Soon Reverend Graham was taking his place at the pulpit. The organist finished the piece she was playing, then settled back, hands folded in her lap. Time for the service to begin.

Most of Hope's ministers were transient. Either they got tired of the town, or the town got tired of them. So far, Reverend Graham had been with them all of three months. His predecessor had lasted six before the congregation kicked him out. Some had thought he was wonderful, just what they'd needed; but most felt he was far too zealous. He believed people had to speak in tongues in order to be true Christians, and most of the congregation had no interest in learning a second language.

The new preacher suited them fairly well, meaning he didn't interrupt evenings at home with pastoral visits. He didn't pry into their private lives. He never criticized people for not coming to church, and he never got after them for having lost the true meaning of Christmas. He minded his own business. He preached Sunday services and officiated at the occasional funeral. His sermons didn't make anybody squirm, and church was always out early enough for the congregation to get to the Hope Cafe before the Presbyterians.

He was just a good old boy, one of the gang. In fact, Maggie was fairly certain he'd put money in the name-the-father pool.

Maggie was pleasantly surprised when he did a better than average job with Harriet's funeral. But then he'd known Harriet and had liked her, plus people had taken him aside to share stories and insights into her character.

Reverend Graham told how Harriet had been deeply loved and respected. How she'd lost both a husband and a son to war, and about how she had started the children's theater.

Fortunately Maggie had come equipped with plenty of tissues, which she soaked quite thoroughly. Her vision was blurred and her throat ached when it came time to sing "Amazing Grace."

The service ended. People slid their hymnals into the slot at the back of the pew in front of them. Everyone filed out in an orderly fashion.

He hadn't come.

A year had passed since she'd last seen him, but the expression he'd had on his face that last day was indelibly stamped in Maggie's memory. Such hurt, such anger.

The cemetery was located two miles from church, on the outskirts of town. If there was one thing Maggie disliked about Hope, or about any desert town, it was the cemeteries. Graves were supposed to be covered with soft green grass and shaded by oak trees. In the desert there was no grass or trees. The Hope cemetery was more desolate than any graveyard she'd ever seen. Only sand, tumbleweeds, and cacti, and the cacti weren't even unique. They were the ugly kind that crept along the ground like parasites.

Away from the shelter of town, the wind was strong. Skirts tangled and molded against legs, heels sunk into loose ground. Sand stung bare skin.

A green tent had been set up over the grave site. Inside were folding chairs with the funeral parlor logo stenciled on the back. Wind blew across the open end of the tent, creating a high-pitched whistle that sounded as though a million people were blowing across pop bottle tops. The tent flaps whipped and snapped with machine-gun speed.

Maggie chose to stand just outside, hoping to avoid the crowd, but people pushed in around her, filling the empty spots.

Reverend Graham took his place in front of the coffin, opened his Bible, and read the 23rd Psalm, followed by the Lord's Prayer.

And then the graveside portion of the service was over. Some of the people drifted away, in the direction of their parked cars. Others stood to the side, talking as quietly as they could beneath the noise of the wind.

Maggie was looking to where her own car was parked at the edge of the road, thinking about picking up Alex from Karen's, when she spotted Johnnie standing by himself on a ridge of ground.

With the exception of a white dress shirt, he was dressed completely in black. Black jacket, black tie, black slacks. The wind was tugging his hair back from his face, pressing his clothes to his chest and legs. The way he was standing, with both hands thrust into the pockets of his pants, made him look as though he'd just stepped from the pages of a fashion magazine.

The urge to go to him was almost overpowering, but she was afraid. Afraid of what she might see in his eyes.

He wasn't looking her way. She followed the direction of his gaze, stopping when she got to Sheriff Cahill—one of Maggie's least favorite people. For some reason, the guy gave her the creeps.

Cahill had probably been good-looking at one time, but the harsh desert sun had faded his eyes until they were almost colorless; years of hard drinking had robbed all the moisture from his skin, giving it the texture of wrinkled leather.

He was someone most of the townspeople would like to say goodbye to. His drinking problem had gotten out of hand. Some said it was so bad that he was often drunk while on duty. Not the person you'd want looking out for your welfare.

At the moment he was on probation and it was probably only a matter of time before he would be relieved of duty. It was just too bad they had to wait for him to do something crazy first.

Johnnie had hoped to slip away without anybody noticing him. No such chance. Cahill was approaching, and judging by the grim set of his face, a slap on the back and a friendly hello wasn't what he had in mind.

"What're you doing here?" Cahill asked when he was close enough to be heard.

Johnnie called upon years of acting to keep his voice nonchalant. "Paying my respects, just like everybody else."

"Respect!" Cahill snorted; the stink of stale booze drifted Johnnie's way. "You don't know what the word means."

The last thing Johnnie needed was a strong dose of Brace Cahill. In order to get to Harry's funeral, he'd missed a night's sleep. He was bone tired, his grief still raw. Under such conditions, it was hard to take a caricature like Cahill seriously. Johnnie decided to ignore the intrusion. For him, Cahill didn't exist.

He turned and was walking away when clawlike fingers dug into his upper arm. Cahill jerked him around to face him. "I'm not finished with you."

A crowd was gathering. Apparently Cahill didn't care, or didn't notice. He was drunk. It was impossible to argue with a drunk, so Johnnie decided to humor him. But as soon as Cahill started talking again, Johnnie regretted his decision.

"You wouldn't even pay for a plot and tombstone for your own mother," Cahill ranted. "You didn't even come to *her* funeral, so what are you doing here now? You're no relation to the old lady."

People moved closer, inching in to get a better view.

Johnnie felt the years pressing in around him—along with an ancient despair.

At that moment, standing in the desolate Hope cemetery, the truth came to him. He'd been typecast. No matter how he tried, he would never be able to escape the part he played in life. He hadn't asked for this confrontation; it had happened because of who he was.

Until that moment, he'd never been able to figure it out. It had just been one of the many things that had always eluded him. He'd never realized that all his life he'd been fighting a losing battle. He'd been swimming upstream, when all along he should have let the current sweep him away.

The only person who'd ever believed in him was dead. And it had taken over fifteen years for him to realize how much Harriet had done for him. Now it was too late. He couldn't do the right thing even when he wanted to.

Last month the owners of her old house had finally agreed to sell. The deal had just gone through when he'd gotten Maggie's message on the answering machine. What was he going to do with a two-story house in Hope, Texas?

Cahill was still going strong, his voice filtering into Johnnie's dark thoughts, his words ringing with a painfully twisted truth.

"How can you show your face around here when your own mother is buried in a pauper's grave?" Shaking with rage, Cahill thrust a stiff arm in the direction of the derelict cemetery.

Johnnie had never done anything to the man in front of him. In fact, he'd always tried to give him a wide berth. So why had Cahill always hated him so much? Yet he knew people didn't always need a reason to hate. Hatred was indiscriminate.

As a kid, Johnnie hadn't been able to stand up to Cahill. The guy had seemed bigger than life with his gorilla size, his glinting eyes, and the gun he liked to load and unload whenever Johnnie was around, giving Johnnie a distinctive dislike for guns.

As a kid, Johnnie had been afraid of Cahill.

Johnnie quit fighting the current. He let it sweep him away. "A pauper's grave was too good for the bitch," Johnnie said calmly, in a voice meant to carry to the crowd. "She should have been left for the vultures to eat." He paused for effect. "But then vultures know better than to eat poison."

Rage lit the faded blue of Cahill's eyes. "Why, you—" He swung one thick arm.

Johnnie had expected anger, but the physical blow took him by surprise. By the time he saw it coming, it was too late. With a sickening crunch, Cahill's fist made contact with Johnnie's face, sending him flying backward. He staggered, then fell to the ground. He scrambled to his feet, sand flying. In less than a heartbeat he swung, catching Cahill in the jaw, knocking the man to the ground.

"Hitting a police officer!" Cahill roared.

"Doesn't count," Johnnie gasped, swaying, trying to maintain his balance in the shifting sand. "You're out of uniform. And you swung first. All these people are witnesses." He glanced toward the crowd.

That's when he spotted Maggie. Her face was white, her eyes anxious. He dragged his gaze away. He couldn't let her distract him.

Cahill shoved himself to his feet and came up swinging. This time Johnnie was ready. He blocked and sidestepped, then brought back his fist.

Cahill went down again.

Was that a murmur of approval from behind him?

With the back of his hand, Johnnie wiped at his bleeding nose, waiting for Cahill to get to his feet. "There's one thing I've always been curious about," Johnnie said breathlessly, his chest rising and falling as he sucked in dry desert air. "Should I call you Daddy?"

A collective gasp rose from the crowd. Cahill shot them a sideways glance, then looked back at Johnnie. He hefted himself to his feet, preparing to charge once more.

At that moment some of the bystanders must have decided enough was enough. They jumped in, grabbing Cahill by both arms. He gave in easily, and Johnnie suspected he was secretly relieved. Johnnie sure as hell was.

"You're no relative of mine," Cahill said through gritted teeth.

Was it the truth? God, he hoped it was the truth.

Johnnie hadn't realized how much he'd missed live performances. Now, to round things off, to lighten things up, he let out a sigh of relief and made an elaborate show of wiping his brow. It got a laugh. Audience approval, something Cahill would never have.

Never losing awareness of Maggie's presence in the crowd, Johnnie continued his performance. "You don't know how glad I am to hear you say that," he said. "I've always dreaded the day when I would find out that my dear old pappy was none other than the town clown."

More group laughter.

To finally find out that Cahill wasn't his father made him almost euphoric. Johnnie felt buoyant, elated.

But just when things were going so well, new sensations crept in, ones he was all too familiar with.

His heart beat a warning in his chest, in his ears. He broke out in an allover sweat. His arms and legs began to tremble.

Hypoglycemia.

He'd missed lunch. Oh, he'd had it all figured out. He would have made it, but he hadn't planned on the extra calorie burn. A person didn't normally exert a lot of energy at a funeral. It was a shame that he was going to blow such a great performance by wimping out in front of everybody.

But suddenly Maggie was beside him—good old Maggie. She grasped his elbow and steered him toward the road, where he could see her Volkswagen parked in the distance. So far away. Miles and miles and miles. Darkness began to creep into the edges of his vision.

He'd never make it.

"Here—" Maggie shoved a Lifesaver into his hand. Without hesitation, he popped the candy into his mouth and chewed it up as fast as he could. Mint saturated his taste buds.

She handed him another.

"Are these the ones that make sparks?" he asked as he crunched.

Behind them, people were starting to move. He could hear the murmur of voices.

"Yeah," Maggie answered.

"Ever tried it?"

"Enough times to know that the Lifesavers have to be fresh. And it has to be really dark."

"You're the first person I've ever known who's actually tried it," he said as she tucked him into the passenger seat of her car. "I like that in a woman."

She gave him a crooked, kind of wistful smile. "Sometimes I do crazy things." She circled the car and got in the driver's side.

"Would you try it with me sometime?" he asked, elation still pumping through him.

She pulled out the choke and turned the ignition. Before she could get to it, he pushed the choke back in. Great teamwork.

"Maybe."

Alone with Maggie, in the dark, crunching candy. Maybe God didn't hate him.

His thoughts went back to the fight. "Think Harriet's pissed?"

Maggie paused, hands on the wheel. Then she looked at him and said with the utmost sincerity, "I think she's somewhere clapping."

Maggie's objective was to get Johnnie home and get some food into him as quickly as possible. In her haste, she disregarded the signs warning of bumps ahead. The little car became airborne as they crossed one of Hope's infamous rain ditches. A yelp from Johnnie had her slowing down.

With her hands gripping the steering wheel at the ten and two o'clock positions, she shot him a quick glance.

In contrast to the black of his jacket, his face was white and covered with a sheen of perspiration. He wasn't going to make it.

Just ahead was a Quick Stop. Maggie swung into the parking lot, pulled out the emergency brake, then shouldered open the creaking door. A minute later she was back with a bottle of orange juice. She unscrewed the cap and thrust the bottle into Johnnie's shaking hand.

Movement was labored, but he lifted the juice to his mouth and took a swallow. As if the effort had sapped him of all strength, he closed his eyes and leaned his head against the back of the seat, bottle resting against one thigh. A moment later he raised the drink to his lips once more. This time he managed to down half of it. By the time he'd finished the entire contents, some of the color was back in his face.

She drove home with a familiar fear wrapped around her heart. It wasn't the constant, irrational fear a mother feels for her child, but rather a valid observation. How had he survived as long as he had?

She'd wanted to see him, and yet she hadn't. She'd needed to make sure he was okay. But she should have known better. He wasn't okay. Johnnie was never okay.

"Where's Alex?" Johnnie asked as soon as they got to Maggie's house.

"Karen's."

He nodded and tossed his jacket over the back of the chair, then headed for the bathroom. When he came out, the blood was gone from his face, his sleeves were rolled up, and his tie had been loosened.

Maggie handed him a plate with a sliced sandwich and an orange. He shook his head, as if the food made him queasy.

She pushed the plate at him. "Eat."

"Since you asked so nicely."

He took the plate. Moving as if he ached, he walked to the couch and sat down.

A half hour ago he'd looked like somebody who'd stepped out of the pages of a fashion magazine. Now his crisp white shirt was bloodstained, his black dress pants wrinkled and dirt-smudged. The knuckles of his right hand were split and swollen. He was like a child who couldn't stay clean for five minutes.

His intentions had been good. She suspected that his intentions were always good. Something just happened to screw things up.

He ate the sandwich as if it were something he had to do, like getting dressed. Then he picked up the orange. He struggled to peel it, then looked up and caught her staring.

"This never happens on a movie set," he said, indicating his injured hand.

She took the orange and peeled it for him. "That's because

movies aren't real," she told him, putting the peeled sections on the plate. When she was done, she said, "Let me see your hand."

He held it out to her, biting into an orange slice at the same time. He chewed, swallowed, then said, "Probably get rabies. I think he got some slobber on me."

"This one almost looks like it needs stitches."

He shook his head, then winced. "Ouch, ouch."

"I'm not even touching—"

"Cactus needles," he said in a rush of breathless words. *"The other side. The other side."*

She turned his hand. The fleshy part of his palm was red and full of needles. He'd taken a punch in the face without as much as a groan, he'd split his knuckles open on another man's jaw, and now he was whimpering about cactus needles.

"I think you're going to need a major overhaul," she told him.

"Sounds like something I might enjoy."

Things were back to the way they had always been, as if they had both silently agreed to keep it light. Which was good. Neither of them was in any shape to deal with an emotional situation.

"I'll get some tweezers," she said. "And if you take off your shirt, I'll put it in some cold water so the bloodstain won't set."

He was agreeable, but his injured hand, obviously stiff, made it awkward. He had a hard time dealing with the buttons.

"Here, let me help," she told him.

His hands dropped. He sat and watched as she unbuttoned his collar, then slid the tie free.

"You break my heart, you know that?" All lighthearted teasing was gone from his face and voice. His eyes were deadly serious. "You do things for me, and make me think you like me. . . ."

Don't do this now. I can't handle this now. "I do like you."

"But then you hurt me. It would be easier if you were shitty to me all the time."

Her feelings for him hadn't changed. He still evoked a rush of love that was more pain than pleasure. Along with it came confusion. How like him to be here now, just when she thought she was putting her life back together. How like him to throw her mind in chaos.

Trying to keep her hands from trembling, hoping he wouldn't

see the pulse she could feel thrumming in her neck, she slid the buttons free, one at a time, working her way down. She tugged the tails from his pants, then slid the cloth over his shoulders and down his arms, leaving him in his pants and white undershirt.

It was unnerving, the way he was calmly watching her. As if he wouldn't object to anything she might decide to do.

With heart beating rapidly, she gathered up his shirt and hurried to the bathroom, closing the door behind her. Safely inside, she stood in front of the sink, his shirt clasped to her.

She shouldn't have brought him here. She should have gotten him a sandwich at the Quick Stop and sent him on his way.

Too late.

She put his shirt in the sink, running cold water over it. Then she searched through the medicine cabinet until she found a pair of tweezers.

When she returned to the living room, Johnnie was examining the flesh of his palm.

She sat down beside him and he gave her his hand. In the light that fell from the picture window, she could see maybe a dozen fine needles. Grasping the tweezers securely, she pulled out the first one.

While she worked, Johnnie asked questions about Harriet, then Alex. Throughout the conversation, there was no mention of the message he'd never returned.

She was too aware of him. Sitting so close, she could hear his steady breathing. When she turned his hand, she could feel the pulsebeat in his wrist, under her fingertips.

He shifted slightly. They weren't quite touching, yet he was near enough for her to feel the warmth of his body.

Gently he tucked a stray strand of hair behind her ear.

"Your hair's gotten longer."

Don't touch me. When you touch me, I come all undone.

She forced herself to concentrate on his hand, concentrate on the needles.

He had beautiful hands, sensitive hands. A long time ago, when Maggie was in college, she'd had a roommate who was into palm reading, enough for Maggie to learn that there were four main lines in a person's palm. The head line, which told how much common sense a person had; the heart line, which told whether or not a person would find true love; the life line; and the line of fate.

The lines in Johnnie's palm were well defined. It was easy to see that his head line was a mess, but his heart line was solid and long, supposedly meaning one true love. But his life line and line of fate . . .

She put a hand over his palm, hiding what she had seen. Total nonsense anyway. But then with Johnnie and his self-destructive ways, it didn't take a psychic to know that his life could end abruptly.

She looked up, prepared to fabricate if he asked what she'd been doing.

He was asleep.

In the glow of afternoon sunlight, the smooth skin that molded the muscles in his arms looked like velvet. Beneath the stretched undershirt, she could see the contours of his chest.

As she watched him, she felt the same sweet ache she felt whenever she watched Alex sleep.

She gave his shoulder a small shake. "Johnnie?"

His head came up. His eyes opened. He took a deep breath and shook the hair back from his face. "All done?" he asked groggily.

"All done."

She could almost feel his exhaustion. "You need sleep. Why don't you go into the bedroom and lie down while I go get Alex?"

"Got a plane to catch."

"Just rest awhile."

She managed to steer him into her room, where he sat down and kicked off his shoes before collapsing across the bed, momentarily back in her life.

Chapter 24

*S*leep was a bad idea.

Even though he was bone tired, Johnnie knew if he allowed himself to fall asleep it would be a deep sleep, a sleep where he'd have no control. He could wake up crying like a baby or screaming like a madman. And he didn't want either to happen. Not in front of Maggie.

She was walking away when he quietly spoke her name. She paused in the doorway.

"Don't go," he said.

She stepped back inside, hesitated, then crossed the room until she was standing near the bed. If he reached out, he could touch her.

He'd worked hard over the past several months, trying to forget about her. But when he'd seen her in the cemetery, everything had fallen apart. All along he'd been telling himself that he was over her, but now he knew it wasn't true. He wanted her just as much as he'd always wanted her.

He reached for her, pulling her to him, spreading his knees so he could bring her between them. He wrapped his arms around her waist and rested his face against the soft cotton of her black dress. Then he took a deep, trembling, stabilizing breath. He relished the scent of her, the purity of her. For the moment he didn't want to move, didn't want to think. About anything.

"I'm sorry," she said quietly. "I'm sorry about Harriet, and I'm sorry I didn't tell you about Alex right from the beginning."

"That's okay." In his mind he'd forgiven her long ago, understanding why she'd done what she'd done.

She closed her eyes. Her hand touched his hair. He could feel her fingertips on his scalp, then against the back of his neck. Beneath her dress, he was aware of the warmth of her body.

She was so real. He'd never known anybody so real.

He wanted to undress her. Slowly. He wanted to drown himself in her, to forget about Harriet and the ache her death had left in him.

His hands fell to her hips. He could feel the sweet curve of her pelvic bones beneath his thumbs. He lifted his head enough to look up at her, his chin resting against her abdomen. "I've missed you, Maggie."

Her eyes opened and he read the sexual awareness in them. He felt himself stir. "Is there any chance you've missed me?"

Her hands were resting on his shoulders. He could feel each fingertip, like small electric impulses traveling through his skin.

"Yes," she whispered.

He thought about how much he'd missed her. He thought about how much she'd hurt him. He thought about the months of hell, of hearing her voice on his answering machine and fighting the urge to call her back. Of lying awake, with his hand on the phone, thinking of her.

He could have her, at least physically, at least for the moment —something he would have been quite satisfied with at one time. Now he understood that he wanted more from her, but he also knew he would take whatever she was willing to give.

To Johnnie, making love was a fine art. He knew all of the techniques. He could make her sigh and make her squirm and cry his name. He could draw out her passion until she sobbed and begged.

He would make love to Maggie as he'd never made love before.

He stood and took her face in both his hands, his fingers sliding through her hair, skimming across her ears. "You don't know how glad I am to hear that."

He kissed her.

A soft sound of pleasure curled in her throat as her lips moved willingly under his. Her mouth opened, her hands tugged at his shoulders, pulling him close. His tongue drove inside her moist, warm mouth, a hand slipping down to the small of her back, pressing her tight against him as he rubbed himself into her. He could feel her breasts, full against his chest. He brought up one hand, filling his palm.

Her dress was two pieces. The top had a row of buttons running down the center. Starting at the neckline, he worked the buttons free, laying the fabric open as he went. With the last button, he tugged the shirt hem loose, pushing the fabric out of the way.

She was wearing a nursing bra.

White. Beautiful in its simplicity. Her breasts straining against the fabric.

He unhooked the clasp above one breast, freeing a dusky rose nipple. He touched the soft bud—some of the softest skin he'd ever touched—watching as a bead of milk formed.

"I've almost got Alex weaned," she said breathlessly, hypnotically.

He couldn't stand it. He brought down his head, licking the bead, his tongue scraping her nipple. Sweet. Warm.

With a slightly trembling hand, he fumbled for the other clasp, opening the panel.

"Johnnie," she gasped, her fingers digging into his hair. "I don't know . . . I don't think . . ."

With the tip of his tongue, he circled the other nipple, then pulled the entire tip into his mouth and sucked. Sweet, warm milk flowed over his tongue.

He'd never been so turned on in his life.

He eased her top over her shoulders until it fell away. Then he reached behind her, unhooking the clasp, freeing her breasts completely, letting the bra drop to the floor. With one finger he circled a nipple, then cupped both breasts in his palms. "I'm amazed at how much . . . bigger they are. Not that I didn't like them before, but there's just something so erotic . . ."

Her skirt had no buttons or zippers. He slipped his hands beneath the elastic band and was easing it down when she stopped him, both of her hands on his.

He looked at her, desire thrumming through his veins. He was steel-hard. He could feel himself fighting the confines of his briefs, needing release.

What's wrong? he asked with his eyes. Was she going to push him away? Could he handle it? Could he pull himself together this time?

"My scar," she whispered.

He saw the fear in her eyes. Something uncomfortably like love blossomed within his chest. He lay an open palm against the fabric that covered her abdomen. "I'll love your scar. I want to see it."

"No. Not now."

"Okay. Shh."

Instead of removing her skirt, he trailed his hands up her thighs, her skin warm and firm against his palms. He slipped a finger inside the leg opening of her panties, stroking along the elastic and inside the crease where hip met body. He teased her femininity, dipping just inside. She was damp and hot.

Her grip on his shoulders tightened. She made small sounds of wanting.

He slid his hands inside the waistband of her underwear, across incredibly soft flesh, moving around to cup the roundness of her bottom.

He was desperate to be inside her, to feel her beneath him, but he was also desperate to make this last, to draw the moment out with torturous skill. With the bed pressing into the backs of his legs, he sat, the mattress giving under him. He pulled down her underwear. With her hands on his shoulders, she stepped free.

She was suddenly as impatient as he. She urged him onto his back, her skirt billowing around and over him. Through the tangle of fabric, she found his belt buckle and managed to open it. Then she went for his zipper.

He lay very still, hardly daring to breathe while she eased the zipper open. Then she placed a small, cool hand against the muscle-hard flesh of his lower stomach.

So close . . .

She touched him. Through the straining cotton of his briefs, she touched him. With a finger she outlined the shape of him, circling, exploring. . . .

His plan fell apart. It had been too long since he'd had a

woman, especially one like Maggie. He'd never had anyone else like Maggie.

Quickly he stripped off the rest of his clothes, then rolled her onto the bed. "The skirt has to go," he told her.

She shook her head.

"Come on, Maggie."

Like someone expecting the worst, she closed her eyes and waited.

He slowly removed her skirt, inch by inch, kissing each newly exposed bit of skin as he went. He kissed her flat navel, then each hipbone, then the soft triangle of hair. Just above it, running horizontally, was a fine red line—a bikini cut, if memory served him right. A little raised, still a little pink, but nothing unsightly. Nothing but sexy.

He slipped off the skirt the rest of the way, past firm thighs and perfect knees and beautiful feet. When he looked up, she still had her eyes closed.

The sight of her naked body made him grow even harder. He wanted to spread her thighs and bury himself inside her.

Instead, he touched the arch of her foot. "You have beautiful feet," he told her.

"I have big feet."

She tried to pull away, but he kept a firm grip, brushing his lips across her creamy arch. Then he caressed her ankle . . . the back of her knee . . . her inner thigh . . . the soft black hair between her thighs. He ran his fingers across her scar. Then he bent and pressed his lips to the delicate tissue.

As soon as Maggie felt his lips there, on the place she hadn't wanted him to see, blessed relief trailed through her. It was okay. He wasn't repulsed.

Maggie felt the warm heavy weight of his body on hers. His hands explored the fullness of her breasts, then moved on to her stomach, her legs.

"You don't mind my scar?" she asked, still feeling the need for reassurance.

"I can hardly even see it."

She could feel his erection pressing against her thigh, hard and throbbing. The thought of him inside her made her weak and hot. "You're just saying that."

"Because I want to have sex with you?"

Doubt ran through her. "That's possible."

He paused. "Damn it, Maggie." He groaned and rolled over onto his back, flinging a hand across his eyes. "Why do you always have to make me into the villain?"

His body, his beautiful naked body, was covered with a sheen of perspiration, his chest rising and falling. He was at the peak of his arousal.

He was giving her a choice. Take him or leave him. She reached. She touched. She wrapped her fingers around him.

"Maggie . . ." he warned through gritted teeth, eyes still closed. "What the hell are you doing?"

"Touching you."

She stroked.

He grew even larger. Her own breath quickened, her pulse racing.

His hand wrapped around hers. His eyes came open, heavy-lidded with passion. "Maggie," he warned again. "No games."

She let go and got to her knees. With her hands braced on his shoulders, she brought a leg over him, her knees against his hips. While his eyes quietly regarded her, she took him deep inside her.

He was a good actor. She would have thought him unaffected except for his rapidly rising and falling chest and the pulse that beat madly in his neck.

"You've . . . always . . . surprised me," he said in a strained, breathless voice. He took in her flushed face and parted lips. His eyes moved down, pausing at her breasts, then moving on to where they were joined, lingering awhile before making their way back up. "Are you going to sit there all day doing nothing?"

She grasped either side of his waist, then slowly rotated her hips. "Maybe."

His eyes closed. He tilted back his head. His hands reached for her hips. "You're killing me," he gasped.

Everything had turned around. He was supposed to be driving *her* crazy; instead she was driving him. But he wasn't so far gone that he didn't know to be careful, now that he was inside her. She'd had a baby. He didn't want to do anything that might hurt her.

On the other hand, she didn't seem worried. "You're okay?" he asked as she continued her slow, erotic rotation. His body screamed for a faster rhythm, for deeper, longer strokes. "I mean . . . physically?"

"I'm fine." She leaned forward. He bent his knees, his thighs lifting her bottom while he filled his hands with her heavy breasts.

He couldn't reach the nipples with his mouth, so he grasped one between his thumb and forefinger, rolling and tugging.

Milk ran free, trailing through his spread fingers, down his elbow, and onto his chest. He could feel himself coming. He fought the urge to roll her over and drive himself into her. Instead, he took two deep breaths and tightened his loin muscles.

She spread herself across him. He could feel himself deep inside her, pulsing, throbbing, aching. He could feel her breath against his throat. She inched up and nibbled his earlobe.

He groaned and rolled until she was under him, his hips pressing into hers, his hands cupping her bottom. He looked at her. Her lips were red and swollen, her cheeks flushed, her body damp with perspiration. He continued to watch her face as he withdrew completely, then used himself to stroke her.

Her eyes glazed over. She cried out his name and reached to pull him closer. He buried himself in her, holding her close while an orgasm shuddered through her. But he didn't give release to himself.

When she was limp, he withdrew. He turned her exhausted body in his arms, cradling her back against his chest, his thighs against her bottom. Then he touched her with his fingers, parting her flesh, stroking, winding her up once more. Soon she was clutching his thighs, arching against his hand, moaning his name.

He turned her and she opened herself to him. He wanted to taste her the way he'd tasted her breasts. He wanted to draw his tongue across her, but with jarring surprise, he suddenly knew he wouldn't make it.

No, this wasn't going as he'd planned. He was supposed to be the one in control, not the one out of it. But then he hadn't taken into account the Maggie factor.

He positioned himself over her, bending her legs, her feet flat against the mattress.

And then he slid inside. "You're sure I won't hurt you?"

Her fingers dug into his arms. "You won't hurt me," she said desperately.

He finally gave in to the rhythm he'd denied himself for so long. Deep strokes, long strokes, hard strokes. Both their bodies were slick with sweat, sliding against each other, stomach to stomach, thigh to thigh. He called her name and moaned in pleasure-filled disbelief.

She cried out, kneading at the muscles of his back. And then he shuddered into her again and again.

Later, while his heart was still pounding against hers, while her damp hair clung to his face, while he lay on top of her with all his weight, unable to move, he remembered something he'd never forgotten before. Birth control.

He didn't know he'd fallen asleep until a movement woke him. He took a moment to marvel over the fact that he'd had no dreams. Then, through his sleep-fogged brain, he noted that Maggie was standing near the door, dressed in shorts and a T-shirt.

"Go back to sleep," she said. "I, ah—" She brought a hand to her hair in a shy gesture that was very unlike Maggie. Color bloomed in her cheeks.

He rubbed a hand across his chest and gave her a crooked smile, not wanting her to be self-conscious about the passion they had shared.

"I have to go get Alex." Her dark hair was tousled, her T-shirt wrinkled. Her legs, below the ragged cutoffs, were long and smooth and sexy.

He loved her.

Sometimes, when he was in that strange state between waking and sleeping, truths came to him. He recognized them as truths, because they revealed themselves to him unblemished, from the honest part of his brain, before he'd had a chance to mix things up and put in a little logic and a little reason, plus a whole lot of excuses.

"You'll stay until I get back?" she asked. "You'll be okay?"

At first he thought she was asking if he'd be okay from this moment on until the end of his life. The answer was no, he wouldn't, not if she wasn't going to be a part of it. But then he understood that she meant for *now*, until she came back with Alex.

He wanted to kiss her, but she wasn't close enough. He wanted to reach for her, but what if she didn't come? His life had been a lesson in rejection and he couldn't take that chance, couldn't put himself in that position.

"I'll be fine," he told her.

She smiled and left.

The last thing he could do was sleep, so he got up and dressed. How could a guy possibly sleep when he realized he was in love?

He was covering new ground here.

On one hand, he was fighting the urge to tell Maggie his feelings and risk a negative reaction. On the other, he was fighting the urge to say nothing and run like hell.

He was still struggling with himself when he heard her Volkswagen pull into the driveway. He opened the front door. Alex! God, was that Alex in her arms? She was dressed in jeans and red shoes and a red jacket with a hood. Like a little person. Not a baby, but a person.

He took the diaper bag from Maggie and tossed it on the couch, then he reached for Alex.

She stared at him with big blue eyes, one finger in her mouth. Very slowly her wet finger fell away, her rosebud mouth came open, and she started screaming.

In that instant his heart broke. It wasn't the kind of screams she used to do, not the pissed-off stuff. This was true fright. Terror. She was terrified of him.

"She's going through a stage," Maggie said, jiggling the baby and making hushing sounds. "She's afraid of strangers."

Stranger? All of a sudden, he was a stranger? She was his daughter. He had sung to her. He had told her corny jokes. He had changed her diapers and talked to her in the middle of the night. Just the two of them.

"Plus she's tired," Maggie added. "She didn't have a nap. I'll go put her down, then I'll be back." Maggie carried the screaming child away, each wail piercing his heart a little more.

Dazed, he wandered into the kitchen, thinking of getting a drink of water, of doing something, anything. Once there, he had another surprise. Boxes. Lots of boxes. Packed boxes. Labeled boxes.

She must have gotten Alex settled, because the crying stopped and shortly after that Maggie showed up in the kitchen.

"What's this?" Johnnie asked, indicating the boxes.

A pause. Then she said, "I'm moving."

"Where?"

"Ohio."

"Ah." He nodded. "Ohio." The word stuck in his throat.

"I've given it a lot of thought and decided it will be better for Alex. And me." She was talking fast, her words coming one after the other as she hurried to get the scene over and done with. "We don't have any family here."

"Where will you live? Do you have a place?"

She wouldn't look at him. Instead, she stared at her tightly clasped hands. "At first we're going to live with Marcella, Steven's mother."

"And later?"

"I don't know." She made a small noise. "Elliot asked me to marry him."

He thought he'd hurt before, when Alex had cried. But this . . . "Are you going to?"

"I'm not sure. I'm thinking about it."

His hand curled into a fist. All the muscles in his body tightened. "Thinking about it? A person usually knows or she doesn't. Want me to get the Ouija board? Would that help? Or maybe Mr. Eight Ball?"

"Johnnie—"

He let out a harsh laugh and shook his head. "You're more mixed-up than I am, you know that, Maggie? You just had sex with me while you were thinking about marrying somebody else. Explain that, will you?"

She looked up, her eyes full of hurt and accusation. "I wasn't messed-up until you came along." Her voice was thick, her eyes filling with tears that she tried to blink away. "My life may have been boring, but it was uncomplicated." She made a gesture of futility with one hand. "Don't criticize me for trying to fix it!"

She was right, he thought numbly. He wasn't good for her. He never would be.

Somehow—he didn't know how—he managed to pull himself together enough to get through the next few minutes. "I think you should move to Ohio," he said in a level, emotionless voice. "I think you should marry Elliot."

"You do?"

Elliot was everything he could never be. "Does he love you?" Johnnie asked.

"Y-yes."

"There you go."

If the last hour of his life were a script, he'd be tempted to say, Wait a minute. Let me get this straight. You've got this mind-zapping love scene, then a realization of love, followed by the guy getting dumped. Doesn't work for me.

But since when did he believe in happy endings? Not since Bambie's mother died.

When would the pain stop? Tomorrow? The next day? Never? He was afraid it might be never.

From the bedroom came the sound of whimpering. Their argument had disturbed Alex. Maggie spun around, practically running from the kitchen.

Johnnie grabbed his jacket off the chair and blindly slipped out the front door.

Chapter 25

*T*hrowing on his jacket over his undershirt, Johnnie left. With no clear idea of where he was heading, only knowing it was away, he walked.

Little by little, he became aware of his surroundings, of cars driving past, of people meeting him on the sidewalk. Most of them said hi or waved. A few in cars stopped and asked if he needed a lift. He just said no thanks and kept on walking.

His car. He had to get his car from the cemetery.

The way there took him past Hope's only park. It covered one square block. Small but nice. It had lots of huge trees and a few swings. In the center was an outdoor stage that was used for just about everything and anything. Political rallies, musical performances by church groups and barbershop quartets. Once Johnnie had seen some little girls tap-dancing their hearts out on that stage.

Back in his high school days, he and Phil and Jake had set up their guitars and amplifiers for an impromptu performance that had rattled the windows in the nearby houses. None of them could sing worth a damn, but that hadn't stopped them. They'd managed to make it through "Whole Lotta Love," and halfway through a particularly loud, shrieking rendition of "Cum On Feel the Noize," when the cops came and pulled their power plug.

It was close to the stage that Johnnie found Phil sitting on the ground with his back to a tree. He had his sketchbook braced against one knee, so engrossed in his drawing that he didn't react to Johnnie's approach.

"How's it going, Phil?"

Phil's hand never faltered. "Drawing a bluebird."

Johnnie watched as Phil shaded a delicate underwing with the edge of his pencil.

"The bluebird carries the sky on its back," Johnnie said.

Phil paused and looked up. "That's beautiful."

"They're not my words, they're Henry Thoreau's."

"I'd like to meet Henry."

Johnnie smiled. Henry would have liked to have met Phil.

"I like all birds," Phil confided as he went back to his work, his wrist looped over the top of the paper at an uncomfortable-looking angle. "Even sparrows. I love to watch birds. Don't you wonder how they do it? Don't you wonder how they stay up in the air like that?"

"They're amazing," Johnnie agreed.

"Wouldn't it be neat if people could fly? Don't you wish you could?"

Johnnie hadn't seen Phil for a while—not since the episode at the tavern. Not one of Johnnie's better moments. If he'd used some control, if he'd used his head instead of his fists, then maybe Phil's drawing wouldn't have gotten ruined. And maybe Johnnie wouldn't have gotten thrown in the slammer—one of a never-ending list of things he'd done to impress Maggie.

Johnnie crouched down beside Phil, an idea forming in his head. "Have you ever tried to sell any of your drawings?" he asked.

Phil looked puzzled. "You mean for money?"

"Yeah."

"I never thought about it. People just give me money."

Johnnie hadn't been able to help Harriet, but maybe he could help Phil. "Your pictures are good enough to sell, maybe for a lot of money, enough to support yourself. I could take some to California with me—"

Phil's hand stopped. He looked up, horrified. "You can't take my drawings."

"How about if we made copies of them on a copy machine? And I just took the copies?"

"I don't know." Phil glanced nervously at his belongings, making sure everything was where it should be. His record player. His records. His box of drawing tools. He picked up the box and put away his pencil. Then he closed his sketch pad.

"Your pictures could be in a book," Johnnie explained. "A book that has detailed illustrations of birds. Just think, if they were in a book, you'd always have them."

"I don't like to see birds in cages. I don't want my birds in a book. They wouldn't be happy in a book."

Johnnie tried to make him understand. "If you sold some of your pictures, you might be able to live in a house. You wouldn't have to sleep outside anymore. You'd have enough to eat. And you'd always be able to buy paper and pencils."

"I like to sleep outside. Birds sleep outside. And I have enough paper and pencils. People give me paper and pencils. You're scaring me."

"Okay, okay."

Johnnie could see he'd made a mistake. Why hadn't he understood that Phil had everything he wanted? Anything more would be too much, would throw him off balance. "Forget what I said. It was a bad idea."

Reassured, Phil calmed down. With long-nailed fingers he opened his box of drawing pencils and took one out. A moment later he flipped open the notebook and began sketching again, his blond hair hanging over his forehead.

Johnnie got to his feet, took out some crumpled bills, and stuffed them into the pocket of Phil's flannel shirt. "Something to eat on." Money. The answer to everything, he thought with self-mockery.

Phil looked up and smiled.

For a moment there seemed to be coherency behind his thick-lashed eyes. For a moment, he seemed to be the Phil Johnnie used to know.

"Where are you going?" Phil asked.

Johnnie looked down the street, past the tree-filled park—an oasis in the desert. "I don't know. Maybe I'll stop by my old place, down by the tracks." He turned back to Phil. "Want to come along?"

Phil shook his head. "I have to finish my bluebird."

Johnnie nodded. "Take care."

"Keep the faith."

Keep the faith. Johnnie hadn't heard anybody say that in years.

He left, heading east. At a corner he stopped and waited for a tan car to cross in front of him, then he continued on his way.

Between the park and the cemetery was Johnnie's old stomping ground. When he crossed the tracks, he turned right, in the direction of the house where he'd wasted too many years of his life.

When he reached the uneven walk that led to the boarded-up front door, he stopped, feeling disoriented. Time seemed to bend and shift. It seemed like yesterday that he'd lived there . . . and it seemed like never. It was real, yet it wasn't. It could have been something from a play, or a book he'd read. Something familiar, yet unfamiliar.

But this time he walked up the sidewalk with the stride of an adult, not a child.

The wind shifted, blowing across the train tracks, bringing with it the strong odor of creosote and burned coal. The smell took him back as none of his other senses could. He felt a soul-deep dread, along with shame, and sorrow, and hope—the boundless hope of a child. How often had he come up the same walk thinking that this time would be different? This time she would be glad to see him?

It hadn't been until he'd gotten into first grade that he'd begun to realize that his mother was different from other mothers. He began to take note of the outward signs of mother love he saw in the kids around him. Combed hair. Not necessarily new, but clean, mended clothes. Money for lunch, or a sandwich in a bag. Nobody else went hungry.

In second grade he'd been invited to a classmate's home after school. The boy's mother had given them milk and cookies, and so he'd learned another sign of love.

In fourth grade he started playing the drums in the school band, but after the Christmas concert, when his mother was the only parent who hadn't come, he quit. By fifth grade he knew what a bastard was, and what a whore was, and he was old enough to know that love wasn't food and clean clothes . . . and yet it was.

Johnnie's thoughts were brought back to the present by the sound of a car turning the corner. A tan Thunderbird, the same car he'd seen near the park. It pulled to the curb, scraping the sidewalls as it came to a jerking stop. The engine was cut, the door flung open. Cahill stepped out.

Seeing him dressed in his cop getup, holster and all, seeing him coming up the walk, his shitkickers scraping across the cement the way they'd done so many times, so many years ago, sent time tumbling backward once again. Johnnie felt the stir of an old fear.

Cahill stopped a few feet away and struck a typical pose. Legs spread, hands on hips.

Johnnie forced himself to relax. He sat down on the steps and leaned back, elbows against the stoop. "Evenin', Sheriff," he said with a strong drawl that Cahill probably wouldn't even notice. It was funny the way people in the Southwest didn't think they had accents.

"You're loitering," Cahill said.

Johnnie laughed and immediately felt better. "Come on, Cahill. Quit with the bad-cop thing. You're really getting on my nerves."

"Insulting an officer."

Johnnie clicked his tongue and shook his head in amazement. "You never quit, do you?" He sat up straight, drawing in his legs, resting his forearms on his bent knees. "Would you tell me something? I'd like to know why the hell you're always on my case. I'd like to know what the hell I ever did to you."

"You were born."

The hate in those three words was something to hear.

"You were a mistake," Cahill added.

Johnnie's gut felt hollow, his mouth dry. "Then you *are* my father."

Cahill looked toward the shanty. His faded eyes became distant. "She was mad at me." He slowly shook his head, remembering. "Told me she wouldn't sleep with me anymore if I wouldn't get

226

a divorce and marry her. She was a tease. Your mother liked to put it in front of me, then take it away. When I wouldn't get a divorce, she went on a binge. Some women eat when they're mad. She went after men. Anybody she could pick up. Anybody she could bring home with her."

Cahill looked directly at him, taking pleasure in his next words. "Your father could have been one of twenty men."

Johnnie felt as though he was going to throw up.

"She wanted to get an abortion. I even made the arrangements, but she chickened out. She was afraid it would hurt, or she'd bleed to death. After you were born she said she wished she'd taken the chance."

Cahill walked past him, to the front door. He pulled off a few rotten boards, then kicked until the door flew open. He motioned for Johnnie to follow him inside.

With an almost morbid, hypnotic curiosity, Johnnie got to his feet.

Rats had eaten holes in the walls, mice had built nests in the corners. Vagrants had left filthy blankets and trash. In the middle of the living room floor was a charred hole where someone had built a fire to keep warm.

Straight ahead was a narrow hall that led to the bedroom where Johnnie had sometimes slept curled in the corner. Inside that bedroom was the closet.

"This is where you're from," Cahill said, his voice barely penetrating Johnnie's dark memories.

Johnnie wasn't conscious of movement, but he suddenly found himself moving forward, stepping over trash, dislodging an empty wine bottle that rolled across the floor.

Maybe it was masochistic, but he walked down the hallway and into the bedroom. He grasped the knob to the closet and opened the door.

Empty.

Strange. He'd almost expected to see himself there.

In the darkness he could barely make out the wooden panel near the floor. He crouched down, ripped the panel free, and felt inside the wall. His fingers touched the hardbound edge of a book. He pulled it out. His poetry notebook.

He got to his feet and thumbed through the dusty pages. Idealistic, innocent ramblings of the person he used to be.

He closed the notebook and was about to toss it back in the closet when he paused, changing his mind. He would take it with him and throw it away somewhere else. He didn't want even a small part of himself left there. He tucked the notebook in the inside pocket of his jacket.

He'd completely forgotten about Cahill until the bedroom door slammed shut behind him, the impact shaking paint chips from the ceiling.

Johnnie pulled his gaze from a curled chunk of stained, peeling wallpaper to look at Cahill. He'd taken his pistol from his holster and was checking the cylinder the way Johnnie had seen him do a hundred times.

"Full load." With a click, Cahill snapped it back into place, gave it a spin, then held the gun out to Johnnie butt-first.

Johnnie didn't move.

"Go on, take it."

The men stared at each other.

Johnnie reached out and took the gun. Better for him to have it than Cahill.

"Ever shot a .38?" Cahill asked.

Johnnie stared at the gun, the metal cold and warm—warm where Cahill's hand had grasped it. It was unusually heavy, like something dead.

"I heard you tried to kill yourself, but somebody happened by before you died. I'll do you a favor. I'll watch while you put that gun to your head and pull the trigger. And I won't call an ambulance until you're good and dead."

What irony that just last week Johnnie had seen his lawyer and had named Alex as his beneficiary. Maybe this was the answer to everything. Maybe it was fitting to have it all end like this. To die in the hovel where it had all started. Like some overacted melodrama. He suddenly wanted to laugh. It was just so stupid.

"What's wrong, boy? Can't do it? No guts? You always were skittish around guns. Always were a chicken. Do yourself a favor. Do the town a favor. The world a favor. Just cock it. That's right. Now, put it to your head."

The smell of steel filled Johnnie's nostrils. He thought about Maggie. And he thought about Alex, about how much he loved them both.

"All you have to do is pull the trigger. Then everything will be fine. Just pull the trigger."

The big goodbye.

Chapter 26

*M*aggie had never had a premonition in her life, but as soon as she realized Johnnie was gone, a feeling of profound dread filled her.

She ran next door and got her neighbor to watch Alex. Then she jumped in her Volkswagen and headed for the cemetery, knowing that Johnnie would have to go there to retrieve his car. She was almost at the park when she spotted Phil shuffling along the sidewalk, his shopping bag clutched in his arms. She pulled up beside him, engine idling.

"Have you seen Johnnie?" she asked, unintentionally startling him.

Phil drew his arms closer and watched her with distrust.

"Have you seen Johnnie?" she repeated, this time keeping her voice casual. She didn't want her own anxiety to further upset him. "Johnnie Irish."

Phil relaxed his shoulders. Then he smiled his angelic smile. "Yeah. Oh yeah," he said, now eager to please. "He gave me something." He dug into the pocket of his flannel shirt and pulled out some wrinkled money. With the handles of his bag looped over one arm, he separated the bills. A couple fell at his feet, then began to tumble down the sidewalk. Maggie set the emergency brake and hurried to help. Together they chased the crunched-up money, finally catching it.

When it was safely back in his pocket, Maggie asked, "Did Johnnie say where he was going?"

"Going?" Phil thought for a moment, then pointed. "Look, a western meadowlark."

"Yes, but what about Johnnie?"

"Home. He was going home."

Frustration mounted. She already knew he would be heading back to California.

"I like to go to Johnnie's house and watch the trains go by."

Trains?

Then it hit her. He was talking about Johnnie's *old* house. Maggie gave Phil's arm a pat. "Thanks." A second later she was back in the car, heading in the direction of the railroad tracks.

The little Volkswagen rattled and shimmied over the rusty rails. It was an area of town she'd never visited, the kind of place where people stared at you from their front porches. The kind of place you wouldn't want to go at night.

She had no idea which house had been Johnnie's, but when she saw a crowd gathered in the front yard of one of the shanties, she slowed and pulled to the curb, a new wave of fear creeping along her nerve endings.

She turned off the ignition and stepped from the car. A boy of about ten was riding his bicycle in her direction, steering with one hand, eating a candy bar with the other.

"What happened?" she asked when he was almost even with her.

He skidded to a stop. "Some guy shot himself." He took a bite of chocolate. "My friend wanted me to come and look, but I've seen a dead guy before." He shrugged, grabbed both handlebars, then sped away.

Maggie ran toward the house, pushing her way through the crowd until she reached the front door.

Voices echoed through a narrow hallway. Images hit her like a series of still photographs. Trash. Crumbling wallpaper.

She stepped over the trash, moving toward the voices. A room. A bedroom.

Blood.

Someone sprawled across the floor. Black jacket. Torn black pants.

Blood.

A hand, its fingers curled. Just beyond the hand, a gun.

Blood.

Johnnie.

No. Oh God, no.

She stood staring, disbelieving, denying, too shocked to move.

As she stared, her field of vision grew, taking in two people bending over him, a man and a woman. Had they been there all along?

Like someone in a trance, Maggie moved forward while hushed conversation drifted around her.

"He just came inside and shot himself."

"He used to live here, you know. The house where he was born."

"I'm not surprised. He's tried to kill himself before."

Maggie dropped to her knees beside him. There was a constriction in her chest. This was it. What she had most feared. She couldn't breathe. A grief-stricken sob rent the air. Somebody was crying. Somebody was hurting terribly.

Make it stop. Make it stop.

There must have been a hole in the roof, because it was raining. Right on his face.

Helluva deal.

Wasn't there a song about that? About dying in the rain?

But the raindrops tasted like salt. How could rain taste like salt?

His eyes were closed; he knew they were closed. He liked them that way, but he suddenly felt the urgent need to open them, to look up at the sky.

It was hard, opening his eyes. His eyelids must have weighed ten pounds each, but he finally managed.

Maggie. Maggie was beside him. And she was crying.

Helluva deal.

If there was one real thing, one real truth in his life, it was his love for Maggie. But love hurt. It was an ache, a rawness of the soul.

He didn't want to see her cry. It hurt to see her cry.

Don't—

Oh God. The pain. It hurt to breathe, hurt to move. But he had to tell her, needed to tell her. . . . He parted his lips, swallowed, and tried again. "Don't . . . cry, Maggie. . . ." His voice was a hoarse croak.

She stared at him, her eyes wide, lit by what looked like joy. That was followed by realization, then panic.

"Somebody!" she shouted over her shoulder. "Somebody call an ambulance!"

"It's already been done," came another voice, a woman's voice, one he'd never heard before. "And the police," the woman added. "They should be here anytime."

Not the police, Johnnie thought. Not Cahill.

Maggie looked down at him, her eyes glistening, her bottom lip trembling. "Y-you . . . scared . . . me. . . ."

It was in his head to say that he hadn't meant to scare her, that all he'd ever wanted was for her to like him. But then somebody else appeared beside her, urging her back.

A cop, but it wasn't Cahill. This guy was younger, with a long face and shaggy blond hair. Johnnie distantly wondered how he got away with a haircut like that in Hope.

"You look . . . familiar," Johnnie said as the cop knelt beside him. He opened Johnnie's jacket and ran his hands up and down his sides.

"Hey, I'm . . . not . . . carrying."

The man laughed. "I'm checking out your injuries. And yeah, we went to school together. I was a year behind you."

"No kidding." Then it came to him. "Rick Thomas. You used to do that . . . trick . . . with . . . your ears."

The guy smiled again.

Johnnie's gaze was drawn back to Maggie. She had moved to the side, watching, a hand pressed to her mouth. He couldn't die without telling her how he felt. Even if she rejected him, even if she pushed him away.

"Maggie—I love you."

He heard her quick, indrawn breath.

"And . . . I love Alex. You'll tell her, won't you? That her daddy . . . loved her?"

She nodded and pressed her lips together.

He let his head fall back, his eyes closed. He could die in peace.

"Why would he do such a thing?" the unknown woman whispered. "What would drive a person to kill himself?"

It hadn't been like that, he wanted to tell them. He was a mess, but there was no way he could kill himself, at least not while Maggie and Alex were alive. His mind spun backward. . . .

For possibly the first time in his life, Johnnie had made a conscious effort *not* to destroy himself. After taking the gun from Cahill, he'd dropped it and moved in the direction of the door. That's when Cahill reached out and slapped him across the face, open-palmed, as he'd done so many times, so many years ago.

"Hit me," he said. "Now that there's nobody here to watch. Like you did in the cemetery." He slapped him again. "Come on, boy. I know what a short fuse you've got." He lifted his hand again.

Cahill knew Johnnie too well. Nobody had slapped him since he'd been a kid. Nobody was going to get away with slapping him now, especially Cahill.

Johnnie swung. Cahill staggered backward, tripping over a pile of trash. But when he hit the floor, he was smiling.

That's when Johnnie saw the gun in his hand. He barely had time to comprehend it all when the gun discharged, the sound deafening in the small, closed room. At the same instant, Johnnie felt the bullet's impact like a kick in the side. He was flung backward, against the wall. There was another discharge and another, in rapid succession, each one slamming into him.

It was like the scene from *Bonnie and Clyde*, where machine-gunned bodies flopped around like rag dolls.

The echo of the blasts was still ringing in his ears as he slumped to the floor. He was dimly aware of a cowboy boot connecting with his rib cage, knocking out what air he had left.

Blackness came, and with it thoughts of Maggie and a deep regret.

Like someone surfacing after a deep, dark dive, Johnnie forced his eyes open. He grabbed Thomas's sleeve. "That son of a bitch Cahill shot me," he gasped, while at the same time feeling an all-too-familiar futility. It was useless. Nobody would believe his word over Cahill's. No, he was destined to go down in history as a suicidal maniac.

"Of course it was Cahill!" Maggie said, dawning realization in her voice. "He was baiting Johnnie earlier today."

That's my Maggie.

"We'll get an APB out on him," Thomas said. "He won't get far. Hell, he's probably at home in front of the TV right now." His cursory examination of Johnnie's injuries complete, he said, "You're one lucky guy."

"Lucky. That's me," Johnnie said. The life was seeping out of him, and the guy was calling him lucky.

"Cahill forgot to replace his target loads."

"Target loads?" Johnnie croaked.

"We use them on the practice range. They're real bullets, but they have a fraction of the gunpowder. That, combined with the fact that at least two bullets hit this—" He held up the notebook Johnnie had stuffed in his pocket earlier.

"Hey, I was shot," Johnnie argued. "It threw me against the wall. I'm in agony. . . . I'm bleeding."

"I'm not saying they're harmless. It looks like you've got some broken ribs. Some pretty nasty bruises, plus a bullet embedded under the skin. Pretty nasty stuff. But not lethal."

Johnnie let his head fall back. His eyes closed. "I'm living a corny movie." But he wasn't dying. *He wasn't dying.*

The wail of a siren could be heard in the distance, growing closer until it stopped outside the house. Two ambulance attendants appeared. They quickly cleared a space next to Johnnie on the floor so they could transfer him to the stretcher. As careful as they were, the movement jarred him. Fire shot across his side, pain ripped through his lungs. He gulped for air and tried not to move.

As he was carried from the building, curious faces swirled in and out of his line of sight. Overhead, the sky was turning orange with the setting sun.

In the confusion he lost track of Maggie. Where was she? He felt himself begin to panic.

"Maggie—" Blindly he reached out . . . and felt her fingers close around his.

Chapter 27

The people of Hope could rest easy. Sheriff Cahill, alias the Mad Marshall, had been arrested and locked away to await trial for attempted murder. He wouldn't be going anywhere for a while. And he would never wear a badge again.

Johnnie got off lucky. His injuries amounted to three cracked ribs, plus some internal and external bruises. He would have been released from the hospital after a night of observation, but because of his diabetes they kept him an extra two days.

While he was there, Maggie came to visit. Johnnie babbled like an idiot and avoided eye contact. A couple of times she tried to get a serious conversation going, only to have him quickly change the subject. Maggie seemed puzzled and confused by his lack of response. But he couldn't help it.

So they stuck to general topics. The weather.

Hot and dry, yep.

Television.

Love that *People's Court*. Yep.

How he was going to get to the airport.

She offered to give him a ride.

No.

She insisted. *Damn.*

Truth was, he was having a hard time facing her. He couldn't quit thinking about his overacted death scene. What to him had been a dying man's confession of love had probably been no more than the ramblings of a lunatic to her. He'd never told a woman he loved her before. And it would never have happened if he hadn't thought he was taking the big trip.

She was better off with someone else, he told himself again. Better off with Elliot. Someone who didn't get into knock-down-drag-out fights at funerals. Someone who didn't puke right in the middle of Main Street, U.S.A. Someone who wasn't a screwup.

Better off.

He hated goodbyes. He avoided them whenever possible. Especially airport and train station and bus station goodbyes.

See you later. That's what he'd tell her, making it seem as if they'd be seeing each other again in a couple of days. But they would both know differently.

When she came to get him, he walked with her to her car, thinking that maybe he should have taken the painkillers the doctor had given him. But painkillers did weird things to his head, and he wanted to be able to keep himself together long enough to board the plane.

As Maggie walked beside him, she took small steps to accommodate his slower gait. They made a strange pair with him in his dry-cleaned, patched-up suit and Maggie in faded jeans, sneakers, and thick green sweater.

She opened the door for him. That made him laugh, then gasp in pain.

"And they say laughter is the best medicine," he said, gingerly lowering himself into the passenger seat, his injuries just another reminder of how wrong he was for her. This will be good, he told himself. Bouncing along in her car.

"Better give up laughing for a while," she said, shutting the door securely beside him.

"Maybe I'll give it up altogether," he said reflectively as she slid behind the wheel.

No comment.

A turn of ignition key. All systems go.

As the car moved away from the curb, he forced himself to breathe shallowly. Pain receded.

Within five minutes they were out of town. No traffic to fight their way through, no stoplights. Fresh desert air rushing in open windows. Good old Hope.

He thought about the way his past bitterness had colored his perception of the town. It had taken him a long time to realize he'd been blaming Hope for his problems, problems that came from within himself. Looking back, he could even recall people who'd been nice to him, who had tried to help him. But he'd had a giant chip on his shoulder. He hadn't wanted their help.

No, Hope wasn't as bad as he'd remembered. All the same, he'd be glad to get away, he told himself. Glad to get back to California. Yessir.

In order to fill every bit of silence, so there was no chance of the conversation getting serious, he talked. He talked about everything and nothing. He talked about theater drink holders and reclining seats. He talked about how the amount of salt in the Dead Sea made people float. He talked about whale songs and human spontaneous combustion.

When he ran out of subjects to bore her with, he asked, "So . . . about this Ohio thing . . ."

The words seemed to bypass the part in his brain that filtered things that shouldn't be spoken aloud. He'd never intended to bring up the Ohio subject. The Elliot subject.

"I'm going because of Alex," Maggie said. "She needs a family."

"You mean a father?" He could hardly choke out the question, hardly stand to think of someone else holding his little girl.

"But I've decided I can't marry Elliot. It wouldn't be fair to either of us. I don't love him. Not that way."

Her voice was cool and level, but the hands gripping the steering wheel were white.

Always before he'd at least been able to visualize Maggie and Alex in Hope. But now . . . To think of them both out there in Ohio, a place he'd flown over lots of times, but never seen . . .

And it came to him that, like Phil and his birds, there were some things a person just couldn't let go of, no matter what.

What if we were a family? he almost asked.

God, what was he thinking? She would laugh right in his face if he said such a thing.

She'd seen him at his worst. He couldn't quit thinking about it. She'd seen him sprawled out on a filthy floor in the dump where he'd grown up.

"I never wanted you to see where I came from," he blurted out. Couldn't he keep his mouth shut? Being with Maggie was like taking truth serum.

They were approaching a roadside stop—one picnic table and a trash can. Suddenly the car veered to the side of the road and skidded to a stop, dust drifting in the open windows. Maggie cut the engine. "Do you think it matters to me where you're from?" she said in a tight voice. "Seeing that place made me realize just how far you've come, what you've accomplished on your own. I'm *proud* of you."

She grabbed her purse, got out of the car, and hurried toward the picnic table.

Away from him, Maggie let her tears flow while she frantically dug through her purse, searching for a tissue. She finally found one, wiped her eyes, blew her nose, then searched until she found another.

When he'd told her he loved her, her heart had been filled with an amazed, wondrous joy. But afterward, in the hospital, he'd acted so strange. She could only assume that he regretted his words, understanding that they'd been spoken during a state of high emotion.

She was saturating a new tissue when she heard footsteps crunching across the gravel, stopping behind her.

"Do you like me?"

Oh God. What a question, spoken like a child who hadn't a clue. *Didn't he know?*

She fingered the tissue, looking for a dry spot. "I love you."

"W-what?"

She turned and looked at him through tear-blurred eyes. "I love you." The words came so easy. A simple statement of fact.

His look of baffled surprise made her love him all the more.

But his silence was frightening. It meant he was thinking.

She looked into the distance, off to the horizon where desert sand met blue sky, and she thought about the old Maggie. "I used to be this very normal person, with a very normal life," she said with a longing for something that could no longer be.

She blinked at her tears, wishing she'd brought more tissues. She should have known. She should have come prepared.

"If you could go back to being the person you used to be, if you could turn back the clock, to before the Hope parade, would you do it?"

She didn't need to think very long. "No," she said quietly. "I wouldn't have Alex." She looked at him. "And I wouldn't have known you." She swallowed at the sharpness in her throat, but it only made it hurt all the more. "I've tried not to love you." She gave a tremulous, self-mocking laugh. "What a joke. I even told myself I didn't love you. But it was a lie. Because, you see, by the time I decided not to love you, it was already too late."

She thought about never seeing him again. Or worse yet, seeing him in movies, someone distant, a stranger with blue eyes and a teasing smile. Someone she had known and loved.

He was going to leave. Her love wasn't enough to keep him. It wasn't enough to make him stay.

She rested her purse on her knee and began digging again. A tissue. Had to find a— Her hand touched the soft, tattered edge of a book. Her fingers curled around it. "I have something I was supposed to give you," she said, holding out the notebook. "Rick Thomas brought it by."

When he saw what it was, he took a step back and his face paled. "I don't want it."

"It's yours. It may have saved your life."

"Throw it away."

Why was he acting so odd? So embarrassed and uncomfortable?

She started to thumb through the book when he jerked it from her hand, spun around, and limped toward the trash container. But for once she was faster. She grabbed the notebook just as he was ready to drop it. Then she quickly moved away, out of his reach so he couldn't take it from her again. Elbows drawn close, shoulders hunched, she opened it.

She didn't know what she'd expected. Certainly not poetry. Certainly not words of wonder and idealism.

In his writing she saw the boy he used to be, and she saw the sensitive man she loved. Even though he would deny it, that idealist was still alive somewhere deep inside him.

"Poetry," she whispered, running her fingers lightly, reverently across a page.

"Go ahead. Laugh. And go ahead and throw it away. The trash is where it belongs."

She hadn't thought it humanly possible to love anyone more than she'd loved Johnnie just five minutes ago. She'd been wrong.

He doesn't know who he is. He can't see his own worth.

In that moment, while the desert sky turned red, she understood that he needed her. This man, this poet, this clown. He needed her to be his mirror, so he could see himself clearly, the way he really was. He needed her to believe in him.

She closed the book and held it safely against her heart, in case he got any more ideas about throwing it away. "Real men don't write poetry. Is that what you're saying?"

"You kill me, you know that?"

"Just because I love you doesn't mean I expect something from you. I don't want you to feel trapped. I don't want you to— Why are you crying?" The sight of his tears broke her heart, the sound of his choking gasp made her feel totally helpless.

The truth hit Johnnie hard. It was like the scene in *The Miracle Worker* where Helen Keller was at the pump and finally realized what Annie Sullivan had been trying to teach her all along.

Oh, *water*.

All his life he'd had a deep-seated fear of rejection. To compensate, he made sure he destroyed anything good before he lost it, before it was taken away, before it could hurt him. Like now. He was getting ready to run like hell, away from Maggie, away from Alex, away from life. . . .

Before Maggie understood what was happening, he reached out and tried to slip the book of poetry from her grasp. She let go. If it upset him so much, she would let him have it to do with what he wanted, even destroy.

She watched as he slapped at the pockets of his jacket, searching for something, finally producing a pen. He bit off the cap, opened the journal, and began writing, his head bent over the page, hair falling forward. When he was done, he turned it around and handed the book back to her.

He'd written a haiku, a Japanese form of unrhymed verse.

> Maggie makes me whole
> I cannot live without her
> Will she marry me?

Chapter 28

$\mathcal{T}$hree days later they were married by Reverend Graham in a private ceremony with Karen and Rick Thomas as witnesses.

When it was over, Maggie, Alex, and Johnnie took a trip by car, what Johnnie called a "see the U.S.A. in your Chevrolet" family vacation. They went from Texas to South Dakota, where they saw the Corn Palace. From there it was on to Ohio, where Maggie had a long, emotional talk with Marcella, and an even more emotional one with Elliot. It was a terrible strain, but worth it. The last thing Maggie wanted was to lose contact with them.

Any sane person would have called the second half of their trip, from Ohio to California, a nightmare. Flat tires, a night spent in a cramped car because motels were filled, changing diapers on the narrow, slanted front seat. To top it off, the grown-ups had a none too brief visit from Mr. Salmonella.

Except for the food poisoning, Johnnie loved the whole ordeal. Mainly because he'd never done anything like it before. And because during their time on the road he and Alex re-bonded.

While they were in California, they took in the premier of Johnnie's movie, *The Big Goodbye*.

Maybe it was because Maggie wanted to shelter him from sadness, or maybe it was because she thought it was his turn to laugh. Whatever the reason, the movie hit too close to home. She cried several times while sitting in the dark theater.

"It's so sad," she told him later.

He gave her hand a gentle squeeze. "It's supposed to be sad."

The reviews were good. Some of the toughest critics raved about the movie, even ones who'd previously said that Johnnie had no acting ability. They used phrases like "comedy's dark side," "tears of a clown," and the one that really cracked Johnnie up: "electric screen presence."

While they were in California they went to see Johnnie's doctor—a specialist in treating diabetes—taking Alex along so both she and Johnnie could have a thorough checkup. Maggie left feeling both better about the disease and overwhelmed by the amount of things she needed to learn.

Before returning to Hope, Johnnie took her to see the ocean. It made her feel the way storms used to make her feel as a child. Awed by the sheer majestic power.

Maggie and Johnnie had been married a month when they moved into Harriet's old house on the outskirts of Hope.

The place was huge, and there was something of Harriet's spirit there, her strength. A more tangible object was her cat, which she'd willed to Johnnie, along with her boat of a car that now sat under canvas in the garage.

To Harriet's son's intense disgust—and to everyone else's glee —Harriet had directed that the rest of her estate be auctioned and the proceeds donated to the children's theater.

At the north end of the house, where the sun poured in, was a room they'd made into a studio. It had a baby grand, where Johnnie worked on setting poetry to music. In the opposite corner was an office area, where together they were working on a screenplay. Johnnie said Maggie was a natural with one-liners. She told him he seemed to bring them out in her.

Even though everything was perfect, Maggie couldn't help but watch Johnnie for signs of boredom. Little by little, she relaxed. Little by little, she came to believe that he was with them to stay.

• • •

On Johnnie's birthday they had company, the way they did so many days, their home just seeming to attract people.

Maggie was in the kitchen making iced tea when she found herself drawn to the screen door, where she had an unhindered view of Johnnie in the backyard tending the grill. For someone who'd never seemed to care one way or the other about his health, he was making a noticeable effort to take care of himself, and she liked to think that she and Alex had something to do with his new outlook.

At the moment he was flipping hamburgers. After living with him for four months, she'd learned that there was the normal way of doing things, then there was the Johnnie Irish way.

As she watched, she heard him explaining every move with an awful French accent, sounding like the chef on Sesame Street.

His rapt audience consisted of three of Sherman's four kids. Cicely, the youngest, was pushing Alex in the swing near the transplanted, thriving catalpa tree. Off in the distance, in the far section of the yard, a tag football game was under way. The players included Karen and her three children, Rick Thomas, plus Sherman and his wife.

Johnnie tossed a hamburger patty above his head, watching as it arced downward, giving a play-by-play, all his vowels distorted. "A double. No, a triple. Could it be . . . a quadruple somersault?"

He lunged, trying to catch the tumbling patty with the spatula, had it, lost it, had it, then lost it again. The patty slid into the grass. Everyone stood staring at it, as if expecting it to get up.

Maggie didn't know Johnnie was aware of her presence at the door, not until he looked up and flashed her a sheepish grin that caused a constriction in her chest. *Love hurt. Even when it was so right.*

Yesterday he'd told her that his life was like a home movie. His words had frightened her, because she'd never much enjoyed home movies. They had always been something boring she'd had to sit through while visiting relatives. She'd asked him if that was good or bad, and he'd smiled a smile that never failed to take her breath away, and told her that home movies captured the real, the good, the true of family life.

He and Alex were inseparable. Every night she couldn't go to sleep unless she spent at least five minutes on her dad's lap, watching Charlie Chaplin videos. They even had their own private greeting—a thing they did with their upper lip and eyebrows.

Yes, Johnnie Irish had mellowed. He wasn't the same person he'd been, and yet he was the same, and more. He still did nutty things. Just last night he'd hung upside down from a tree limb, making monkey noises while scratching his armpit. Alex had been his audience—a comedian's dream, he called her. She could always be counted on to shriek in delight at everything her father did.

His psyche was fragile. That was the one thing people didn't know about him, didn't understand, what she hadn't understood at first. But she was strong, and if there were times when he sometimes got lost, she would find him. She wouldn't let him stay lost. Because she knew that although he didn't always believe in himself, she believed in him.

Johnnie watched Maggie disappear from the kitchen doorway. "Here." He handed the spatula to Sherman's oldest son. "Take over, will you?"

He strode to the house, the door slamming behind him. He came up behind Maggie and wrapped his arms around her, pulling her back to his chest, his fingers spread across her softly rounded abdomen. He bent his head and pressed his lips to her neck, inhaling the scent of her. "How's my little groupie doing?" he asked, patting her stomach. She covered his hands with hers.

"Fine."

"No queasiness?"

He knew she probably wouldn't admit to being sick, especially if it meant ruining Sherman and Judy's visit. "You're sure?" he asked.

She turned in his arms and smiled up at him. "I feel fine."

Sometimes it was all so perfect that it scared him. He didn't deserve so much.

Before they'd realized what was wrong, before they'd found out she was pregnant, she'd scared the hell out of him. For weeks she'd walked around with dark-rimmed eyes, unable to keep anything down. He thought she was dying, that he was going to lose her. Unthinkable.

Then they discovered she was pregnant and he was scared all over again. He didn't know if he could go through another childbirth. The first time, when they'd both been blissfully ignorant, had been rough enough. But Maggie had assured him it was easier the second time and he believed her. Either that or go crazy.

And then there was Alex. Even though the doctors had told him that she wasn't at risk, he constantly watched her for any signs of diabetes. He didn't think he'd be able to handle it if he knew he'd passed the disease on to his daughter. But there were tests now that could detect it early, before it even struck. In such cases, the disease could sometimes be kept at bay. Progress was being made. There was hope. Someday there might even be a cure. Not for him, but maybe the next generation. Maybe Alex's generation.

"The gas station pool is running three to one in favor of a boy," Maggie told him, leaning back against the cradle of his arms.

"What do they know?"

"Earl Cramer says if your features change, it means you're having a boy. Something to do with male hormones."

"Personally I think Cramer's full of it."

But she did look a little different. More delicate. Her skin had a transparent quality it hadn't had before. And there was a sleepy look to her eyes. Again he felt that tug of fear. Love was scary as hell. "Sure you're okay?"

She smiled. "I'm *fine*." She slid her hands up his T-shirt, her fingers gliding across his ribs and chest, touching the diabetic dog tags he now wore on a chain around his neck—a symbol of how much he'd changed, how much he credited Maggie with his new-found desire to live.

She smiled up at him. "I'll show you just how fine later on."

He pulled her closer, settling himself in the warmth between her thighs. "You don't scare me."

She laughed up at him—a wonderful, unrestrained sound. Outside, Johnnie could hear Sherman's deep voice, then the laughter of the children, followed by Alex's delighted squeals. Music he'd never grow tired of.

There were no more nightmares, but there were still periods of self-doubt. No, he wasn't a hundred percent. Was anybody? But he'd found a measure of peace. He'd found what could almost be called contentment. And sometimes—not often, but sometimes—he even dreamed he could fly.